"Guren Ichinose!
    Hey, I'm talking to you! Why are you ignoring me?!"

"I'm not human anymore, Guren…
I can't be with you any—"

"NGG…AGGGGGHHHHHHHH!!"

"If it'll help you…even a little…
I'm okay with it."

Seraph of the End

Guren Ichinose: Catastrophe at Sixteen

2

Story by Takaya Kagami
Art by Yamato Yamamoto

Translated by James Balzer

VERTICAL.

CONTENTS

Book Three

Book Four

Book Three

Night and Day

The first time they introduced him to his fiancée, Shinya was ten years old.

It was weird to think that he would be meeting his future spouse—his partner for life—at only ten years old. Still, when they told him he was about to meet her, his heart began to beat faster in his chest.

What kind of girl was she?

Was she cute?

Was she kind?

Would they get along?

"…"

It would be a lie to say that some of these romantic thoughts hadn't occurred to Shinya.

They had.

Thoughts of the future.

A fantasy of the happy times they could spend together.

"…"

But those thoughts weren't what caused Shinya's heart to pound in his chest.

After all, it was hard to get too worked up over the prospect of falling in love when it was with a girl he had never even met. His heart was beating faster for a different reason.

It was something else that was causing him to tremble in excitement.

So I survived… I get to live.

That was the thought Shinya had when they told him he was about to meet his fiancée.

The realization that jolted his heart into beating faster.

Shinya was ten years old, but he had already killed his fair share of people.

The ones he had killed had been like him. Potential fiancés, to Mahiru Hiragi.

In other words, they had been selected as possible stud horses, to mate someday with Mahiru Hiragi and create another generation of genetically superior children for the Hiragi Clan.

The competition, to beat the other candidates and become the Hiragis' stud horse, began for Shinya when he was five.

At first, the process hadn't been so terrible.

How fast could he run?

Did he learn new languages quickly?

Have a gift for magic?

Shinya had been a student at one of the Order of the Imperial Demons' many kindergartens throughout the country.

The Order of the Imperial Demons was a magical syndicate led by the Hiragi Clan. Shinya was selected by the school to join a special group of exceptionally gifted children.

At first, he was happy for the extra attention. He was more talented than the other children. Better. Special. He was special. Every day they told him how great he was, and pretty soon it went to his head. Being better than the other children gave him satisfaction. It became important to him.

He enjoyed growing stronger, and learning new spells.

Until one day, when the principal of the kindergarten broke the news to him.

"Everyone's so impressed with how hard you work, Shinya!" he said, in a singsong voice. "Even the head clan has taken notice. They want you to come to Tokyo! Isn't that great? You'll be transferring schools tomorrow. Are you excited?"

Shinya wasn't allowed to go home that day, or ever again.

His parents were given 300 million yen in compensation, and their position in the Imperial Demons rose by several ranks.

Supposedly, his parents went practically out of their minds with joy over being singled out by the head clan. Shinya only heard about their reaction secondhand, however. He wasn't allowed to see his parents. Not anymore.

Shinya cried and he screamed. He didn't want to go away. But none of the adults listened. It was an honor, they told him. He was being selfish, they said.

The new life that waited for him was terrible and cruel.

Tokyo.

Shibuya.

Once he was transferred to the new school, there was no more time for crying.

Tests were held once every three months. If he didn't make it into the top thirty percent he would be "disposed" of.

He and the other students were also forced to fight each other in violent matches every year. The losers were eliminated.

Win or die.

Win or die.

Win or die.

Only one of them would be allowed to survive in the end.

Shinya couldn't remember how many of them there had been in the beginning.

It had been a constant race against time.

To learn new spells.

Master new illusions.

Perfect new fighting techniques.

Sometimes he made friends. When they both survived, they were happy for each other. But if a friend couldn't make it into the top thirty percent he was eliminated.

Watching friends die only motivated everyone else to work harder.

They were afraid the same thing might happen to them.

Make friends.

Watch friends die.

Make friends.

Watch friends die.

Stop making friends.

Still watch them die.

In order to juggle the terrible stress, Shinya began to constantly grin. It seemed to help. He was able to learn new spells faster than those who scowled all the time or sank into depression. It seemed to make him more productive and efficient. Sometimes his smile would even enrage his opponents, making them slip up and cause their own downfall.

So Shinya kept smiling as he clung to survival.

The competition grew stiffer and stiffer each day, and the matches more desperate. Still Shinya hung on, a smile plastered to his face.

"..."

Until finally, one day—

Shinya showed up at the training ring. But the other candidates, whose faces he had grown used to seeing, were no longer there.

An old man, the instructor from the Hiragi Clan, came up and spoke to him. Until yesterday the man had only ever spoken to Shinya and the other candidates in angry shouts. Today, suddenly, he was respectful. He bowed his head as he spoke.

"Congratulations, Lord Shinya Hiragi. You have been selected as Lady Mahiru's fiancé."

Hiragi. The old man had called him Shinya Hiragi.

Shinya had been trained in the teachings of the Order of the Imperial Demons—the religious sect led by the Hiragi Clan—ever since he was five. And now Hiragi was his name as well.

It was almost off-putting how quickly the instructor's attitude toward him changed.

He seemed to be in genuine awe, even afraid, of Shinya.

"So then...I don't have to compete anymore?" Shinya asked,

grinning as always.

"That is correct, sir."

"I survived?"

"Yes, sir."

"I…I see."

At first, Shinya didn't feel much of anything. The news was too sudden. Having spent so much time competing, day in and day out, left him unsure of how to react.

The instructor, though, was oblivious to his discomfort.

"By the way, sir," he said, "your fiancée, Lady Mahiru, will be arriving shortly. It was her personal request to meet you… It seems Her Ladyship is very interested in meeting you."

"…"

"You and Lady Mahiru will lead the Hiragi Clan one day. I offer my humble wishes that these first introductions prove most felicitous."

Having congratulated Shinya one last time, the instructor left the room.

Shinya was left alone in the empty training hall.

It was where he was going to meet his fiancée, Mahiru Hiragi.

The very same hall where he had spent so many years fighting to the death.

When he was told she was on her way, the truth finally sank in.

"…"

He had survived.

At some point along the way he had begun to feel as if this life of incessant competition would never end. But it was over. And he was alive.

Just then, a young girl appeared at the entrance on the other side of the hall. A part of Shinya couldn't help but wonder…

What kind of girl was she?

Was she cute?

Was she kind?

"…"

Mahiru came closer.

Her appearance surpassed anything Shinya had imagined.

She had long, ashen hair, which was sleek and shining, and strong, commanding eyes. Her skin was pale and ethereal.

While her appearance was graceful and soft, her voice was cold and clear.

"So you're the one who survived, to plant a seed in me?"

Shinya bowed his head.

"Yes, my lady. It's a pleasure to meet you."

"What is your name?"

"Shinya."

"Shinya... What characters do you use to write that?"

"The ones for 'deep' and 'night.' As in 'midnight.'"

"That's a very unusual name."

"Is it? I guess I never noticed."

Of course, since he was five Shinya had spent his entire life at the Shibuya training facility. He had never had time to think about his own name.

Shinya. Once he thought about it, he had to admit the name was a little strange.

"Mahiru means 'midday,' doesn't it?" asked Shinya, smiling. "You shine like the midday sun, my lady. Shinya seems like the perfect name for someone like me, lucky enough to breathe in your shadow."

Mahiru narrowed her eyes slightly. She looked displeased.

"I didn't think you'd grovel so much."

She seemed to dislike the way Shinya had spoken to her. But it was important that she was happy with him. The only way he was allowed to continue to exist there was as Mahiru's fiancé.

She was the one who had come to meet him, so she had to be at least a little interested in getting to know him. Shinya needed to get her to like him while he had the chance.

He tried to think. What sort of attitude did she prefer? What kind of man did she like?

"Forgive me… I only learned just now that I've survived. I'm not really sure what the appropriate way to act in front of a Hiragi—"

Mahiru cut him off.

"I have no interest in you. Please just be yourself."

Shinya peered into his fiancée's face. He was trying to read her expression, to figure out what she was thinking.

She was a member of the Hiragi Clan.

To members of the Order of the Imperial Demons, Mahiru was a goddess by divine birthright. She was probably used to everyone sucking up to her.

In that case, a different approach was probably needed if Shinya wanted to get her to like him…

Before Shinya could finish his thought, however, Mahiru spoke again.

"My heart already belongs to somebody else," she said. "There's no room left for you. That's what I came here to tell you today."

Shinya finally understood.

He stared back at Mahiru.

"…"

And fell silent. He had to be careful. One misplaced word could spell disaster. Mahiru was rejecting him. But if she rejected him, his existence was worthless. Up until the day before, everyone he knew who had failed to prove their worth to the clan had been eliminated.

"Relax, you can speak freely," Mahiru said, almost as if reading his thoughts. "I made sure that no one would be spying in on us."

"So you say. It's a little hard to trust you…"

Mahiru smiled faintly.

"Are you being yourself now? That's fine. You can be straightforward with me."

"Is that what you prefer?"

"I suppose. It still won't make me like you, though."

"It won't? That puts me in a spot. You've been my whole reason for living."

"That's too bad."

"Am I that awful?"

A smile tugged at the corner of Mahiru's lip.

"I wouldn't know," she said. "This is the first time we've ever met."

"Then I still have a chance?"

"No," Mahiru dashed his hopes immediately.

Her voice was gentle as she spoke, but also firm. Shinya got the sense that nothing was going to change her mind.

And that meant...

"Am I...going to be killed today?" he asked.

Mahiru shook her head.

"No. I'm going to act like I like you, and pretend we're a couple."

Shinya thought for a moment. Why would she want to do that? Why had she bothered to come here and meet him today?

The answer occurred to him immediately.

"You mean you're in love with someone whom the Hiragi Clan doesn't approve of."

Mahiru's eyes widened slightly in surprise.

"You are clever, aren't you?" she said.

"And you chose to have me cover your tracks."

Mahiru smiled.

Her whole face lit up. Just thinking of that person she loved seemed to fill her with joy.

"Now I get it," Shinya said. "When they told me you were coming I wondered what you would be like. I never expected that someone from the Hiragi Clan would be a run-of-the-mill, lovestruck little girl."

Mahiru laughed.

"That's me. Just a run-of-the-mill, lovestruck little girl. Unfortunately, I was born into a family where love isn't a run-of-the-mill affair."

"You don't mind calling yourself a lovestruck little girl?"

"Ahaha. All I ever wanted was to have a normal life."

"..."

"To be a normal girl who can fall in love with anyone she likes."

21

Shinya understood. He had wanted a normal life, too.

Kill or be killed. Be the best or be eliminated. He had never wanted a life spent constantly battling fear.

"It's better this way, isn't it?" conspired Mahiru. "I won't force you into a relationship with someone you don't really love."

"Well, when that someone is as pretty as you are—"

"I really don't need your flattery," Mahiru cut him off.

Shinya grinned.

"I meant it. You're very beautiful. I may not have been interested before, but now that you tell me I can never have you it makes me want to try."

"..."

"After all, I've never lost at anything before in my life."

Shinya gestured toward the training hall. It was where he had spent his entire life since he was five, competing against others.

Mahiru smiled faintly.

"True. If you had lost here, I suppose you would be dead by now."

"All right then, I've decided. I don't mind being your cover for now, but someday I'll make you love me. That's my next challenge."

Mahiru was still smiling, but she looked at Shinya with something like pity in her eyes.

"Why wait? Now is as good a time as any for you to experience losing," she said.

"What?"

"If you lose for once, it might make it easier for you to give up on trying to win me over."

"I don't understand..."

But before Shinya finished speaking, Mahiru had already made her move. She was headed straight toward him.

Her movements were graceful... But they were also slow.

Shinya watched her dubiously.

"I expected more from a Hiragi..." he muttered.

He could hardly believe that he had been risking his life all this time for someone so weak. Contempt boiled up inside him. His interest in Mahiru, and his desire for her, quickly began to dissipate.

Mahiru swung her fist. It would be easy to block. If she'd been in the training facility in Shinya's place with that level of skill, she'd have been eliminated ages ago.

Shinya raised his hand into the air and reached out to intercept her arm.

But the moment he thought he had her…

"…"

…she suddenly disappeared.

He felt someone tap him on the back.

It was Mahiru. She whispered in his ear.

"Ha. You thought you could plant your seed in me? You'd have to lay a hand on me first."

She was on a different level.

A whole different level from the battles he had been fighting until yesterday. She was a dangerous opponent.

Shinya cursed his own stupidity.

He realized that she had placed a *fuda*—a paper charm inscribed with a spell—on his back.

She leaned in close, and whispered.

"*Explode.*"

Shinya reacted immediately. Swinging his arm back as fast as he could, he pasted a counter-*fuda* onto his back to try to ward off the damage.

Then he took a step forward and spun around.

Mahiru was smiling.

There was a sadness to her smile.

She gave off a presence completely unlike moments ago.

She suddenly seemed invulnerable.

Which of them was stronger?

The answer seemed pretty obvious…

"I guess…I just lost, didn't I?" remarked Shinya.

Mahiru smiled.

"Was this your first time losing?" she said. "Think of it as inspiration, to grow stronger."

Shinya laughed.

"I think I've actually been on the losing end ever since I got here," he said.

Since his parents had sold him.

To this place he couldn't escape.

To a fiancée he couldn't refuse.

He had been defeated long ago, the moment he'd lost his right to live free.

But not Mahiru.

She was different.

She had come to see him today because she was determined not to lose. She would love the boy her family had forbidden her, determined to rely on her own strength and to choose her own life.

"Can I ask you one question?" requested Shinya.

"What is it?"

"The boy you like? Is he even stronger than you are?"

Mahiru grinned in response. There was a twinkle in her eye.

She really did look like just a run-of-the-mill girl in love.

She tilted her head to the side, as if thinking.

"Hmm… I'm not sure. But whether Guren is strong or weak, my feelings for him won't change."

"Well, that's discouraging. It doesn't leave a lot of room for me, does it?"

Mahiru smiled again.

Her smile was gentle and bright, like the afternoon sun shining on a quiet day.

"I'm pretty sure Guren is strong, though… He's probably much stronger than me."

"So that's why you like him? This Guren guy?"

"Yes."

"Because he's strong?"

"Yes."

"I see… Fine, then. I'll be your cover. Use me as a shield until you can be together with the guy you really love."

Mahiru grinned.

"Thank you. Here's to our futures, Lord Shinya Hiragi."

"You can just call me Shinya. And I'll call you Mahiru. That will attract less suspicion than calling each other 'lord' and 'lady,' don't you think? Anyway, to our futures, Mahiru."

Mahiru smiled again.

She had a very pretty smile.

"…"

For the first time, Shinya felt it.

Although he had never even met him, Shinya began to feel a little jealous. Of the boy named Guren Ichinose.

Chapter One

A Demon's Paw

Guren Ichinose watched the blood as it drained from his arm.

The dark, carbon dioxide-rich fluid was being drawn out of his vein through a needle.

"Sir?"

Guren turned in the direction of the voice. The woman who'd spoken was in her early twenties and dressed in a white lab coat.

Her name was Mitsuki Iori. She was one of the occult researchers at the Order of the Imperial Moon—the religious sect led by the Ichinose Clan.

"This is the last of the samples," she said, removing the fifth and final syringe from Guren's arm.

"Huh? Okay, thank you."

Guren nodded. He rolled his sleeve back down.

"When will you have the results?" he asked.

"Our researchers are already working around the clock to figure out what's happening inside you, sir… In fact, we've already gotten results back for several of the tests we did earlier."

"And?"

"Your toxicology tests came back positive…"

"What kind of poison is it?"

"…"

Mitsuki smiled sheepishly.

"We're not actually sure…but it appears to be man-made. It's interwoven with magical energy, but so far we haven't been able to pinpoint the strain of magic being used."

"If you guys don't recognize it, then it must be some pretty sophisticated stuff."

"That seems like a safe assumption…"

"Do you think you'll be able to identify it?"

"Of course! You can count on us. We won't rest as long as that poison is inside you, sir!"

Mitsuki couldn't look more enthusiastic.

Guren stared at her blankly. He was thinking of something else.

Of the face of the girl who had placed the poison in him in the first place.

The beautiful face of Mahiru Hiragi.

Mahiru was trying to perfect cursed gear, a task that everyone else thought impossible. It was a type of magic that involved sealing a demon directly into a weapon.

She had already made significant progress.

Guren had even watched her trade blows with a vampire noble. Vampires were incredibly powerful—nearly untouchable compared to humans.

Which meant that Mahiru's progress on cursed gear had already greatly exceeded any previous technological or magical research.

"…"

Guren recalled the day.

The smile on Mahiru's face.

The things she had said.

…You're not really human anymore. Could a human arm reattach itself after it had been sliced off? The demon has already tainted a piece of your soul…

…In the end, you'll fall. Your heart will grow black and twisted, just like mine. Do you see, Guren? We just can't stay apart. We'll keep each other company on the road to hell…

The demon.

The demon's poison.

27

The poisonous demonic curse.

Guren touched his right arm lightly. He had cut it clean from his body after it had happened. But he could move it freely now as if it were as good as new.

"Sir?" said Mitsuki. "There's something else we need to discuss."

"What is it?"

"You know that there are many ardent believers in the Order of the Imperial Moon. We need your permission to select a few to experiment with the poison."

"..."

"I know the order doesn't currently allow human experiments, but..."

Guren shook his head.

"No," he said.

"But sir, if we're going to get to the bottom of this..."

"I said no. I won't permit it. You already have me to experiment on. Isn't that enough?"

It wasn't just that he wouldn't permit it. He couldn't. Human experimentation was an indispensable part of research such as this. But that was precisely why this research was forbidden.

And it wasn't really the Imperial Moon who had forbidden it.

It was the head clan—the arrogant and despotic Hiragi Clan.

If the Ichinose Clan's pursuit of human experimentation and forbidden research came to light, the Imperial Demons would treat it as a declaration of war.

The Imperial Moon would be crushed immediately. It had no hope of resisting the Hiragis. The difference in strength between the two organizations was too great.

That left only one course of action...

"Use me. Say it's treatment for my injuries. It will give us cover for our research."

Mitsuki still wasn't persuaded. She tried to argue with him.

"It's not enough. We can't just sit back while the poison is eating away at you, sir. Time is of the essence…"

"I said no!" Guren shouted angrily.

Mitsuki clamped her mouth shut.

"If we start conducting human experiments," Guren continued, "where will it stop? New magic, new research, new powers. Power, power, power… And then what? What happens after we turn our own comrades into human guinea pigs? Will we be swallowed whole by our own lust for power, or will the Hiragis crush us beneath their boots? Either way, it's a disaster in the end."

Guren thought of Mahiru again.

She said she loved him.

But she had been driven mad by power. She was coming apart at the seams.

I love you. You're just like me, your loyalties lie in madness and depravity…

"Mitsuki, now is not the time," cautioned Guren. "Not yet. No human experiments."

"…"

"I'll be your guinea pig for now. Do your experiments. We don't need to perfect the demon's curse. All we need to do is find a way to neutralize the poison."

Mitsuki's frown suddenly gave way to a smile.

"Sir?" she said.

"Yeah?"

"Did you know we have the same blood type? Type A."

"Huh?"

What was she talking about?

Then it dawned on Guren what she was about to do.

"Stop!" he shouted.

But it was too late. Mitsuki was still holding the syringe in her hand. The syringe full of Guren's blood. She jabbed it into her own wrist.

"You're too important to use as a guinea pig, sir," she said.

She pressed down on the plunger, injecting the blood.

"You fool!"

Guren reached out and smacked the syringe from her hand, but half the blood had already entered her arm.

It was possible that nothing would happen.

Maybe she would be fine, even with Guren's blood inside her system.

She grinned. Nothing seemed to be happening.

"There… Now our research can move forward. We can use my body, too, for—"

"…"

Mitsuki broke off, mid-speech.

Her expression changed.

Her entire body shook. She clamped her right hand over her left wrist, where she had injected the syringe.

"Wh-What is this… So much p-power. I… Ah… Eeeeek!" Mitsuki began screaming.

Her left hand swelled and bulged. Dark tendrils of magic surrounded the hand, and the nails began extending into sharp talons like a demon's claw.

"N-No… I can't control it…"

Guren drew his sword.

It was Hoarfrost, the enchanted sword he had received from Kureto Hiragi. He swung down hard.

The strike connected. Mitsuki's left hand was severed clean from her body. But it continued to mutate, growing enormous before their eyes. Spidery legs arched from the severed end. The decapitated hand suddenly stood upright.

It was already larger than the lab's hospital bed.

Three huge eyes sprouted in its palm.

Next, a mouth formed beneath the eyes. It was lined with rows of fangs. The mouth stretched open in a gaping maw, ready to devour Mitsuki.

"Die!" shouted Guren.

He swung his sword once more, using every ounce of strength in his body. The blade hit the creature between the middle and ring fingers, slicing it in two, through the palm and down to the wrist. Guren didn't let up. He reversed his blade and took a second sideways strike at the creature.

The three massive eyes rolled sideways in their sockets, staring wetly at Guren.

The creature's mouth opened, and it spoke in a deep, croaking voice.

"What is this? You're a demon too?" it said.

"Shut up, you freak!"

Guren's sword sliced clean through its middle, from left to right.

The hand finally fell silent. It toppled to the floor, chopped into four pieces.

Just then, the door to the lab swung open. Several scientists in white lab coats came rushing in.

"Sir!"

"Lord Guren!"

"I'm fine," said Guren, turning toward them. "Take care of Mitsuki's wound!"

She sat slumped on the floor. Her arm was gone, but a *fuda* had already been plastered over the wound. Apparently she had managed to stop her bleeding herself.

The other researchers tried to lift Mitsuki up and carry her out of the room.

But she wouldn't listen to them. She was staring at her own severed hand, which had been mutilated by the demon's poison. It lay in massive pieces on the floor.

"A-Amazing... What was that? There was so much power... I've never seen anything like it... W-We have to research this..."

She had just lost her arm...

And she had been completely powerless to control what had

happened...

But her face seemed almost ecstatic as she spoke.

Guren remembered what Mahiru had said.

You won't resist it. You thirst for power. You need it. You're just like me. You've fallen deep, and there's no climbing back out.

It was going to spread.

The madness and greed were going to spread like an infection.

Several of the researchers were already staring in fascination at the pieces of demon corpse lying on the floor.

One of the researchers reached out to touch it.

"Don't," said Mitsuki. "It's infectious. We'll need to wear hexmat suits from now on."

The other researchers helped her to her feet.

She bowed toward Guren.

"I'm sorry you had to witness that, sir," she said. "But this had been a huge breakthrough for our research. I promise you, I'll find a way to unravel whatever secrets this curse is hiding."

Guren sighed in disgust.

"You just lost your arm and already you're talking like that..." he said.

Mitsuki mistook what he said for a compliment.

"Yes, sir. If the human race is ever going to take the next step forward—if the Order of the Imperial Moon is ever going to grow powerful under your leadership—then sacrifices such as these are necessary."

Had any Hiragi spies been in the room to hear her words, the entire order would have been marked as subversives and destroyed immediately. Fortunately, all of the faces in the room belonged to researchers whom Guren had known since childhood.

After all, they were in a small village in the mountains of Aichi Prefecture, far away from Shibuya and the Hiragi Clan's main base. The village's inhabitants were all members of the Imperial Moon.

They were currently in one of many rooms in a huge laboratory located in the basement of the Ichinose Clan compound, which was situated in the center of the village.

"The human race? You're starting to sound pretty full of yourself," chided Guren.

Mitsuki laughed.

"We scientists are all that way…. Okay, everyone. Let's get started. We've finally got a lead on our research. Oh, by the way, Lord Guren."

"Yeah?"

"It's time."

Guren glanced at the clock hanging on the wall.

The time was 1:00 a.m.

Guren attended a school run by the Hiragi Clan. If he was going to make it on time for classes tomorrow they would need to start driving soon.

Guren nodded.

"I'll be back. Keep up your research…"

"Yes, sir. I promise you we'll get results."

"Just be careful. If you're going to take any risks…"

"Make sure the Hiragis don't find out, right? Don't worry, I know," Mitsuki assured. "I got a little carried away today. But I wanted to produce some solid evidence while you were still here, sir."

Solid evidence.

In other words, she wanted to carry out serious research into demonic curses, but had not been granted permission. So instead she had forced the project forward in the presence of the future head of the clan. In fact…

Guren turned toward the other researchers.

"Are you all on board with this as well?" he asked.

"…"

They stood by with nervous expressions on their face.

Their nervousness was understandable. They knew very well what they were trying to do.

Their own comrade—Mitsuki Iori—had just knowingly risked her life for the project.

Guren glanced toward the door. Several fully armed Imperial Moon soldiers stood outside the room. Guren recognized their faces. They were all very capable fighters.

"Lord Guren," said Mitsuki, "if this research succeeds, it could be an answer to the Imperial Moon's prayers, a way to—"

"Be quiet, Mitsuki," Guren cut her off.

He already knew what she was going to say.

An answer to the Imperial Moon's prayers—a way to finally pry themselves free from beneath the Imperial Demons' boots.

A way to escape the constant ridicule, persecution, and oppression they faced.

A new power had suddenly fallen into their laps. One that seemed to make all those dreams possible.

"…"

It was that possibility that had caused Mitsuki to act so recklessly.

The same thing had happened to Mahiru. She had been completely infected with madness.

If they continued this research, the Hiragis were sure to catch wind of it at some point. Once that happened, the Imperial Demons would attempt to kill each and every one of them. The scientists in the room, however, understood that.

"Do you really want to declare war on the Hiragis like this?" Guren asked.

"None of us intend to make you fight this battle on your own, sir," Mitsuki replied.

"…"

"Your father, Sakae Ichinose, is a moderate. Our parents' generation were all content to follow him… But we are with you, Lord Guren."

"…"

"When the Hiragis tortured Lord Sakae, we made up our minds. We won't let them keep humiliating us like this…"

"Enough, shut up," Guren said. "I understand."

"But…"

"I'm saying I'm with you. I'll do as you wish."

Mitsuki's face lit up.

Joy spread on the faces of all the other researchers as well.

The decision, however, was suicide.

They were planning to fly in the face of an organization whose power dwarfed their own at least a thousand times over.

If they were going to pull this off, it would take madness.

It would require a demon's strength.

But...

"I want you to avoid human experimentation as much as possible... If we're going to win this, we're going to do it with our reason intact."

"But sir..."

"No buts. That's an order. If the Hiragis catch wind of what we're doing too soon it would be disastrous. You need to keep things low key."

"..."

"And I'll decide the timing for when we actually declare war."

"But if we move too slow..."

"If we do it, we'll do it this year."

Looks of surprise flashed across the faces of the researchers.

It was already mid-August.

That meant, at the very latest, they would be going to war in four months.

But that was probably about as long as they could keep what they were doing a secret from a group as powerful as the Hiragis.

Plus, there was what Mahiru had said.

The truth is, this year at Christmas, the world will come to an end.

The trumpets of the apocalypse will sound, and a virus will spread. When that time comes, a new world will arise. One that, more so than ever, requires power.

There was a chance that a virus—a biological weapon—would be released. On a scale wide enough to bring the word to its knees. Everywhere, all at once.

Guren didn't know what the Brotherhood of a Thousand Nights would achieve by doing something like that, but common sense suggested that they already had an anti-virus if they were willing to release the virus.

It could be a way for them to blackmail the entire world.

That was one possible scenario: Follow us, or everybody dies. The Thousand Nights were a fairly large, worldwide syndicate. If anyone was capable of pulling off something like that, it was probably them.

It would also help explain why the Thousand Nights had launched their war.

If there wasn't much time left until the world came to an end, then the Thousand Nights could afford to wage war with the Imperial Demons without worrying about the cost to their own forces.

Guren smirked. "Hmph… So an angel is going to alight at Christmas, trumpet in hand, to kick sand in the world's face? You gotta be kidding me. This is modern-day Japan we're talking about."

Either way, the Order of the Imperial Moon needed to build up its own strength before it was too late.

Time was running out.

No one needed to remind Guren of that fact.

He turned toward Mitsuki. "Fine," he said. "Do it. Be discreet. Be careful. But work fast."

"Yes, sir!" the researchers cried in response.

They immediately went to work.

It was probably too late to turn back now.

Their rebellion against the Hiragi Clan had already begun.

◆

As Guren left the lab his two bodyguards pushed through the throng of soldiers and rushed to him. The pair was never far from his side.

Their names were Sayuri Hanayori and Shigure Yukimi.

They both looked extremely worried.

"Master Guren!" shouted Sayuri. "Something happened in there while we were gone, didn't it?!"

While Sayuri was talking, Shigure peeped into the room. The researchers inside were all scurrying around in a frenzy.

"Mitsuki Iori's arm is missing," she said, turning back toward Sayuri. "And the body of some strange monster is lying on the ground."

Sayuri glanced at Shigure quizzically before turning her eyes back toward Guren.

"Master Guren... Is there something you're hiding from us?" she said.

Guren shook his head.

"It's nothing you two need to know—"

"That's unacceptable," Shigure interrupted him. The expression on her face was stone cold. "Our duty is to protect you. How can we do that if we don't understand what is going on?"

"It's the only way you can do it. You're my personal bodyguards, serving at my very side, at a school run by the Hiragi Clan, in order to protect me. Whenever possible, I have to avoid letting you overhear any information that could cause problems if it got leaked to the Hiragis. If you knew anything that we didn't want them to become aware of..."

Sayuri nodded. "That wouldn't be a problem. If they captured us we'd just kill ourselves first."

Shigure nodded in agreement. "So you see—"

Guren cut her off with a laugh and said, "At your level, do you think you'd even have the chance to kill yourself? Don't underestimate the Hiragis. If the two of you knew what was going on, I would never let you leave this compound again. I'd find two other guards to serve me. Do you understand? If you want to stay by my side, then keep those ears covered."

Sayuri and Shigure exchanged glances.

"If that's what it takes to stay by your side…"

"…then that's what we'll do."

Guren turned his back to the two and began walking.

"We're heading back to Tokyo. Is the car ready?"

"Ready and waiting."

"Then let's go," he said, satisfied. "We've got school tomorrow."

Chapter Two

The Mice Will Play

—Look, it's Guren Ichinose…

Guren overheard the other students whispering.

He was in one of the classrooms, at First Shibuya High School.

Until just recently, the school had been a hive of enemies.

They had called him names, bullied him, thrown bottles full of cola at his head. Lately, however…

The door to the classroom opened. He could hear several students whispering to each other in the hallway.

—I heard Lord Kureto chose him as one of his personal operatives.

—I heard that he was hiding his true strength, but then Lord Kureto recognized how powerful he really was.

—I heard he's friends with Lord Shinya, and there are even a couple of students from the Jujo and Goshi Clans who respect him.

—Hey…weren't you the one who made fun of him and called him an Ichinose mongrel?

—You did it too!

—I did not! You don't know what you're talking about, you liar!

Overhearing their idiotic conversations, Guren slumped over his desk, head in hand. He was still sleep-deprived.

He had spent the night in the back seat of a car as it sped along the Tokyo-Nagoya Expressway, at 95 mph, from Aichi Prefecture to Tokyo.

But he hadn't been able to sleep well. As they drove, he couldn't stop thinking of what might happen in the days to come.

"…"

Guren stared out the window with a sleepy expression on his face.

It was fine inside the classroom, with the air conditioner set on full, but the weather was so hot outside that the landscape seemed to shimmer before Guren's eyes.

It was the twentieth of August.

Normal schools were in the middle of summer vacation. Not First Shibuya, however.

The temperature had reached record highs for several days in a row. The news stations had all been making a big fuss about it. Why was it so hot, lately? If global warming continued at this pace, they said, abnormal climate patterns might start leading to food shortages.

Of course, if the world actually was going to end at Christmas, then there probably wasn't much point in worrying about food supplies.

"Hey, Guren… Guren!"

Someone was calling his name.

He ignored the voice and continued to stare out the window for a little while.

That just made the speaker angry. She slammed her hand down on his desk.

"Guren Ichinose! Hey, I'm talking to you! Why are you ignoring me?!"

Guren turned toward her with an annoyed expression. She was one of the girls in his class.

She had distinctively beautiful crimson-red hair, fiercely slanted almond-shaped eyes, and pale milky skin.

Her name was Mito Jujo. She was from the revered Jujo Clan.

"You've been lying around like a slob every day lately instead of training," she said. "You think you can afford to slack off just because Lord Kureto has taken a shine to you?"

"Slack off?" muttered Guren. "Is someone slacking off?"

"You are!" scolded Mito. "You act like you're too good for class, and you never show your real potential during sparring or magic exams. Just what do you think you're doing?!"

Guren wasn't really sure how to answer. The truth was that the classes at the school were all too easy for him. There wasn't really anything he could learn from them.

Besides, the other students at the school were all his enemies. There was no reason for him to let them see his true strength.

Which was why he continued to act lazy and shiftless. But that probably wasn't the kind of explanation that would pass with Mito.

Lately, his reputation and standing among the Hiragis had begun to rise—a cause for celebration as far as the other students at the school were concerned. In Guren's place, they would have hardly been able to contain themselves.

From Mito's point of view, Guren should have been over the moon at how lucky he was.

Guren wondered if he should try to fake that a little. But what was the point? After all, Kureto was already aware of Guren's true strength. And of his bad attitude.

While Guren was still thinking…

"Yaawwwwnn…"

…a huge yawn escaped his mouth.

Mito nearly had a fit.

"When are you gonna get serious?!" she shouted.

"If you're gonna shout like that, would you mind not doing it so close? You're hurting my ears."

"First of all, I saw how easily you lost last period when you were sparring with Kaizuki… Explain yourself! I know you could beat him easily if you tried."

Guren shrugged.

"No, I'm pretty sure that was my best."

Mito narrowed her eyes.

"You don't get it, do you? I'm the one who gets put on the spot when you act that way!"

"Huh? You get put on the spot? What for?"

"What for?!" cried Mito. "Some of us on your team are from real clans. Haven't you realized that when you slack off our reputations suffer?"

So that was it.

As one of Kureto's operatives, Guren had been placed on a special squad with Mito Jujo and Norito Goshi. Mito was worried that if Guren appeared weak, it would reflect poorly on the other members of the squad.

Guren smirked.

"Why should I have to take care of your reputation?" he said.

"Because... Because we're both under Lord Kureto's command! We're a team. We should do our best, and help each other out. As friends..."

Guren stopped listening.

A team?

Friends?

They were under the command of Lord Kureto.

Chosen, by the great and magnificent Lord Kureto Hiragi.

"Hmph," snorted Guren. He yawned again and rested his head on his hands.

"Are you listening to me, Guren?!" shrieked Mito.

The boy sitting at the desk next to Guren's grinned at her.

It was Shinya Hiragi.

"You should just leave Guren be, Mito. It's not like his acting rude and lazy is anything new."

Shinya was a son of the Hiragi Clan by adoption. Mito bowed at him sheepishly.

"B-But, Lord Shinya..."

"Besides, for someone as strong as Guren, these lessons must be really boring. Isn't that right, Guren?"

"..."

Guren ignored him. That just got Mito fired up all over again.

"What do you think you're doing, ignoring Lord Shinya when he's talking to you?!"

The students in the hallway heard Mito's shouting. Guren could overhear them whispering to each other again.

—See? The rumors were true! Look at how friendly Lord Shinya and that girl from the Jujo Clan are being...

—But the Ichinoses are just a branch family. I heard they were all troublemakers. Why would the Hiragis, or Lord Kureto, be interested in them?

"..."

Guren stared out the window. He bit his lip as he listened to the students in the hallway.

Once upon a time, the Ichinose Clan had been the most loyal, and most powerful, of all the great families serving the Hiragis.

But five centuries ago, they had split from the Hiragis and formed a new religious sect known as the Order of the Imperial Moon.

Not much was known about that time.

But they did know the reason for the split.

Believe it or not, it all boiled down to a love story. And a very tragic one, at that.

The eldest daughter of the Ichinose Clan at the time had been very beautiful. The first and second Hiragi sons had competed for her affections, but after many twists and turns, it was the younger brother who succeeded in winning the girl's heart.

Unfortunately, the eldest son was unwilling to forgive them.

According to legend, one fateful night he violated the girl, impregnated her, and then castrated his brother.

Afterward, he banished his brother and the girl—who was pregnant with his own child—from the clan.

The younger brother proceeded to form a new sect with the Ichinose girl. It came to be known as the Order of the Imperial Moon.

The eldest son could have easily crushed the new organization if he wished.

He was heir to the great Hiragi Clan, after all.

To the Order of the Imperial Demons.

But instead, he let the sect remain.

He did it to humiliate them.

The Ichinose girl had spurned him, and his brother had defied him. It was his way of mocking them. He wanted their disgrace to live on for all eternity.

They would live in shame—they, and their children, and their children's children, and so on and so forth, until the end of time.

Since the brother had been castrated, obviously he and the girl could never have children together.

But due to the rape, she had become pregnant with a child belonging to the leader of the Hiragi Clan. The two decided to keep the child and raise it as the future leader of the Imperial Moon.

For the rest of his life, the brother was treated as an object of ridicule.

As was the girl.

They still had their love.

But everything else had been taken from them.

The other houses all laughed at them. Sneered openly.

The two had brought it upon themselves.

For daring to defy the Hiragi Clan.

That was what all the members of the great houses were taught growing up.

The Ichinoses were and always would be filthy mongrels.

It was their fate by birth.

As time passed, however, those events became a hazy story from a distant era.

A story that had little to do with Guren, the Hiragis, or the present day.

It was why Kureto felt comfortable making use of Guren now. Apparently, the eldest Hiragi was finally willing to forgive the Ichinose Clan.

Maybe it flew in the face of tradition, but it was the rational thing to do. Nobody was interested anymore in some moldy old love story about the bones of their ancestors.

There were nine other houses:

Nii. Sangu. Shijin.
Goshi. Rikudo. Shichikai.
Hakke. Kuki. Jujo.

The Ichinose Clan, which rounded out the number to ten, was actually the largest and most powerful of these.

Kureto establishing control over them was actually a big deal.

Maybe Kureto had maneuvered Guren into his pocket out of political motivations...

Just then, break ended and class began.

Mito headed back to her seat still fuming at Guren.

Norito grinned at her as she walked past.

"You just don't learn, do you?" he said. "Why do you care so much what Guren does, anyways? Do you have a crush on him or something?"

"You shut up!"

Mito punched Norito in the arm.

Norito laughed.

Naturally, no one else in the classroom did. Mito was from one of the storied clans. They were scared that if they laughed at her she might come after them.

They all just tried to look agreeable instead, plastering fake smiles across their faces.

Both the Jujos and the Goshis were clans to be feared.

The teacher stepped up to the front of the class and began her lesson.

Today's was about countering Western magic. None of it was of any interest to Guren, however.

Shinya suddenly leaned over and tapped Guren on the shoulder.

"Hey, Guren…"

"…"

"Hey…"

"Be quiet."

"Huh? I guess you're right. I should try to keep my voice down, since we're in the middle of class and all."

"That's not what I meant…"

But Shinya ignored him, scooching his chair over. He leaned in close and whispered in Guren's ear, "How's this? Is this quiet enough for you? Ms. Aiuchi won't get angry now, will she?"

Guren sighed and turned toward him in annoyance.

Just as Guren suspected, Shinya had a huge grin on his face. The guy knew that none of the teachers at the school would dare yell at a Hiragi. He was just pulling Guren's chain.

Guren didn't say anything. Shinya was always trying to get a rise out of him. Guren wasn't about to start encouraging him now.

Undeterred by Guren's sullen frown, Shinya leaned in and whispered into his ear once more. "The Thousand Nights want to make contact somewhere tonight. I think we should meet them."

Guren's eyes shot open in surprise despite himself.

He glanced back at Shinya.

They were in a classroom at a school run by the Order of the Imperial Demons. It wasn't a safe place to say something like that.

If anyone heard them, Guren and Shinya would almost certainly be arrested, tortured, and summarily executed.

Shinya just grinned like he couldn't care less. He had probably already taken precautions to shield them from being overheard.

Still…

"…I don't like being surprised like that," Guren said.

Shinya laughed.

"That's what you get for pissing off Mito and ignoring me."

"Be serious. I don't have time for your games..."

Shinya narrowed his eyes. The expression on his face was earnest.

"I'm not playing. I don't have any more interest in foolish games than you do."

Guren stared back. Shinya flashed him his usual toothy grin.

Guren still didn't feel ready to trust him.

Shinya had handed over the piece of the chimera—the so-called Four Horsemen of the Apocalypse—that Mahiru had left behind, so maybe he could be trusted to some degree. But there was plenty Guren stood to lose by trusting too easily, and very little to gain.

Which was why he needed to stay cautious when it came to Shinya.

"..."

Guren remained silent.

Shinya placed a scrap of paper on Guren's desk without waiting for an answer. It gave the location of tonight's meeting.

The note was in Shinya's handwriting. If Guren were to hand it to Kureto, the Hiragi Clan would be able to attack the meeting place. Shinya would probably be killed before the day was through.

The guy was deliberately putting himself in a vulnerable position. Again.

Guren stared at him quizzically.

"Why do you trust me so much?" he said.

Shinya laughed.

"Why do you mistrust me so much? I think that's the question."

"Maybe I just don't like your face."

"Haha. How could anyone dislike a face as friendly as mine?"

"Shut up."

"Anyway... Maybe you don't know much about me, but I've been hearing about you for as long as I can remember."

"..."

"Ever since I was a kid, every time I met Mahiru, all she ever talked about was you."

"So what? It drove you crazy with jealousy? You weren't actually in love with her, were you?"

Shinya smiled.

"Mahiru? I guess I did like her, a little. But I don't think I was ever crazy in love with her."

"Hmph…"

"I was jealous of you, though."

"Huh? What do you mean?"

"I kept imagining what you'd be like. I imagined fighting you if you ever showed up in person, just to see which one of us was stronger. Sometimes I'd imagine what you'd look like. That sort of thing."

Guren recalled the day he and Shinya had met.

It was the first day of school. Shinya had attacked him out of the blue.

Of course, there was no way of knowing if what Shinya was saying now was true, but Guren had the feeling that at least part of his story could be trusted.

If they were living in a world where words like "trust" actually carried any weight, that is.

Guren picked up the scrap of paper that Shinya had placed on his desk. He slipped it into his pocket, careful not to smudge Shinya's handwriting.

Noticing how careful Guren was to preserve his handwriting, Shinya laughed.

"Cagey as always."

"What can I say? I'm just a loser, born and bred. I've always got to watch out for who's going to kick me next."

Shinya had a dissatisfied look on his face as he stared at Guren.

"Sometimes you sound like a sniveling dog… I can just imagine what Mahiru would think if she heard you say something like that. I wonder what it is she sees in you."

"Maybe I'm the one who has the friendly face," quipped Guren.

Shinya rolled his eyes at him and chuckled.

"Heh...heheh..."

Guren turned his eyes back out the window.

The courtyard continued to bake under the blazing sun.

It was summer.

The very heart of summer.

If the world was going to end at Christmas, that made this their last summer ever.

◆

After the last class of the day they had homeroom. As soon as it was over, Guren's phone rang.

The name on the screen was Kureto Hiragi's.

Kureto was in the running to be the next leader of the Hiragi Clan. He was also president of the student council. No one at the school was powerful enough to go up against him.

Guren pressed the talk button and placed the phone to his ear.

"What?"

"Hmph. You should answer, 'Thank you for your call, Lord Kureto. How may I serve you?'"

"I didn't know you expected your followers to grovel like that."

"Don't worry, I'm just joking."

"Jokes are supposed to be funny. I guess you're so used to being kissed up to that it's rotted your brain."

"Ha! Are you trying to get yourself killed?"

"If you wanna kill me then just go ahead and do it. There's nothing stopping you, after all."

"Hmph... I have to admit, I do like that attitude of yours."

"I'm not sure I know what you mean."

"Your manners are terrible, but you understand your position. You know you're no match for me."

"..."

Guren didn't reply. It was the truth. As things stood now, he was no match for them.

Not so much Kureto, but the Hiragis as a whole.

The Ichinose Clan was powerless against the Hiragi Clan. And the Order of the Imperial Moon was powerless against the Order of the Imperial Demons.

This wasn't some playground brawl. Even if Guren crossed swords with Kureto and came out the winner, such a victory would be entirely meaningless.

For instance, if Guren were in love with somebody, and one day Kureto suddenly decided to rape and impregnate her, there was really nothing on earth that Guren could do about it.

The situation between the two clans was the same as it had been five centuries ago. Not a thing had changed.

Mito and Norito were ready to leave. They sauntered over in Guren's direction.

Norito glanced at Guren. A smirk crossed his face.

"Ooh, look who's getting phone calls as soon as the bell rings. Who is it? Let me guess, your girlfriend?"

"What?!" Mito jerked her head up in surprise and glared at Guren.

Guren ignored her and continued his phone conversation.

"Well? What are you calling about?"

"Come to the student council office tomorrow during lunch."

"I'd rather not."

"Ha. Too bad you don't have a choice. I'll see you tomorrow."

"Tsk," Guren clicked his tongue in annoyance and hung up.

Shinya was still sitting at his desk. He stared up at Guren.

"Was that my brother?" he asked.

"You heard Norito. It was my girlfriend."

"Hold on a second!" cried Mito, still fuming. "With the way you've been slacking off during training, what makes you think you have time for a girlfriend?!"

Guren was starting to wonder if Mito had lost her mind.

He rolled his eyes at her and then sighed. Mito's cheeks flashed red as she continued to glare at him; it looked like steam was about to come out of her ears. Norito couldn't help but laugh.

Guren just picked up his bag and made to leave.

Mito angrily called after him. "What, you have to rush off as soon as your girlfriend calls? I never knew you were so whipped!"

Shinya began laughing as well.

"I'm pretty sure that phone call was from my brother, Kureto," he said.

"Huh? It... What? It was?"

"Are you headed to the student council office?" Shinya asked.

Guren shook his head.

"No. He told me to come tomorrow, during lunch."

"Wait a second!" screamed Mito, even louder than before. "Forget about being lazy. What were you thinking, talking to Lord Kureto that way on the phone?!"

"Man, give it a rest already."

"Don't tell me to give it a rest, I'll have you know!"

Mito continued to shout at Guren from behind as he left the room. He had a feeling that now that he was out in the hallway she would just start screaming louder, so he shut the door behind him.

Sayuri and Shigure were already waiting outside. They had been assigned to the classroom next to Guren's.

Sayuri smiled happily. Her face shone with anticipation as she watched Guren approach.

"Master Guren! How was class?"

"Those Hiragi scum didn't try anything today, did they?" added Shigure in an icy tone.

Moments ago he had been getting an earful from Mito about proper manners when speaking to "Lord Kureto." His own bodyguards, meanwhile, were standing there referring to the whole Hiragi Clan as "scum."

The contrast was almost enough to make Guren laugh out loud.

"Nothing much happened today," he said. "Just the same routine."

Sayuri scrunched her face up in worry.

"What do you mean, the same routine? Did someone throw another cola bottle at you?"

"If they did," said Shigure, narrowing her eyes, "we'll murder every last one of those Hiragi punks."

Shigure slipped a blade from the sleeve of her uniform into her palm. She meant what she said.

But Sayuri seemed to have other things on her mind and ignored this. "By the way, Master Guren," she said, raising her eyebrows, "what would you like for dinner today? I'll make anything you like, just name your pick…"

"Curry and rice."

"Again~?!"

Suddenly, the door slid open. Mito was about to enter the hallway when she noticed Shigure glowering menacingly at no one in particular.

"Oh wow, Shigure! You looked so scary just now. Is something wrong?"

"No, nothing in particular."

"This is perfect timing, though. Could you talk some sense into your master for me? Tell him how much his bad manners and attitude toward Lord Kureto are hurting his chances in life."

Shigure stared up at Mito coldly.

"I don't think there's any problem with Master Guren's attitude," the loyal bodyguard said.

"You shouldn't go easy on him just because you're one of his retainers…"

"I'm not interested in hearing someone from another clan complain about Master Guren's manners. Maybe you should consider keeping your opinions to yourself."

Mito didn't know what to say to that. She turned awkwardly toward Guren as if he might salvage the situation.

"What are you looking at me for?" Guren said.

Mito's cheeks flushed red again, for some reason.

"I-I was only trying to help you…"

"Well, no one asked for your help."

Norito suddenly poked his head out from behind Mito's back.

"Okay, folks! Enough ganging up on Mito! Don't tell me you forgot? Today we all get chummy-chummy and go hang out at Guren's place, so try to play nice!"

This was the first time the supposed host had heard of it. "Huh? What the hell are you talking about?" spat Guren.

Norito laughed.

"Hey, we're all teammates on Lord Kureto's squad, right?" he pushed his luck. "Don't you think it's about time we got to know each other a little better?"

"No, I don't. I don't think that at all."

"Exactly, I knew you'd agree! And what better way to get to know each other than to go hang out at your place!"

"Quit messing around! Didn't you hear what I just said?"

Shinya joined them in the hallway and butted in on their conversation.

"Hey, that does sound pretty fun. Count me in."

Guren shook his head in disgust and turned from them.

"You're both morons. I'm going home."

Guren began walking, his two bodyguards in tow.

Sayuri, however, kept casting furtive glances behind them as they went.

"All three of them are following us, aren't they?" asked Guren.

"Yes, sir."

Guren sighed.

"Don't tell me they're serious about this…"

Shigure glanced up at Guren.

"Would you like me to kill them, sir?" she said.

"How are you going to do that when you barely managed a draw fighting just Mito?"

"Well yes, that's true. But… Augh. I'm sorry, sir. If only I was stronger…"

"It's fine. I'm not really angry."

Guren thumped his hand on top of Shigure's head and stroked her hair lightly. As soon as he did so, she jerked her head in his direction and opened her eyes wide in surprise. Her face, usually expressionless, blushed ever so slightly.

Sayuri, meanwhile, nearly did a triple take.

"Auugh?! H-Hey?! What's the deal? What about me?! I want you to stroke my head, too, Master Guren!"

Shigure shoved Sayuri back perfunctorily.

"You had your turn. Master Guren stroked your hair after you confessed your love to him the other day. This time it's my turn."

"But… No fair! I want Master Guren to stroke my head too!"

"No."

"B-But…"

Despite their antics, Guren could tell from the pair's expressions that they understood what was going on.

Guren had slipped the scrap of paper he'd received earlier from Shinya behind Shigure's ear while stroking her hair. All the note contained was a time and place.

2:00 a.m.
The tennis courts
Hikarigaoka Park

It was where the meeting with the Brotherhood of a Thousand Nights was scheduled to take place. Obviously the words "Brotherhood of a Thousand Nights" weren't included anywhere on the note. If Guren was going to meet with the Thousand Nights, he needed to be ready first. He would need weapons and equipment. Those preparations would have to be made in secret. No one could find out.

"Joking aside," said Shigure, "I was planning on picking up our dry cleaning on the way home today. I need to split. What about you, Sayuri?"

"I have to go to the supermarket. Will…they all be coming over?"

Guren glanced behind them.

"Maybe," he said. "Those three are pretty pushy. I'm not sure they'll take no for an answer."

"I see. I'll pick up enough for everyone then, just in case."

Norito saddled up beside them.

"You mean I get to taste your home cooking, Sayuri?" he said. "This must be my lucky day…"

Sayuri turned toward Guren and smiled, giving Norito the cold shoulder.

"I'll go buy what we need to make curry and rice, just like you asked, Master Guren," she said. Spinning around on her heel, she hurried off together with Shigure.

"Man, you're one sneaky dog, Guren," teased Norito, standing next to Guren and watching them go. "What's the deal, picking two such cuties as your guards?"

Shinya joined them and said, "You could get some cute guards of your own if you really wanted, Norito."

"O-Oh, Lord Shinya… The truth is, my younger brother is the important one in our family. My parents don't have very high expectations for me…"

"But you're under Kureto's command now. That's gotta count for something…"

"Well yes, that's true. You should have seen how quickly everyone's attitude toward me changed back home. It kinda pissed me off, to be honest… And now my brother's acting prissy about it, too…"

The two continued to walk with Guren as they spoke.

"You two weren't serious about coming to my place, were you?" Guren asked.

Norito nodded emphatically.

"Of course we were! What's the problem?"

"Ohh, I get it," said Shinya, grinning. "You're worried we'll see all the porn you've got lying around."

Of course, it wouldn't really matter to Guren if there had been any. Porn mags aside, he was careful to leave nothing compromising in the apartment should the Hiragis decide to come and sniff around.

Guren wondered, however, what had suddenly given Norito the idea of coming over. Shinya was probably curious about that as well.

After all, they were thinking of meeting with the Thousand Nights.

Could it be that Kureto had realized something was up?

What if ordering Guren to come to the student council office tomorrow was just a ruse, and Kureto in fact already knew about their meeting tonight?

Guren decided to ask Norito point-blank.

"Norito... Did Kureto tell you to keep an eye on me or something?"

Shinya glanced at Guren. Indeed, Shinya seemed to have been wondering the same thing.

Norito, though, just shrugged his shoulders.

"No. Lord Kureto didn't tell me to do anything."

"Then why did you suddenly conjure up this idea of coming over to my place?"

"Why not? I mean, we're friends, aren't we?"

"Huh?"

"I mean, we're classmates. If this were a normal school, we'd be smack dab in the middle of summer vacation now."

"What's your point?"

"I just thought we should all hang out for once. Yeah?"

Guren shook his head, confused.

"I have no idea what you're talking about."

Norito laughed.

"You don't? Anyway, the truth is, my parents said something yesterday."

"Your parents? You mean they told you to make friends with the

Ichinose kid, now that Kureto Hiragi has taken an interest in him?"

Norito shook his head.

"The opposite, actually. They said you were just an Ichinose in the end, a degenerate and a traitor. And that you'd show your true colors before too long. They told me not to get too close."

Secretly, Guren couldn't help but think that Norito's parents sounded pretty perceptive. But apparently Norito meant to defy their wishes.

"You should listen to your parents. You don't want to be a delinquent."

"What's wrong with being a delinquent?"

"What, you're a rebellious teenager now?"

"Haha! Maybe. Why don't we steal a motorcycle and go on a joyride? Make it a summer to remember?"

"Get lost."

"Haha!"

"Do you have a license?" Shinya asked Norito.

"No. How about you?"

"Me neither. I did learn to ride, in case I ever need to."

"Yeah, me too. Do you think it would be better to get a real license? There's actually this sweet bike I've been wanting."

The two continued walking with Guren as they conversed. It looked like they really were planning on coming over to his place, invited or not.

While Shinya and Norito went on about motorcycles, Mito joined Guren on his other side.

"Could I ask you something?" she said. It looked like she was planning on tagging along, too.

"What is it?"

"Just now, when you patted Shigure on the head…"

"Yeah?"

"Umm… Well…"

"What is it?"

Mito fidgeted, as if she was having trouble saying what she was thinking.

"Are the two of you…going out?"

"Huh?"

"I mean, unless you're always that touchy with your bodyguards. Y-You don't go into their rooms at night, do you?"

"What are you talking about?"

"They're your retainers, so they can't say no. A-And that's terrible. I can't believe you would do something like—"

"Man, what is wrong with you?"

Guren sighed, tuning her out.

He wasn't sure what had gotten into everyone today. They were talking about stupid things and acting out like kids from some normal high school. Guren wasn't even sure what it meant to "hang out with friends." Once they all got to his place, what were they going to do?

Play cards?

"What did I do to deserve this…" he muttered.

The four exited the school building.

It was still sweltering outside.

There were students in the schoolyard, training. Which was typical. After the Thousand Nights' attack, their numbers had dwindled, but no one was taking any time off. First Shibuya wasn't that type of school.

The Imperial Demons were keeping a lid on things. Except for a few higher-ups, no one actually knew they were at war with the Thousand Nights.

Nevertheless, the first skirmishes had already begun. There was fighting going on between field offices, not just in Japan, but in countries around the world.

As the Imperial Demons' headquarters, Shibuya still had to be one of the most peaceful locations worldwide.

Not even the Thousand Nights could mount a direct attack on Shibuya that easily.

The attack on the school had been an exception, of course. They'd had inside help for that.

As Guren stared at the schoolyard, his mind drifted to thoughts of Mahiru. She was his childhood friend, and she had stained this very schoolyard crimson with the blood of their classmates.

Noticing Guren's gaze, Mito said, "Hard to believe how quickly time passes, huh?"

Guren wondered if she was remembering the same images he was. Of the schoolyard. Awash in blood and bodies.

"It really is," he said.

Guren had made almost no progress yet. Time seemed to keep rushing past him while he continued to stand still.

"We've known each other for such a short time, but already you've saved my life twice," Mito said.

"It was just coincidence."

Mito smiled awkwardly and glanced at Guren. "Was it just coincidence that you got so beat up you wound up in a coma for a month?"

"I guess I'm clumsy that way. Besides, I needed to catch up on my sleep."

"You always take everything so lightly. But Guren?" Reaching at his back and grabbing his shirt, she said, "I really am grateful... I want to repay you."

"Repay? What do you mean?"

"Well...I could help support you while you earn more recognition from Lord Kureto and rise up in the Imperial Demons' ranks."

Thanks but no thanks, thought Guren. He kept the sentiment to himself, though.

"I mean...given the Ichinose Clan's current standing, there's no way my father would ever permit anything more..."

"Huh?"

"Nothing. Just thinking out loud."

Mito took a step away from Guren. She seemed a little flustered, but Guren wasn't sure why.

He just couldn't figure out what was going on inside her head.

Or in Norito's, for that matter.

Why were they both so interested now in hanging out with the Ichinose loser?

Back in Aichi Prefecture he had initiated research into forbidden magic. If the Hiragis caught wind of it the punishment would be swift. But for some reason these two trusted him as if it were the most natural thing in the world.

Were they his comrades? His friends? Earn recognition from Kureto? In any case, it seemed pretty foolish.

He was a degenerate and a traitor, just like Norito's parents had said. It would be safer for them if they kept their distance.

Instead, though, they were trying to be his friend. Just because they were in the same squad under Kureto's command, they wanted to get to know each other better. Norito and Mito didn't seem to suspect Guren in the slightest. They were oblivious, just two privileged kids from the top clans.

"..."

Guren stared at the two laughing together and wondered. Would he be able to kill them when the time came?

They were enemies, after all. Enemies of the Ichinose Clan. Sooner or later, he would have to get rid of them. But would he be up to it when the time came?

He hadn't been in Ueno. He should have killed them then, but he hadn't. He still wasn't sure if he'd made the right decision. It wasn't a matter of right and wrong, or what he believed in. It was what he should have done, but he hadn't been up to it.

I just couldn't...

"..."

The words echoed in Guren's head. He remembered what Kureto had said to him earlier on the phone.

Your manners are terrible, but you understand your position. You know you're no match for me...

Was that the truth?

Did all his ambitions boil down to empty posturing? If something ever happened—for instance, if Sayuri and Shigure were taken hostage—would he just crumble and fold?

Maybe he was a coward. The type who chickened out in the end, shying away from killing even the likes of Mito and Norito.

If so, it would be better if he just abandoned his ambitions up front. After all, he had already begun dragging his Ichinose Clan allies into the fight.

A war was starting.

Had already started.

Norito, though, didn't seem to have a care in the world.

"Hey, Guren," the guy said, smiling, "is your place far?"

"If I said yes, would you go home?"

"Nope."

Guren sighed. Feeling a little tired already, he answered, "No, it's not too far…"

"We're live, on scene! As you can see, efforts by firefighters have all been in vain, and the fire continues to rage on unchecked!"

A reporter on TV was shouting in an excited flurry. Apparently, some apartment building somewhere had gone up in flames and the responders hadn't been able to put them out yet.

Aerial shots, taken from a helicopter, filled the screen. The six o'clock title call played, and the image transitioned to the studio, where a female newscaster bowed toward the screen. There was a grave expression on her face.

The six o'clock news had just begun.

Which meant it was evening.

And yet, for some reason…

"Check!" shouted Shinya.

They were sitting in the living room of Guren's apartment. A miniature shogi—or Japanese chess—board, which they'd bought at the convenience store, was set in front of Shinya. Across from him, on the other side of the board, sat Mito.

"Hmm… Hmmm… Hold on, just let me think for a moment!"

She sat with her arms crossed. A look of panic appeared on her face as she tried to figure out what move to make next.

Norito was sitting on the sofa, drinking a cola. He was counting down the time.

"Better make it quick," he said. "I'm keeping track, and you don't have much left."

"I know already, just shut up!"

"Let's see, you've got…"

"I said shut up!"

The three seemed pretty into the game. Guren was sitting a little further away from them at the dining room table.

"Hey, when are you guys going to go home?" he said.

"Everyone, be quiet!" Mito shouted angrily.

None of them had actually known the rules for shogi. Whether that was because, with their kind of childhoods, they had never had time for games, or just because the opportunity to play had never come up, it was hard to say. Either way, Guren didn't see the point of buying a game they didn't even know how to play. But Norito had picked it out and looked up the rules online. As a result, they had all wound up playing a shogi tournament against each other.

The first match was Norito vs. Guren. Guren lost quickly.

The second match was Shinya vs. Mito. The match was still in progress and Mito was struggling.

Shinya began humming.

"Hmm hm hmm… If I were you I'd just give up…"

"J-Just, hold on a second, Lord Shinya."

"I'll wait as long as you like. How many seconds left, again?"

"Forty," said Norito.

"Augghhh…" groaned Mito.

Her pupils flared in concentration. She was really invested in the game. Guren could understand how she felt.

Once they got started, shogi turned out to be more interesting than he'd expected. You had to anticipate your opponent's next several moves and build a plan in advance. They were all beginners, so none of them knew any theory behind the game. They just had to throw themselves in and figure it out as they went along.

During his own match, Guren had racked his brain to learn how to lose as quickly as possible without letting Norito catch on that he was doing it on purpose. Apparently Guren had succeeded. Norito had been practically through the roof when he'd won. Mito had felt compelled to console Guren.

He had a feeling, though, that Shinya might have noticed he had lost on purpose.

Playing games was a stupid waste of time. He just wanted to end it as quickly as possible so that he could get them all out of his hair. But Shinya and Mito's match was dragging on much longer than he had hoped.

Glancing over his shoulder at Guren, Shinya flashed a mischievous expression.

"…"

Judging from that look, Guren had guessed right. Shinya knew exactly why Guren had lost.

"Jackass," Guren muttered under his breath.

Shinya grinned. "I didn't hear what you just said, but I'm pretty sure I got the sentiment."

"Twenty seconds left," said Norito.

"Would someone turn off the TV please?!" wailed Mito. "I can't concentrate!"

Norito glanced toward the television.

"Man, that fire's really going though, isn't it?" he said.

Images of the blaze continued to fill the screen. The reporter on the scene was shouting something. A crowd of onlookers stared up at the building, which by this point was just a hunk of concrete spewing flames.

Suddenly, a lone woman broke free from the crowd and came rushing forward.

She looked to be about twenty-five.

"Yuu! Yuichiro!" she cried.

Apparently her child had been left inside the apartment. One of the firefighters moved forward to stop her.

"Ma'am! Calm down! Leave this to us!"

"Let me go! Yuu! Yuu's in there!"

"Hey! Point the camera this way! Get this on film!!"

The camera zoomed in, and the mother's face showed up on the screen. She was a pretty woman with black hair, but right now her face was twisted up, and her hair was in disarray.

Norito fell silent, mid-count. Mito stared at the screen as well. They were all transfixed by what they saw.

The firefighter began shouting.

"Somebody, give me a hand! She's got some kind of crazy strength... Please, calm down!"

"Yuu! Yuichiro!"

The woman was holding something in her hand. The camera was shaking too much to tell what it was, but she was trying to lift it up.

"Ma'am, calm down..."

The woman suddenly swung her arm and punched the firefighter square in the jaw.

"Ngh... What the hell are you doing?!"

The firefighter grabbed her arm. There was a brief glimpse of the object in her hand. Was it a lighter? The firefighter hadn't noticed. No one else on site did, either.

The woman began screaming.

"Don't put out the fire! He's a demon! That boy is a demon! I have to kill him! I have to kill him today! Aiiieeeeeee!!"

She raised her left hand into the air. There was a plastic bottle in that hand. Some sort of liquid poured from the bottle's mouth onto the woman's head.

"It's gasoline!" hollered the firefighter. "She's got gasoline!"

The woman began flicking a lighter in her other hand, but the spark didn't catch. One of the fighters reared up, just in time, and punched the woman in the face, knocking her to the ground.

Several firefighters tackled the woman and held her down.

Still she continued to scream.

"He's a demon! I have to kill him! I have to kill him!!"

A man in a hooded sweatshirt suddenly came walking toward the screen. The camera momentarily caught his face.

Guren recognized the man.

It was Saito.

The man from the Brotherhood of a Thousand Nights.

He was the man who had attacked First Shibuya High School, together with Mahiru. That meant that whatever was going on there, the Thousand Nights was wrapped up in it somehow. It also meant that it had been an accident. If the Thousand Nights had known what was going to happen in advance, they would have made sure that no television cameras were around to capture it. They probably would have covered up the fact that a fire had happened at all.

The TV screen suddenly went black. The visuals immediately switched back to the studio. The female anchor was caught off guard and quickly tried to find something to say.

—*A truly shocking scene.*

—*Chaos at the scene.*

—*We'll bring you more, as soon as the story is updated.*

Et cetera, et cetera.

But Guren knew the story would never come on again. Not unless they ran something fake instead.

Mito spoke.

"What do you think all that was about?"

As far as Guren knew, Mito and Norito had never seen Saito's face. They probably didn't realize that the Thousand Nights was involved in whatever was happening.

Shinya, of course, had noticed. More importantly, the Imperial Demons had probably noticed as well.

Surely they were already gathering intelligence behind the scenes.

Chances were the Imperial Demons were already working overtime to investigate what the Thousand Nights were up to. Just like they had done with the incident in Ueno. Maybe Guren and the others were about to be summoned by Kureto again.

"Something about that kinda creeped me out," Norito said.

"Anyway, I forgot to keep counting. Are you still thinking, Mito?"

Mito shook her head.

"No, I guess you win, Lord Shinya. By the way, Guren, before we start the next match…"

"Yeah?"

"I'm getting kind of hungry."

"Go home."

Sayuri and Shigure still hadn't gotten back. It looked like the preparations for tonight were taking longer than Guren had anticipated. After what had just happened, though, it was possible that the meeting with the Thousand Nights would be called off entirely.

On the other hand, as long as the Imperial Demons were distracted by the incident, it might actually be easier for them to meet up.

Was it better to go, or to call the whole thing off?

Shinya stood up.

"All right, I guess it's about time we packed it in. There's something I've got to do, anyways."

Finally. Shinya probably wanted to look into the incident himself a little, too. That made sense. If they were going to meet with the Thousand Nights later, they couldn't go in clueless.

Once Shinya stood up to go, Mito and Norito fell in line without ado.

"Whatever you say, Lord Shinya."

"Let's have a rematch next time," Mito said, standing up. "Hopefully I'll be better prepared."

She was still talking about shogi. Shinya grinned at her.

"You got it," he said. "This was really fun. We should all play again some time."

They began leaving. Shinya had left his phone on the floor. Guren glanced at it out of the corner of his eye but didn't say anything.

"I wish we'd had a chance to talk with Shigure and Sayuri, too. We're in the same squad together, after all," Mito regretted once they were at the front door.

"Yeah, I really wanted to try some of Sayuri's home cooking," added Norito. "I guess there's always next time."

"You're not planning on coming here again, are you?"

"Is that a problem? We could all go to my place next time, instead."

Guren just gestured toward the door, ushering them out. He obviously wasn't interested in prolonging their conversation.

"All right then, it's been fun," said Shinya, opening the door.

Shinya, Mito, and Norito finally left the apartment.

Guren locked the door behind them. He went back to the living room, picked up Shinya's phone, and glanced at the screen. The phone wasn't locked. It was opened to email, and something was written in the message field:

—Oi! Who said you could look at other people's phones, Guren? You creep! LOL

"Don't be LOL-ing me," Guren muttered with a sigh.

He closed the mail screen and checked to see if there was anything else of interest on the phone, but it was empty.

The phone was a dummy.

Guren walked back toward the front hallway.

Just as he arrived, someone knocked on the door. Guren turned the lock and opened the door. Shinya was standing there with a grin on his face.

"I forgot my phone," he said.

Guren held it up in his right hand.

"Did you peek?"

"Of course. I'm a creep, after all."

"Haha!"

"You forgot your phone on purpose, didn't you?"

"Yep. And you lost at shogi on purpose, didn't you?"

"I don't know what you're talking about."

"You don't? How about next time we play each other? Then we can settle once and for all which of us is the real mastermind."

"I'm not interested."

"Uh-uh, don't try to worm your way out of it."

"For whose benefit would we be trying to prove ourselves?"

"Hmm… In our case, I guess it would be Mahiru."

"Now I'm even less interested."

"Is that so?" said Shinya, laughing. "Anyway…"

Shinya glanced past Guren's shoulder, meaningfully. The TV set was still audible in the background. Obviously he was thinking of what they had just witnessed a moment ago, when Saito's face had flashed on the screen.

Guren figured Shinya had forgotten his phone on purpose so he could come back and discuss things with Guren. Specifically, whether or not they should go meet with the Thousand Nights later.

"All right, Guren, you're the tactical mastermind," Shinya said. "What do you think we should do?"

"I don't think we should go meet them," answered Guren. "It's too dangerous right now."

"Hmm. You might be right."

"We should look into what caused that fire. We need to figure out what's happening and get a grasp on the situation before we make our next move."

"I see… By the way, Guren?"

"Yeah?"

"You're gonna have trouble keeping your friends if all your tactics involve lying to them. You were actually planning on going and meeting with the Thousand Nights on your own, weren't you?"

Guren nodded. He didn't try to deny it. "You're not my friend," he said.

"Haha. You are going to meet with them, then."

What other choice did Guren have?

They needed more information. But they wouldn't make any progress if they stopped to investigate first. Maybe they could inch forward bit by bit if they took things slow, but they simply didn't have the time for that.

The war between the Imperial Demons and the Thousands Nights was accelerating, day by day.

And some act of terrorism dire enough to bring the world to an end might occur in December.

If they were too afraid to take risks, then everything would be over before they even played their hands.

Either that, or they'd be crushed before they managed to maneuver themselves into a better position.

They needed to make a move.

The Thousand Nights said they were going to share what they knew about cursed gear and the chimera with the strange, unidentifiable DNA—genetic material that was supposedly from the enigmatic Four Horsemen of the Apocalypse.

The reason they were willing to share that information now was that Mahiru had betrayed them. She had disappeared, taking the chimera with her.

The chimera was an extremely valuable research specimen for the Thousand Nights and they wanted it back. Hence they were willing to share what they knew, on the condition that Guren and Shinya also shared any information they might have on Mahiru.

That also meant that the Thousand Nights were still unaware that a piece of the chimera's body was in Guren's possession. He had to gain information while he still had the chance. He needed to know what that thing was.

After all, the chimera had aroused even the attention of the vampires, who usually displayed little interest in humans and almost never meddled in their affairs. But the Thousand Nights, Mahiru, and the vampires were all fighting over this creature.

If they could just find a place to start, researching the chimera might uncover something truly powerful. However…

Guren glanced toward Shinya.

They had split the chimera sample into two smaller pieces. Both he and Shinya were holding onto one half.

Guren's half had been sent to Aichi Prefecture where it was currently being studied by Imperial Moon researchers. So far, though, their analysis seemed to be going nowhere.

Guren had no idea what Shinya had done with the other piece.

"About that research…" said Guren, broaching the subject.

Shinya shook his head. "You're going to have to take care of it. I don't even have my own lab, so there's no way for me to look into it on my side."

Guren wondered whether he was telling the truth.

"You know," said Shinya, a dissatisfied look on his face, "we don't have many allies, and our opponents are a lot more powerful than us. Do we really have to keep playing games?"

"The research hasn't gone anywhere yet," Guren confessed. "I've kept it to a small group of people that I trust, to make sure what we're doing doesn't get leaked. So maybe that's why. But it doesn't seem like they have any idea what it is yet. Which is exactly why…"

"…we need to meet with the Thousand Nights tonight?"

Guren nodded. They were interrupted, however, before they could speak any further.

"Lord Shinya, did you find your phone?"

It was Mito.

She and Norito appeared outside the door.

"I found it," said Shinya, turning around. "It looks like it slipped underneath the sofa."

Norito smiled.

"Lucky you found it," he said.

Guren thrust his hand out, passing the phone to Shinya.

"Fine, all of you can go home now."

"Roger that! Let's do this again next—"

Guren slammed the door without waiting for Shinya to finish his sentence. He went back to the living room.

The time was 6:17 p.m.

The news was still playing, but no matter which channel Guren turned to, no one was covering the fire. The Thousand Nights had already gotten to the media.

Guren thought back to the woman—the mother—he had seen on the screen moments ago. Out of her head, she had been dousing herself in gasoline.

She had screamed about needing to kill the demon.

"The demon..." muttered Guren.

What in all hell had she been talking about?

It was possible the woman was just crazy, and the things she had been shouting had been meaningless.

December.

Christmas. The end of the world.

A virus.

The angel of the apocalypse.

The Four Horsemen.

What was it with all the religious terms?

Were they actually alluding to something biblical, or was it just code for some sort of biological weapon or terrorism?

A commercial began playing. Some famous woman was stuffing fried chicken into her face like it was the most delicious thing she'd ever tasted.

Guren stared absently at the screen for a few seconds, then glanced down at the shogi set that had been left on the floor in front of the TV.

Shogi is nice and easy, Guren thought. The only opponent you had to worry about was the one right there in front of your face.

All you had to do was put together a strategy to deal with that one opponent. Plus, the opponent had the exact same amount of tactical strength that you did.

The real world wasn't so easy.

In the real world, enemies were usually a lot more numerous or powerful than you. And more often than not, there was more than one group conspiring against you.

In the real world you had to form alliances and choose your battles. You had to know when to double-cross and when to remain faithful.

A single mistake could prove fatal.

And once you made a move, there was no way to take it back.

"..."

Guren stared at the cheap shogi board. Unlike Western chess, in shogi you could replay pieces you took. He picked up one of the pawns that Mito had scored and placed it in front of Shinya's king.

Even after that move, however, Mito still lost. Shinya would be able to take Mito's king on his next turn.

According to the rules of shogi, at least, Mito lost.

But the real world wasn't shogi. Even if the king died, his organization would go on.

Guren pushed the pawn forward.

Killing Shinya's king.

"..."

Guren needed to find a way to kill the Thousand Nights' king.

He needed to find a way to kill the Imperial Demons' king.

It didn't really matter if he died, too, in the process. He was already prepared for that. The results would be worth it. But what would actually happen once he was gone?

Would his comrades survive him? What ambitions did he harbor that he hoped would remain even after he was gone?

What did he want to accomplish so badly that he was willing to stake his own life, and that of his friends, on doing so?

"..."

Guren reached down to pick up an empty cola bottle from where it had been left on the floor.

As he did so, he heard the front door open.

"I'm home!" cried Sayuri.

She came into the living room holding a shopping bag in each hand. When she saw Guren stooping over to pick up the empty bottle, she rushed over in a panic.

"Ahh, you shouldn't be cleaning up! Leave that sort of thing to us!"

She snatched the empty bottle from Guren's hand.

Shigure came into the living room after her.

"I'm back," she said, bowing.

She began cleaning up the potato chip bags scattered all over the dining room table.

Guren stared at the two girls.

"…"

What would it mean to him to have to carry on, Guren wondered, after they were tortured and killed?

Obviously it was too late to turn back now. Things had already been set into motion. They had embarked on research forbidden by the Hiragis.

Besides, if the world really was going to end in December, he couldn't just sit around twiddling his thumbs while he waited for the apocalypse to happen.

Nevertheless, Guren had to wonder…

"…"

What was he trying to protect?

What was most important to him?

Shigure glanced at Guren.

"I put it in the usual locker," she said.

Guren nodded. There was a rental locker they kept stocked with spell *fuda* and battle gear.

It also included many items of forbidden magic, all customized specifically for Guren's use and created via schools of enchantment unknown to the Hiragi Clan.

The locker was also where they kept things they couldn't leave lying around the apartment in case the Hiragi Clan ever came to check up on them.

"About tonight…" said Shigure.

"You're not coming. I'm doing this alone."

"But…"

"You'll just be in my way."

"Ah…"

Shigure fell silent. She looked remorseful.

"If I'm not back by morning," said Guren, staring at her, "then you two should return to Aichi Prefecture."

Shigure and Sayuri both glanced Guren's way. From the moment they had begun preparing his equipment, they must have been aware that he might die tonight.

If he did, it wouldn't pose any real problems for the Ichinose Clan. He wasn't their leader yet. If someone was going to risk his life, it might as well be him.

Sayuri stared at Guren for a moment, then forced herself to smile.

"I'm making chicken curry…" she said.

"Sounds good."

"I have to use instant today, though…"

"It's fine. As long as you make it I know it will be delicious."

Sayuri blushed and flashed Guren a happy smile. He had other things on his mind, though.

"Shigure," he said. "I'm going to change. Bring me some street clothes."

Shigure nodded.

"Yes, sir," she consented.

The taciturn follower disappeared down the hallway.

Sayuri, meanwhile, went to the kitchen and put on her apron.

Guren glanced at her for a moment before turning his eyes to the clock once more.

It was 6:30 p.m.

There were still seven and a half hours left until the meeting with the Thousand Nights.

"I guess I should try to get some sleep," he muttered.

He glanced at Sayuri, who was already moving briskly about the kitchen. He supposed it could wait until after they ate.

◆

1:30 a.m.

Nerima Ward, Tokyo.

The Thousand Nights had specified Hikarigaoka Park for their meeting. Directly adjacent to Hikarigaoka Station on the Toei Oedo subway line, it was huge.

If Guren entered from the station side, however, there was a chance he would be caught on the surveillance cameras. Instead he rode a motorcycle around to the park's west side where the groves and lawns were located. That way he could slip in among the shadows, shielded from sight by all the trees.

He parked along a footpath near the edge of the park, switched off the engine, and set down the kickstand. He pulled off his helmet and peered toward the park. It was dark inside. The surrounding trees blocked what light there was from the moon.

Guren hung his helmet on the bike's handlebar. He pulled the sports bag on his back around to his chest and reached inside.

He took out a pair of night-vision goggles. He would need them to see in the park. He also pulled out several *fuda*—paper talismans inscribed with spells—and slipped them into his sleeve. He shoved several more into his pockets before slipping his bag back onto his back. He shortened the straps so it wouldn't sway as he moved.

Just as Guren was getting off his bike, another large motorcycle pulled up nearby. It parked next to him.

The driver was Shinya.

Shinya turned off his engine, removed his helmet, and smiled.

"I should've figured you'd enter from this direction too… Judging from the map, it's the only good way in."

Shinya was right. Guren had checked the map, and this spot had clearly stood out as the best point of entry.

It was surrounded by trees and hidden from prying eyes.

The tennis courts where their meeting was scheduled to take place were located on the east side of the park. By approaching from the west they could scout out the area as they went and secure an escape path behind them.

"They'll probably be expecting us to come from this direction, though," Guren noted.

"That's true. By the way, do you have a motorbike license?"

"No."

"So you're driving without one. Where'd you get the bike?"

"I stole it."

"Then it's just like Norito said—taking a joyride on a stolen bike."

Guren laughed. "I guess we're just a bunch of rebellious teenagers after all."

He slipped on his night-vision goggles. The darkness took shape, appearing green through the lenses.

Next to him, Shinya got off his bike and chuckled.

"I don't know if creeping into a park with night-vision goggles is quite what Norito had in mind," he said. "You see anything good? Any couples making out in the dark?"

"It is summer, after all."

"What? Let me see?"

Ignoring him, Guren headed into the trees.

"Ah, hold on a second. I'm coming too."

Guren heard Shinya switch on his own night-vision goggles behind him, but didn't turn around. He was keeping an eye out for traps as he walked.

Behind him, Shinya's movements seemed well practiced. His footsteps barely made a sound. He was moving not only quietly and carefully, but also very quickly. He had probably undergone specialized training.

"We still have a little time until the meeting," whispered Shinya from behind. "Were you planning on getting there first and lying in wait?"

Guren shook his head. "No, I thought I'd check out the situation from a distance."

"That's a good idea. Those tennis courts are too out in the open. It's a bad spot for skulking."

That was probably why the Thousand Nights had chosen it for their meeting.

"Where are you going to set up?"

Guren checked his wristwatch. The time was 1:38 a.m. There were still twenty-two minutes until the meeting.

He stopped walking.

They were still in the groves, surrounded by trees. The meeting place was further ahead, past the open lawns. Once they stepped out, there would be nowhere left to take cover.

That left just one option...

"We should go up in those trees, there..."

"You mean so you can check out all the couples getting it on, don't you?"

"Sure."

"...You're killing the gag, Guren."

"Huh?"

"Never mind..."

Guren began preparing. First he pulled several *fuda* from his bag and pasted them onto the tree he was going to climb. He was setting a trap just in case they were ambushed. Once the *fuda* were in place, he climbed the tree and picked out a thick branch to perch on.

The tree next to him shook. Apparently Shinya had climbed that one. When Guren glanced his way, Shinya waved back and then pointed east, in the direction of the tennis courts.

"..."

Guren nodded and turned that way. It was late at night, but through his night-vision goggles the park appeared fairly bright. The stars overhead twinkled with unnatural luster and shone down on the trees below.

Guren turned up the magnification on his goggles and adjusted the focus for their target destination.

A footpath stretched out past the grassy lawns. A little farther along there was an area with several pieces of playground equipment, and past them a practice wall.

That was where the tennis courts were.

Eight people in suits were already standing there—and they obviously weren't there to make out. They were all men and appeared to be highly trained. The suits they wore were the same as the ones the soldiers from the Thousand Nights had been wearing when they'd attacked First Shibuya.

If the men in the tennis courts were as powerful as Saito, then they were a dangerous group indeed. If a fight were to break out, Guren and Shinya probably wouldn't make it back alive.

"..."

Guren checked his watch once more.

The time was 1:45 a.m.

Fifteen minutes left.

This was his last chance to decide whether to meet with them or return home.

Guren looked up from his watch and redirected his gaze toward the Thousand Nights soldiers.

Something was wrong. They were shouting. They closed ranks and fell into battle formation.

For a split second Guren froze, worried the men had noticed them. But the soldiers' panic seemed to be caused by something else.

All of a sudden, something came flying from the shadows. Whatever it was, it went straight for one of the suited men.

The man's counterattack was amazing. Chains immediately sprouted from his body. Guren was right. The men's bodies had been altered, just like Saito's. One of the chains went hurtling at the thing from the shadows.

But it easily dodged and grabbed the man by his neck. And then tore his head clean from his shoulders. In the next instant, it did the same thing to another of the men…and then another, and another.

One of the other blacksuits tried to run. The thing grabbed him by his hair and latched onto his neck. The man's body shook like a stiff doll, then went limp.

The thing was sucking out his blood.

"Not another vampire," Guren groaned.

Unlike the one he had met in Ueno, this vampire didn't appear to be a noble. You could tell from its clothing. But the way it moved, it clearly wasn't human, either. If it really was a vampire, then the men from the Thousand Nights were as good as dead.

Vampires were too powerful for humans. They were in a whole different league.

Fighting one off was hopeless, especially in the dark like they were.

"…"

The battle was over.

Almost as soon as it had started.

Indeed, the vampire had killed all of the soldiers from the Thousand Nights.

Guren stared at the tennis courts, transfixed. The wheels in his mind were spinning, trying to figure out what had happened.

A vampire had just killed the soldiers from the Thousand Nights. But why? What did it all mean? Vampires usually didn't take any interest in human affairs. They saw people as mere livestock and rarely cared about their food's squabbles.

So why was a vampire here, now? Why did vampires keep interfering?

What was going on?

The bloodsucker probably hadn't noticed them hiding in the trees. The distance between them was still pretty far. But if Guren and Shinya had gone straight to the meeting and not stopped to scout out the situation first, they'd be dead by now. A chill ran up Guren's spine.

"…"

Suddenly, the vampire turned their way.

A female.

A beautiful one with long flowing hair.

She was staring directly at them.

It couldn't be. There was no way she could see them from that distance.

The vampire's mouth opened in a grin. Her mouth was stained with blood. Guren could see fangs.

She fell into a crouch and began running toward them.

"Guren!!" Shinya shouted.

"I see her!"

Guren leapt from his tree. The goggles were blocking his peripheral vision so he tore them off and tossed them away.

And then he ran, as fast as he could.

Ducking and weaving through the trees, until finally he stumbled clear of the park.

He grabbed the motorcycle key from his pocket…

Then he leapt onto the bike, thrust the key into the ignition, and kicked up the stand as he turned the key.

And just as the engine sputtered to life, the vampire lunged out onto the street in front of him.

Guren gripped the accelerator and revved hard. The 1,000 cc engine screamed, and he lurched forward with his front wheel up in a wheelie. Like a bullet from a gun, he hit the vampire full force, intending to mangle her beneath his wheels…

But the vampire caught the bike easily by its front wheel. She smiled at Guren.

"Dammit!"

Her claw pierced the tire. There was a crunching sound as spokes were crushed in her grip.

Falling from the bike, Guren drew his katana from his waist in one fluid motion.

He swung wildly, but the vampire dodged his blade without difficulty. He'd never be able to hit her. She lifted up the heavy bike with one hand, high into the air, and tossed it straight at him.

There was nowhere to run.

He was going to die...

"Guren, give me your hand!"

It was Shinya.

Guren flung his arm out blindly in the direction of his voice and was yanked back hard.

Shinya, speeding past on his own bike, had caught Guren's arm. Dragged along behind, Guren kicked the ground several times and scrambled on, behind Shinya and the wrong way around.

The motorcycle the vampire threw went crashing into a taxi cruising down the opposite lane. The demolished car rolled over on its side in a heap.

It was chaos.

The vampire was still giving chase. Guren pulled several *fuda* from his bag and scattered them behind him.

The moment the *fuda* hit the ground they burst in staccato explosions. One caught the vampire's foot, and her leg burst into flames, but it regenerated as fast as it burned. She ran through the *fuda* heedlessly. Her clothes had caught fire, but she didn't seem to care. She wasn't even trying to put it out.

Shinya was concentrating on steering.

"Hey," Guren called out to him over his shoulder.

"Yeah?"

"I think she's gonna catch up to us."

"You're kidding! We're going almost fifty miles per hour..."

"Here she comes!"

As Guren yelled, the vampire launched herself into the air. She was leaping straight for them, but she wasn't as lightning-quick as she would have been if they were standing still. Guren and Shinya were speeding away in the opposite direction, as fast as 65 mph by now.

Shinya pulled the accelerator even harder. The vampire's outstretched hand approached them nonetheless.

If Guren could just ward off the first attack, they might still be able to get away. Once the vampire hit the ground again, she would have to make another jump. She'd probably lose some of her momentum when she did.

The bike, on the other hand, would accelerate further.

It was just one blow.

If he could just evade one blow.

"..."

Guren gripped his sword in his right hand. Reaching backward with his left hand and holding tight onto Shinya's shoulder, he took a deep breath, then exhaled forcefully.

The vampire stretched its arm out toward him.

Guren swung his blade at the creature's hand.

She tried to catch it, but Guren wasn't about to let her. He had to carry through with his swing without letting the creature's claws get in the way. A strike that she mustn't grab.

If he failed, they were dead.

If she caught the blade, they were dead.

He only had once chance…

"Eat metal!" he yelled.

He arced the blade down hard. The vampire reached for it with her claws…and missed.

Guren's swing severed the vampire's arm from her body.

"I got her! Go, Shinya! Go!"

"I'm going! I'm going!"

The vampire glanced down at her severed arm with a blasé expression. The injury barely seemed to bother her.

But she stopped chasing them.

She landed back on the ground and watched them go.

The bike shot away at breakneck speed. They were probably going at least ninety at this point. If they slowed down now, the vampire might resume her pursuit.

Swiftly disappearing from her line of sight would make her give up. But with how fast they were going, they couldn't even turn safely. Crashing at that speed meant certain death.

Guren was still holding onto Shinya's shoulder. He swiveled around, facing forward. As he turned he caught a glimpse of a red traffic light, but they sped into the intersection.

A truck slid out in front of them to make a right turn.

A taxi was already blocking the other lane.

Shinya veered to the side, trying to slip through the gap between the two.

"Hold on, Guren!" he shouted.

"Dammit, this isn't our lucky day!"

Guren hugged Shinya's body with his left arm.

The bike's side mirror hit the truck and broke off. A piece of it came flying toward Guren's face. Instinctively, he brought the pommel of his sword up to protect his eyes. The piece still struck him on the face, and Guren felt his skin slice open.

They were safe, though. The fight was over.

"…"

The vampire wasn't chasing them.

The streets were almost empty, given the hour, and they could keep driving at a daredevil speed. But the vampire probably couldn't catch up to them now. Which meant they needed to mind a different sort of risk…

"Hey, Shinya, slow down!" warned Guren. "We don't wanna get noticed by the cops, do we."

"What about the vampire?" asked Shinya.

"I think she's gone."

"What, really? All right!"

"Just slow down already!"

Shinya laughed. "We've got no helmets on and you're holding a katana… I think they'd arrest us even if we weren't speeding. I bet we look like old-school biker-gang hoodlums!"

Guren glanced at the sword in his hand and laughed as well. "You've got a point… But after all the trouble we went through to get away, I don't think I wanna get killed by your crappy steering."

"Hey, I've never been in a single accident, you know."

"You don't even have a license!"

"Does that really matter at this point? Anyway, if I slow down now we're going to stick out like a sore thumb. Riding double, with no helmets… Two guys, for that matter."

"Whatever, just slow down."

"Fine, fine."

Shinya began to decelerate. He turned off into a dark one-way alley and parked the bike.

"Are you sure she's not chasing us?"

Guren nodded. "I think so."

"You think so or you know so?"

"You wanna go back and check?"

"Thanks, but no thanks. By the way, Guren…"

"Yeah?"

"You're hurt," he said, gesturing toward Guren's forehead. "Did the vampire do that?"

"No," Guren replied, getting off the bike, "that was from your crappy steering. It was a sneak attack from the side mirror."

"Haha. It's your own fault for not moving out of the way."

Guren let that pass and touched the cut on his brow. There was a lot of blood. Cursed blood. When Mitsuki had injected that same blood into herself, her arm had transformed into a monster that sprouted legs and hopped around the room.

Guren didn't know how much blood a person needed to swallow or inject before succumbing to the curse. Either way, coming into contact with his blood was dangerous.

"Here, let me bandage that…" offered Shinya.

"It's fine. I'll take care of it myself."

"But the cut's on your forehead. You can't even see it."

Ignoring him, Guren held a piece of gauze against the wound.

"Quit being such a tough guy. If you don't bandage it properly it'll scar."

"Will it? Your concern is appreciated."

"No man's gonna wanna marry you if you've got scars all over your face."

"Haha, very funny. Just shut up, already."

"Hah…"

Shinya laughed for a second, and then took a deep breath. He sighed slowly, the tension finally unwinding from his body.

Then he said, "That was a pretty close call, though, wasn't it? What do you think that was all about? Why would a vampire show up?"

"How should I know?"

"Well, it killed all of the men from the Thousand Nights, in any case."

Guren checked his wristwatch.

It was finally 2:00 a.m. The time they were originally supposed to meet the men.

They couldn't go back to Hikarigaoka Park to meet them now. The men the Thousand Nights had sent were all dead. And the vampire might be lurking there.

The fact that the two of them were still alive was nothing short of a miracle.

They had just gotten lucky.

If it weren't for a string of coincidences, they wouldn't be standing there now.

Vampires were just too powerful for humans to take on. If the vampires ever got it into their heads to wipe out mankind, they could do so in a heartbeat.

For now, however, they tolerated humanity. To the vampires, people were no more than braying cattle. It didn't matter to them whether there were a few more or less in the world.

That was why vampires generally didn't interfere in human affairs. It was extremely rare for anyone to even catch a glimpse of them.

"..."

Lately, however, Guren found himself crossing paths with them on a regular basis. Apparently, they were none too happy with the forbidden research the Thousand Nights were getting up to.

Guren recalled what Ferid—the vampire noble that had traded blows with Mahiru—had said about the chimera.

This is frightening stuff, you know. I have no idea what you humans were thinking, meddling in this sort of thing. If you keep playing with forbidden magic like this you'll bring the whole world crashing down on our heads.

The chimera was dark magic, capable of bringing the whole world to an end.

In other words, the secret behind whatever forbidden magic the Thousand Nights were hiding must lie in the piece of chimera in Guren's possession.

But that secret was also what the vampires were so upset about.

They weren't going to stand idly by while mankind let their greed get the better of them and destroyed the world.

"It won't matter how big the Thousand Nights are," said Shinya, apparently thinking the same thing. "If they run afoul of the vampires they'll be crushed."

That was definitely a possibility. However, Guren wondered...

"You really think the Thousand Nights would ever openly oppose the vampires? They know they have no chance of defeating them."

If the vampires ordered the Thousand Nights to call off their research, then the Thousand Nights' only choice would be to comply.

"Then what do you suppose is going on?" asked Shinya. "Why do all these vampires keep butting in?"

Guren didn't know. Right now, that seemed to be true of most things.

The motives of all the different groups were so tangled up together that it was impossible to pick out the truth.

He did know one thing, though...

"..."

Shinya glanced at Guren, who suspected that they were both thinking the same thing. Someone behind the scenes was pulling all the strings. Throwing the Thousand Nights and the Imperial Demons into chaos. And they both knew who.

"..."

Mahiru Hiragi. She was behind everything.

The woman behind the curtain, calling all the shots.

There was no way of knowing whether she'd instigated the massacre that had taken place just moments ago, but still...

"If we keep sitting around doing nothing, this whole thing is gonna play out without us," Shinya lamented with a sigh.

Guren knew how he felt. Mahiru was so far in the lead, it was hard not to get discouraged by the sight of her running in the distance.

Guren removed the gauze from his wound. The bleeding had stopped. Luckily, the cut was close to his hairline. If he pushed his bangs forward, he would be able to hide it.

He put the bloody piece of gauze into his bag and began walking away.

"Hey, where are you going?" Shinya said.

"Home," answered Guren.

"You're gonna walk?"

"How else are we going back? You're not planning on riding around in the open with no helmet on, are you?"

"Well, no..."

Shinya hopped off the bike, abandoning it where it was parked. Apparently he, too, had stolen his ride.

"But we're all the way in Nerima Ward. It's gotta be a whole dozen miles back to Shibuya."

"What's your point?"

"Maybe we should steal some bicycles. I guess we should take separate routes back, though, huh?"

"Obviously."

"I guess this is where we split up, then."

"Yeah," Guren said without turning around.

"I'll see you tomorrow at school."

"Sure."

"Good night!"

Guren stopped walking. He turned around for a moment to stare at Shinya, who was waving goodbye.

"Shinya?" he said.

"Yeah?"

"..."

"What is it?"

"You saved me today," Guren said at last. "If you weren't there, I'd have been a goner for sure."

A faint look of surprise appeared on Shinya's face. "Huh? It's not like you to say thank you. But hey, if you think you owe me something—"

"I don't," Guren cut him off. "If I hadn't been there, you'd have been a goner too."

"Well yeah, I guess that's true…"

There had been no call, though, for Shinya to save Guren. He had taken a big risk coming in on his bike to grab Guren's hand like that while the vampire was attacking. The smart choice would have been to just ride away and leave Guren behind.

But Shinya hadn't done that.

Guren wasn't sure how much that meant, but it did mean something.

"I guess I can trust you a little after all…" he admitted.

Shinya smirked. "Just a little?"

"Yeah, just a little."

"Well, thanks. Is that all?"

"Yep."

"I'll see you tomorrow, then."

"See you tomorrow."

And with that, Guren began walking in the direction of Shibuya.

◆

It was after 3:00 a.m. by the time Guren got home.

Shigure and Sayuri were still awake.

"Master Guren!" they both cried, rushing toward him as he came through the door.

They looked like they were about to cry.

"Why are you two in your pajamas?" Guren asked, staring at them. "I told you to go back to Aichi if I wasn't back by morning—"

"We knew you'd come back alive," Shigure interrupted him.

"I gave you a direct order—" Guren tried to remind her.

Sayuri cut in next, staring up into his face and bursting into tears. "Ahh, Master Guren! Why are you covered in blood?!"

She ran with her arms out as if to cradle him.

Catching them, however, Guren held her back.

"Stay away... My blood is infected."

"I don't care!"

"Well, start caring! Shigure, ready a bath. I need to wash all this blood off."

Shigure didn't move. Tears began to well up in her eyes, too.

"Uh... Uhhh... Forgive us... If we were only stronger, we could've been there for you..."

When she saw Shigure's tears, Sayuri began bawling even harder.

"If you didn't come back, I don't know what we would have done... We were so worried. Why are we so weak? We should've been there to help you..."

Guren was still standing in the front hallway. He let out a tired sigh.

"Can't this wait until another time?"

"You're out there risking your life," Shigure insisted. "At the least,

we should be at your side. I hate staying at home waiting like this. Maybe we're too weak to help, but if nothing else, we could take a bullet for you. I…"

Shigure's voice trembled, and she fell silent. It was unusual to see her cry.

They'd been worried for real.

Wailing with tears in their eyes, they rushed forward and hugged Guren.

"What's wrong with you two? I told you to stay back!"

But they didn't care. They wrapped their arms around Guren, holding him tight. As they did so they came into contact with Guren's blood. Hopefully it had dried.

Nothing happened. Apparently it wasn't enough to infect them. Maybe the demon couldn't spread through contact alone. Or maybe there just wasn't enough blood. Were there certain conditions that had to be met for the demon's curse to spread?

"You two are going to get a talking-to later," growled Guren. "I told you to stay back but you disobeyed me. For now, you're going to have to return to Aichi, immediately, to get checked out."

"W-Will you come with us, Master Guren?" asked Sayuri, staring up into his face.

"No. I'm staying here."

"But we have to stay by your side, Master Guren…" pleaded Shigure.

"You need to follow my orders, that's what you need to do."

"No, I want to stay here."

"Me too. I want to stay with you!"

"You two are making me angry."

"Wahhh!"

They scrunched their faces up. Tears formed in their eyes again.

"…"

As Guren stared down into their faces, he couldn't help but be thankful that he hadn't taken them with him.

They would both be dead now. Guren was certain of it.

He began to think. About what it would mean to him if his friends died.

About his own weakness.

Mahiru was prepared. To abandon anyone, anytime. To watch her friends and comrades die.

Guren recalled what Shinya had once said.

You could never be like Mahiru, Guren... But I don't think that's a weakness. After all, if you were willing to make the same choice that she made, we wouldn't be trying to save her in the first place. Would we now?

Was Shinya right?

Or was that just the kind of excuse that weak people made for themselves?

Sayuri and Shigure wouldn't hesitate to give up their lives if it was for Guren's sake.

But was that strength, or weakness?

Was risking one's life, not for some greater goal or ambition, but for the sake of another, a sign of weakness or strength?

"Hey? How long are you two going to hang onto me like this? I'm tired. I just want to take a bath and go to sleep."

His two bodyguards exchanged glances. For some reason, Sayuri blushed.

"I-If you need someone to scrub your back..." she said.

"Be quiet," shushed Guren.

By the time Guren got out of the bath it was already past four.

It was hard to believe, but school was going to begin in just a few hours. To make matters worse, he had to go to Kureto's office that day during lunch. That meant he couldn't simply sleep in instead.

"Just my luck..." muttered Guren.

He threw himself down onto his bed with a groan. Somehow, though, he couldn't seem to fall asleep.

It was morning.

Guren was at First Shibuya High School, in the same classroom as always.

Today's fourth period was independent study hall. But since fourth period was right before lunch, it ended up being an extra-long recess. Most of the students had already left the room.

At First Shibuya, however, no one dared to slack off. Independent study meant independent study. The students were all busy, somewhere, with something. If they didn't do well in the regularly held qualifying exams, they risked being expelled without notice. In fact, since the exams took the form of violent spell duels, slacking off could even get you killed.

As a result, the students at First Shibuya took their studies very seriously.

Besides, if they did well in school, they could earn a good position in the Order of the Imperial Demons after graduating. With all the expectations their families placed on them, they had little choice but to try their best.

About half the students had already left the room.

But Guren had stayed. He was too tired to move. He hadn't gotten nearly enough sleep the night before.

Shinya lay slumped over at his own desk, fast asleep. Apparently he hadn't gotten much shut-eye either. Unlike Shinya, however, Guren couldn't afford to take a nap. As long as he was at First Shibuya, he was surrounded by enemies and needed to remain on guard.

Shinya was breathing peacefully. Guren stared at him through heavy lidded eyes, feeling a little jealous. Eventually, he cast his gaze out the window.

As he turned his head, he caught sight of a certain annoying redhead coming his way.

It was Mito.

She was holding a shogi board under her arm. Apparently she was hoping to play again.

As she came closer, she hid the shogi board behind her back. Guren considered telling her that he'd already seen it. He opened his mouth to speak…

"Yawwwwn"

…and a huge yawn escaped instead. He immediately lost track of what he was thinking.

"What's wrong with you?" asked Mito. "Didn't you get enough sleep last night?"

"What? I guess not…"

"You know it's our duty, as members of the Imperial Demons, to always be healthy and well-rested. You should take better care of yourself, Guren Ichinose."

Mito had annoying down to an art form. Guren nodded meekly. Telling her to shut up was more trouble than it was worth at this point. He was too sleepy. He didn't want to get roped into one of her long-winded conversations.

"Yes, Mito. You're right, Mito. I'll try to be more careful next time," he said.

Mito seemed a little taken aback by Guren's response.

"Well… Good…" she said. It was almost funny how easily she was satisfied. "I'm just glad that you finally understand. As servants of the Hiragis, it's important that we students remain humble and diligent in our…"

Blah blah blah blah blah.

Guren was exhausted. The more Mito talked, the sleepier he became.

She suddenly took a step closer.

"By the way…"

"Yeah?"

"Y-Yest…"

"Yest?"

"Y-Yesterday was a lot of fun…wasn't it?"

Mito seemed embarrassed. Guren wasn't quite sure why.

For his own part, his most salient memories of the day before were of almost getting killed by a vampire.

"Was it?" he said.

"D-Didn't you have fun too, Guren?"

Her face suddenly sagged. She seemed to want to hear Guren say that he'd enjoyed himself.

"Sure. Yeah, I guess it was fun," he said.

"Right?"

Mito's face lit up. She was really wearing her heart on her sleeve today.

"If we're gonna be on Kureto's squad together," she went on, "I think it's important to build team spirit."

Guren didn't really agree, but he nodded anyways.

"Sure."

"That's why I thought, maybe soon, we could all do something like that again…"

"Sure, okay."

"So then…"

"Sure."

Mito suddenly narrowed her eyes. She leaned in close and glared at Guren.

"You're not really listening to me, are you?"

Whoops.

Now Guren had done it. He had agreed too quickly without waiting for Mito to finish. He couldn't help it. He was just so sleepy.

"When are you going to clean up your act, Guren Ichinose?"

"Would you stop screeching—"

"I do not SCREECH! You listen to me, mister. All I'm trying to do is to look out for your best interests so—"

"All right, all right already. I get it."

"No, it's not all right! You know what—"

"Mito."

"What?!"

"I had fun yesterday too. It's not often I get to hang out like that. Shogi was a lot more fun than I thought it would be, and those potato chips really were delicious... Well? Was there anything else you wanted to hear?"

"Ah... D-Did you really have fun?"

"I did."

Guren was actually telling the truth.

It had been kind of fun to just horse around for a change, drinking cola, eating potato chips, wasting time. Norito and Mito were real numbskulls, talking about how they wanted to help Guren because he'd risked his life for them. Real numbskulls.

Maybe Shinya was the same. After all, he had risked his life to save Guren.

"..."

They were comrades.

They were a team.

Guren wasn't sure that communicating with each other was worth it given their different affiliations—Ichinose, Hiragi—but precisely to the extent that it was pointless...

"...yeah, I guess it was fun."

Mito burst into a grin.

"Right?" she said happily. "I know I had fun. I told you, it's important to build team spirit that way!"

When push came to shove, Mito was a nice person. Almost to the point of being a ditz about it. A real "good girl" who felt like she should pay Guren back for saving her life.

She was still smiling as she pulled the shogi board from behind her back.

"Ta-daa! I actually bought it this morning at a convenience store. Me and you still haven't played each other. How about a match?"

At first Guren wanted to refuse because of how tired he was. But it wasn't like he could sleep at school anyways.

He accepted her challenge.

"Where should we play?"

The boy sitting in front of Guren leapt to his feet in a fluster.

"P-Please, take my seat, Mito!"

"Thank you." Mito nodded at the boy as if it were only natural that he should give up his seat for her.

She sat down across from Guren and set the board down on his desk.

Norito sauntered over from across the room.

"Picking up where we left off?"

"Are you gonna play for real today?" asked Shinya, without lifting his head up. He hadn't been asleep after all. "If you are, then I wanna watch."

"Huh?" Norito glanced at Guren. "You mean you weren't playing for real yesterday?"

"He was barely trying. You know Guren. He's a born liar…"

Norito crouched down next to Guren's desk and said, "Hey, don't underestimate me like that. You owe me a rematch. But this time you have to play for real. Mito, get out of the way."

"No way," she complained. "Today it's my turn to play Guren."

Shinya lifted his head up.

"You know what, if Guren is going to play for real then I think it's my turn."

That sounded like a challenge.

Mito and Norito exchanged glances and quickly backed off.

Guren glanced at Shinya, who still appeared to be pretty sleepy, and said, "What exactly are you trying to prove?"

Shinya grinned in reply. "My brother wants to see you during lunch, right? I just figured I'd help wake you up a little bit before you go."

"You think you're good enough to wake me up?"

"Naturally."

Guren smiled. "In your dreams."

"Prove it."

Mito leaned in close to Guren and whispered, "You shouldn't talk to Lord Shinya that way…"

"Fine," Guren replied to Shinya, ignoring her, "I didn't have anything to do until lunch anyways. Let's play."

Shinya sat up. He took a deep breath and then exhaled. His usual grin appeared on his face. "All right then. What should we make it? Five seconds per move?"

"Let's make it three."

In a real fight, a moment's hesitation could spell death. Five seconds was too much time to spare.

Shinya nodded. The match began.

Over the next hour, Guren and Shinya played seven matches against each other.

Guren won four and lost three, meaning he came out ahead, but just barely. Under different circumstances, or with luck, the results could have easily gone either way.

He also won all his matches against Mito and Norito. But halfway through, one of their classmates, who was a shogi buff, joined them. His name was Tanaka. He was too good for them, and they all lost handily.

They had a good laugh about it.

In the end, if you wanted to win at a real fight, you had to train for a real fight, and if you wanted to win at shogi, you apparently had to train for shogi.

Which begged the question: Were they really training properly for the coming war?

"…"

Just then the bell rang.

Fourth period was over.

"Looks like I won for today," Guren said to Shinya, who was still sitting next to him.

Shinya laughed and said, "I thought Tanaka won?"

"You know what I mean. Wasn't this between you and me?"

"Fine, but I'll win next time. I'm gonna brush up on some moves."

Mito and Norito both chimed in.

"Me too!"

"Yeah, me three!"

"You're all starting to sound obsessed," Guren said with a sigh.

He stood up.

The others stared up at him.

"Are you going to see Lord Kureto now?" Norito asked.

"Try not to say anything rude…" cautioned Mito.

Guren nodded.

"I'll be on my very best behavior," he said.

"Do you promise?"

Guren retuned Mito's gaze. She looked worried. Worried for Guren's sake, even though it had nothing to do with herself. The same applied to Norito. He had a look of concern on his face. All for Guren's sake.

Guren nodded.

"I'll be careful, I promise. So lay off already, okay?"

Guren stopped by his locker to get his katana, which he strapped to his waist.

Finally prepared, Guren set off to answer a summons from the person in the highest position of power at the school.

He set off to the office of the student council president.

◆

A lone girl stood in front of the door to the student council office.

Supposedly she was in Guren's class, but he almost never saw her there.

Like Mito, she was a beautiful young daughter from one of the great houses.

She wore her golden blond hair in two tresses. Her name was Aoi Sangu, and she had been waiting for Guren.

"I'm here to see your master," Guren said, eyeing her.

"Yes, I've been waiting for you."

"Isn't Kureto in his office?"

"Come with me, please."

Aoi began walking, gesturing for him to follow.

Guren followed her from behind. The skirt of Aoi's First Shibuya High School sailor-suit uniform was short. She didn't appear to have any weapons hidden there. Guren could tell from her bearing that she was a fairly capable fighter, but since she didn't seem to be armed, he guessed that she was primarily a spell caster.

She was probably at about the same skill level as Mito and Shigure. If she decided to turn around suddenly and attack Guren, he had a feeling he would be able to kill her without suffering a single scratch.

"You're in the same class as me, aren't you?" asked Guren, satisfied with his assessment. "Don't Kureto's lackeys have to show up for class?"

Aoi barely attended class. Guren had only seen her a total of three times since the first day.

"I don't like to waste my time on pointless things," Aoi said.

"Are you saying attending class is pointless? I guess I can't argue with you, there."

"No," said Aoi, without turning around. "I meant this conversation."

"This conversation is pointless?"

"Precisely. You have no interest in me. And no intention of speaking honestly. Correct? We have no reason to talk to each other."

No reason to talk? In truth, that applied to almost everyone at the school. So why were Mito and Norito always so intent on bothering Guren?

"I have no intention of speaking honestly with you, either," Aoi continued. "What would you propose we discuss in that case?" She glanced over her shoulder and smiled faintly. "How about the weather? It's been awfully hot lately, hasn't it…"

Guren smiled. "You have a point."

"Then be quiet, please."

"Hmph."

"Lord Kureto is currently in the basement of the gymnasium."

Guren remembered the basement. He'd been tortured by Kureto in a small room located in that very basement.

"He's not planning on torturing me again, is he? I'm starting to suspect he gets a kick out of it."

"It is the most effective way of extracting information."

"So he's going to torture me again?"

"No. Someone else is currently being interrogated," Aoi said, turning around. "Mahiru Hiragi's younger sister. Shinoa Hiragi."

Aoi watched Guren's expression carefully.

Guren, however, didn't flinch.

The moment she'd turned around, he knew she was springing something that she hoped would shake him.

Guren didn't let the information get to him.

Or, at the very least, he didn't let it show.

"Who?" he said.

As soon as he spoke, the phone in Aoi's skirt pocket began ringing. She pulled it out and put it to her ear.

"Yes, this is Aoi Sangu. Of course, sir. Understood, sir."

She hung up and turned back toward Guren.

"There was a camera recording your expression just now… Apparently, you passed. There was no indication that you were lying."

"I passed?"

"The test, to confirm whether or not you have been in contact with Shinoa Hiragi."

"What are you talking about? Why test me about something like that?"

"Lord Kureto will fill you in on the details. Come with me to the interrogation room."

Aoi continued walking.

Guren was on thin ice.

He had to keep acting like he didn't know who Shinoa was.

Like he hadn't seen Mahiru since she disappeared.

But pretty soon, just acting wouldn't be enough. He was going to have to start moving faster. The tide was turning faster than he thought.

Kureto was already on Mahiru's trail. The fact that he was torturing Shinoa probably meant that he suspected Mahiru of betraying them.

Mahiru had confided in her sister.

She had confided about Guren.

About her feelings.

About what she was up to—

Her plans to acquire enough power to crush the Hiragi Clan.

How she had joined with the Brotherhood of a Thousand Nights to betray the Hiragis.

How she meant to betray the Thousand Nights in turn.

Mahiru had told all of this to her sister.

Because of that, Shinoa risked being tortured and killed.

Or held as a hostage.

If Shinoa talked, Guren would almost certainly be killed as well. The fact that Kureto had just tested him probably meant that she hadn't spilled any information yet. But it was probably just a matter of time.

Shinoa was still young. She would talk. In which case…

Guren needed to kill her first. He needed to kill Shinoa Hiragi and make it look like an accident.

Was he capable of that?

More importantly, was it actually the right decision?

"…"

Aoi and Guren continued to walk down the hallway.

They were getting closer and closer to the interrogation room.

Guren had no way of knowing how things were going to unfold once they were inside. He didn't have the information he needed for that. Instead, he found himself thinking of Mahiru.

Was she capable of abandoning even her own sister if that's what it took? The one person in whom she had always confided?

Mahiru.

Kureto.

The Imperial Demons.

The Thousand Nights.

This wasn't like shogi. There were too many opponents in the game, and they all had their own motives. Guren, meanwhile, was stuck in the middle. Where a single wrong choice could result in death.

"I just wish I knew what was going on…" he muttered.

He thought he'd spoken too softly for anyone to hear, but Aoi turned around.

"Did you say something?"

"It's nothing. I just said you're right, it's really hot out today."

"Yes, it certainly is. I hear we've been getting record highs this summer."

"You don't say?"

"Yes, but enough small talk."

Enough, indeed.

Aoi and Guren continued walking down the hall.

Toward the torture chamber located in the basement of the school gym.

◆

As soon as the door to the interrogation room opened, the smell of blood filled Guren's nostrils.

A single chair had been placed in the center of the tiny room.

There was someone bound to the chair, at both her wrists and ankles. She was just a young girl.

She looked to be about seven or eight.

She bore a beautiful likeness to Mahiru—had the same clear, cold eyes. Her name was Shinoa Hiragi.

Blood trickled from her fingers and toes. The nails on her hands and feet had been torn out.

There was also a huge bruise across her face. It looked like someone had beaten her.

She glanced up as they entered, turning her round eyes toward Guren.

She grinned.

"Not another torturer," she said. "I haven't done anything wrong, so maybe you should just let me go already."

Her tone was flippant.

But Guren understood what she was trying to say. She hadn't talked. She hadn't given them any information about him. Guren, however, realized that he had let his own expression slip for a moment.

The moment he set eyes on her.

He couldn't stop his face from blanching with hate when he saw how they'd tortured Mahiru's little sister.

"Your expression just now was very interesting, Guren. Would you mind explaining what it meant?"

The voice came from the rear side.

Guren lifted his head. A lone figure was standing in the shadows.

Cold, expressionless, he had an intelligent air.

His name was Kureto Hiragi. He represented the pinnacle of power at their school.

Kureto stood by the wall with his arms crossed, staring at Guren. A katana hung from his belt.

Whether he had been there all along or entered partway through, Guren couldn't say, not having noticed him. If Kureto had chosen to

attack him by surprise, Guren would have been killed for sure.

Kureto was very good.

His eyes betrayed no emotion. He stared at Guren from the shadows, silently appraising him.

"I just don't like to see little kids tortured," Guren said, meeting Kureto's eyes.

"Nor do I."

"Then what the hell are you doing this for?"

"This level of torture is nothing to a Hiragi. Just look at her. She's smiling."

It was true. There was a grin on Shinoa's face. She had been trained to withstand torture. This level of questioning was probably just a cakewalk for her. Still...

"I don't like the way you do things..."

Kureto laughed. "I don't require your approval."

"I guess you don't."

"Either way, here we are. Even if I torture Shinoa, it's unlikely she'll talk. All Hiragis undergo training to that end."

"..."

"Which obviously makes this questioning useless. Anything I do to her would be pointless. She would die before she told me what I wanted to know."

Did all the Hiragis really undergo such brutal training? Or was Kureto lying when he said Shinoa wouldn't talk, just to put Guren off guard?

Guren suspected the first was true.

The whole place was twisted. The Imperial Demons was a sick organization run by broken people. Shinoa, Mahiru, Kureto, and even Shinya must have been trained to withstand any torture.

Kureto stared at Guren.

"Even if she doesn't talk, though," he said, "there is something precious that we can take from her. Something that can never be recovered once it's lost. Isn't that right, Guren?"

"…"

"Shinoa is only eight years old. She's never even been in love. Maybe she should lose that precious 'something' right now… What do you think?"

"…"

"If you don't like seeing children tortured, I imagine you must want to protect her."

"You sick son of a bitch…" groaned Guren.

Kureto only smiled. "Your opinion of me doesn't matter. You don't plan on lecturing me now about what an ugly, dirty world we live in, do you?"

"…"

"Let's move on, then," Kureto said, abruptly launching into the reason he had summoned Guren. "The Brotherhood of a Thousand Nights contacted me recently. They said that Mahiru was the traitor. Is this true?"

Kureto eyed Guren, watching calmly for any reaction.

Guren remained silent.

Kureto narrowed his eyes and said, "Should I take your silence as a yes?"

Guren wasn't sure how to answer. He didn't know what the right choice was.

How much information did Kureto already have?

He had to say something, though. The wrong choice might get him killed. If he remained silent, he would still be killed.

"I'm not sure…" he said.

"You're not sure of what?"

"Mahiru. I'm not sure whether or not she's a traitor."

"Are you a traitor?"

"Of course not. The Ichinose Clan isn't powerful enough to betray the Hiragis. Even if we did betray you, we wouldn't be able to cause any harm."

"That is true. If you betrayed us, we could simply kill you and be done with it. Fine. I believe you aren't the traitor. But you knew about Mahiru's betrayal."

"No."

"Mahiru was in love with you. She told you everything, didn't she?"

"Not that I'm aware of."

"Are you sure? Because Shinoa, here, told me that Mahiru was confiding in you."

"That's a lie."

If it wasn't a lie, and Shinoa really had broken under torture, then Guren was about to be executed as a traitor.

Likewise, if the Thousand Nights had told Kureto that Mahiru and Guren had been in contact, then he was probably just moments from death.

Kureto, however, just smiled faintly and said, "I suppose you wouldn't fall for something as simple as that, would you?"

It looked like Guren had chosen correctly. But he was walking a thin line. Apparently, the Thousand Nights had told Kureto about Mahiru's betrayal, but nothing else.

The most obvious scenario seemed to be that the Thousand Nights were trying to squash Mahiru now that she had crossed them as well. But it was possible that she was still working with the Thousand Nights and that her betraying them was a lie. In that case, was Mahiru, herself, circulating the information that she'd betrayed the Hiragis?

While Guren was no longer sure what was true and what untrue, he was stuck in the hot seat, and one wrong choice could get him killed.

"First of all," Guren said, "do you really believe everything the Thousand Nights tells you?"

"Huh?"

"We're in the middle of a war. Don't tell me the Hiragis buy into every single bit of intelligence their enemies put out."

"No," assured Kureto, "I only believe what I see with my own two eyes. That's why I haven't killed you. Or Shinoa. We need to figure out what the Thousand Nights' motive is for sharing this information, instead of letting their propaganda turn our heads. We tried to get answers out of the messenger from the Thousand Nights, but unfortunately our interrogator got carried away with the questioning. The messenger died prematurely."

Kureto glanced sideways.

He was gesturing toward the next room.

It was where Kureto had waited while Guren was being tortured. A bright red liquid was seeping toward them from beneath the door. Apparently that was where the smell of blood had come from. There was a body on the other side.

"Did you get a little thrill from making a kid look at the body?" spat Guren.

Kureto laughed. "I didn't realize you Ichinoses had such a compassionate streak. That must be why you can never seem to beat us at anything."

"We never had any intentions of trying."

"Ha. That's what I like about you, Guren. You always remember your place."

Kureto took a step forward. He stood behind Shinoa, stroking her head. He suddenly released her shackles from behind the chair.

Shinoa was free.

"May I stand?" she asked, staring up into her brother's face.

Kureto shook his head.

"Stay seated," he said.

"..."

Guren stared at Shinoa. Her tiny legs were covered with horrible injuries. Her toenails had been ripped out, and the skin had been flayed. She really didn't look like she was capable of standing...

"Her injuries are all makeup," divulged Kureto. "Shinoa hasn't been tortured. I would never subject my adorable little sister to something so pointless, Guren. After all, it's not as if she would talk."

Shinoa jumped to her feet and grinned.

"I told you to stay seated," Kureto ordered.

"But I'm tired of this boring act."

"That's too bad, because I'm bringing in Shinya next. I don't want you messing up your makeup."

"..."

Shinoa glanced awkwardly at Guren. He tried to read something from her expression, but he was unable to decipher whatever lay hidden in those eyes.

"Are you telling me this whole thing was just a test?" he said.

Kureto shook his head. "It was to gather information. When you're fighting an enemy as massive as the Thousand Nights, sometimes it can become difficult to separate truth from fiction."

"Well? Did you come to any conclusions?"

"I've decided to trust you," he said. "You are one of my most valued retainers, after all."

Guren had no idea what had led Kureto to that conclusion. Was it based on some aspect of their conversation?

"You still don't understand?" asked the student council president.

Kureto's cold gaze seemed to pierce right through. It was almost as if he knew what Guren was thinking.

Guren's expression remained set in stone, but his fingertips twitched, ever so slightly. He was slowly inching his hand toward the sword on his belt, to be ready to react whatever happened.

Kureto remained calm, his expression unchanged. However...

"We already know that you and Shinoa have been in contact," he said. "But we're going to kill Shinoa first."

"Ahh!"

The girl tried to move. Before she could, however, Kureto reached out and grabbed her around the neck.

Guren was now rushing toward him. He drew the sword from his hip and swung.

Kureto countered easily, sliding his sword halfway out of its scabbard to block Guren's strike.

"Don't make another move, Guren, or I'll break Shinoa's neck..."

"…"

Guren froze, still holding the edge of his blade against Kureto's.

Kureto laughed.

"Haha. You should see your face. This is why I trust you, Guren. Because of your humanity. Because you couldn't abandon Shinoa just now. By the way, I actually announced Shinoa's death sentence last night. I did it through channels that I knew the Thousand Nights, and anyone else keeping tabs on the Hiragi Clan, are aware of. Of course, I also made sure that you and Shinya wouldn't catch wind of the verdict. In any case, what do you suppose happened?"

Guren glared at Kureto. Why would he make such an announcement? The answer was obvious. It was a trap to lure Mahiru out into the open.

"She ignored you?" he guessed.

Kureto laughed again. Letting go of Shinoa, he thrust his hand into his pocket and pulled out a phone. It was opened to the email screen.

The sender was listed as unknown.

But the subject line read "Mahiru Hiragi."

The body of the message simply said:

—Do as you like.

Guren stared at the text. There was his proof. Mahiru had abandoned her sister as easily as if she meant nothing to her.

Of course, there was no way for Guren to know whether the message was really from Mahiru. He was surrounded by so many lies at this point that there was no telling anymore what was true.

He suspected, however, that the email really was hers.

It seemed like something she might do.

The sort of thing she was capable of doing.

At least, when Guren met her in Ueno, it seemed as if the demon had already possessed her far enough to render her willing to say such a thing.

Shinoa stared at the phone in Kureto's hand. Her eyes quivered slightly. It was the first time Guren had ever seen her display a childlike emotion. For a moment, her face was that of an ordinary eight year old.

One who had been abandoned by her sister.

By a sister she had believed in.

She quickly regained her composure, however, and the fretful look was gone from her face—too late to avoid Kureto's notice.

He pushed with his own blade, and Guren stepped backward.

As far as Kureto was concerned, their fight was over. He returned his sword to its sheath.

"Can you believe that?" he said, his expression half-exasperated, half-whimsical. "I never even gave her this address. I have no idea how she got it."

" . . . "

"Her control of the situation is amazing, isn't it? She truly is smart. With this one email she made me question everything I was thinking. Was it wise to kill Shinoa? To kill you? To kill Shinya? Who are my enemies, and who are my friends? How much of this scenario has she engineered? Am I being played? We've been getting caught with our pants down since the very beginning of this. Too many lives were sacrificed the day the Thousand Nights attacked the school. And Mahiru's been the one in the driver's seat all along."

" . . . "

"Mahiru is frightening. She always has been. Not at all like you, Guren. You're the kind of person who draws his blade in the heat of the moment because the little sister of some girl you like is about to get killed. But that's also why I trust you. You have humanity. You would never betray your friends. You're not one of the people at the center of all this. You're just some slob fool who got used by a woman."

" . . . "

"The truth is you've already met with Mahiru. Haven't you, Guren?"

Guren didn't respond.

But Kureto didn't seem to care. "You don't need to answer. I wouldn't believe you no matter what you said. But I will give you a piece of advice. You shouldn't trust Mahiru. I know that she's very beautiful…but she's a monster, Guren."

A monster.

That much was probably true.

But Guren didn't understand what had caused her to become one. When he and Mahiru were young, they had promised to be together. She had been a normal, endearing little girl. Maybe a little conceited, but also lonely. Normal.

What had happened?

What happened to her after that day? After they had been ripped from each other's arms under a clear blue sky?

"If you think you can control that monster, though…" Kureto carried on, "give her a message from me. She cares about you. She might actually listen to what you have to say."

"What's the message?" asked Guren.

"Tell her to come back. Back to the Hiragis. I won't oppose a marriage between the two of you."

"Huh? Why on earth would Mahiru and I get married?"

"You're lovers, aren't you?"

"We were just kids."

"But she is in love with you."

"What's that got to do with—"

"Either way," Kureto interrupted, "if there's any part of you that wants to save her, you'll do it, Guren. None of that other stuff matters to me anymore."

"…"

"I'm not interested in outdated conventions. What harm would come of a Hiragi and an Ichinose being united? We're too bogged down with unproductive fights as it is. If you are all going to be under my command in the end, then I see no reason not to accept you into our fold. Do you understand what I'm saying, Guren? If you find Mahiru, hold onto her tight and don't let her go again."

"..."

"And if you can't do that, kill her. Because if you don't, she'll bring death to everyone around her. Do you want to know how many people died in the Thousand Nights' attack on the school?"

Guren shook his head. "I don't care."

"If you didn't care, would you have saved your friends? Norito and Mito both had some very nice things to say about you. About how kind you are, and how you can be trusted. They said you're a good guy."

Considering the circumstances, Guren wasn't sure if Kureto was complimenting him or mocking him.

"That's why I decided not to kill you today. You and Mahiru are two different kinds of people. Someone with as much self-control as you, who values the lives of his friends, could never be a threat. If you could just learn to listen to your superiors and let yourself be put to good use, someone with your abilities could really shine."

Guren stared at Kureto. One thing he had said was definitely true. Guren had no chance of defeating the Hiragis.

Not now, at least. Not yet.

"You're laying this on pretty thick..." observed Guren. "Something must have really scared you to make you come on so strong."

Kureto laughed. "Two of the only people in the world with any chance of getting in touch with Mahiru are standing in front of me right now. At the very least, that has to up the chance that this conversation will get back to her."

So in other words, Kureto was saying all of this for Mahiru's benefit.

Kureto glanced towards Shinoa, who was still listening calmly.

Guren put his sword back in its scabbard. "Why don't you send Mahiru a message yourself?" he said. "I don't even have her email address."

"Haha. Do you think Mahiru would really listen to anything I have to say?"

"Do you think she'd listen to anything I said?"

"You certainly stand a better chance of persuading her than I do."

Kureto pressed a few buttons on the phone in his hand. Guren's own cell rang in response.

Guren pulled it free from his pocket. A message had arrived from Kureto. It contained an email address he'd never seen before.

It had to be Mahiru's.

"This is an order. Meet with Mahiru and talk some sense into her."

"What if I said I didn't want to?"

"I already told you, it's an order."

Guren glanced at his cell again.

"Can I ask you one thing, Kureto?" he said.

"What is it?"

"Which one of you was stronger? Between you and Mahiru?"

"Mahiru," Kureto replied without hesitation.

"…"

"Mahiru is brilliant. But a genius who is ignorant of ordinary human suffering is no choice for a leader."

Guren couldn't but laugh. "And Lord Kureto understands ordinary human suffering?"

"Compared to Mahiru, at least. Which is why I know how you feel, Guren. I understand you so much that it pains me. Crawling around in the dirt like a worm is hard, isn't it?"

"Asshole," Guren muttered.

He glanced down at his cell again. At Mahiru's email address.

Guren still wasn't sure if the address, or the message Kureto had received, were even real. It could all be a lie cooked up to confuse Guren and Shinoa.

But if Mahiru had sent the message…she really was a monster.

"All right," said Kureto. "Get started. Send her a message now."

"I hope you're not expecting too much from me and Mahiru's relationship…"

"Enough, just send the message."

It was an order.

Guren's fingers began tapping.

The message he wrote was simple. It read:

—This is Guren. Send a reply.

They waited for a moment, but no answer came.

Guren raised his head and stared at Kureto. "Satisfied?" he asked.

With a calm nod, Kureto said, "If she makes contact, report it to me immediately. And tell her not to forget who her real enemies are. The Hiragis are on her side."

"If the Hiragis are on her side, then why did she have to betray you?"

"Exactly. That's where you come in, Guren. It's your job to make her understand. She's broken. She's lost her way. But, together, you and I are going to tame that love-crazed fool."

Guren glanced at his phone once more before shoving it back into his pocket.

"Are we done?" he asked.

Kureto nodded. "Yes. You can go."

Shinoa stared up at Guren, but he didn't meet her eyes. He wasn't sure what she was thinking, but it was dangerous to make eye contact at the moment. Not even the slightest change in behavior would escape Kureto's notice.

Guren made to leave.

Just then, it rang. His phone.

Everyone there was staring at Guren's pocket.

He took out the phone. The call was from a number he didn't recognize.

"Mahiru?" asked Kureto.

Guren shrugged.

"It could just be a telemarketer."

"Answer."

" . . . "

Ignoring the call was no longer an option. Guren pressed talk. A voice came over the line. It was a woman's, sweet and clear.

"Who is this?" it asked.

"That's my line," Guren objected.

They both knew who they were talking to as soon as they heard each other's voice.

The call was from Mahiru.

"So you're still alive?" she said. She sounded amused.

"Don't be so quick to kill me off. How did you get my phone number, anyways?"

"Love has its ways."

"Shush."

"Haha." Mahiru seemed genuinely happy to be talking to him. "What about Shinoa? Is she alive?"

"She's right beside me."

"Her corpse is?"

"No, her."

"Put her on."

"I wouldn't recommend that."

"Is Kureto there, too? Is he listening in? Thank you for looking out for my sister, Guren. You were always kind. But put her on. It will be fine."

" … "

Guren moved the phone away from his ear, glanced up, and said, "She wants me to put Shinoa on."

Kureto seemed to think for a moment. "Put her on speakerphone," he ordered.

Guren pressed the button, and Mahiru's voice filled the room.

"Shinoa, are you all right?"

Shinoa glanced at the phone through lidded eyes and chuckled.

"That depends on what you mean by all right."

"Just in general terms… Are you hurt?"

"No, I'm not hurt. Just as you planned, I'm sure…" Shinoa bit her lip petulantly. "But I think my maidenhood was in danger for a while.

121

I'm only eight, you know."

"Hmm? I never knew Kureto had such a Lolita complex."

"You don't really sound worried at all… I saw the email. It said, 'Do as you like.'"

"Haha. I did write that, didn't I? Did I hurt your feelings?"

"No," Shinoa said with a shake of her head. "I know you didn't have any other options. They didn't really torture me, anyways."

"I didn't think so. Kureto wouldn't waste his time with something so inefficient. It's one of his weaknesses. But I'm glad you're all right. By the way, are we on speakerphone?"

"Yes."

"Who's listening?"

"Guren, Kureto, and some blond girl I don't know."

"Must be Aoi Sangu. What about our father? Is he there yet?"

Kureto stepped in to answer. "Father doesn't even know that you've disappeared."

"Kureto? Is that you?"

" … "

"It's so nice to hear from you, br—"

Kureto cut her off. "Enough with the pleasantries. You betrayed the Hiragis and ran away. Because of you, countless friends and comrades of ours are dead. What was the point of all that killing? Why did you disappear?"

"Haha," Mahiru laughed amusedly. "I'm sorry, Kureto, but I don't have anything to say to a liar like you."

"What are you talking about? What lies have I told?"

"Father doesn't know that I've disappeared? Really? Father, who has spent so much time doting on me?"

"It's the truth."

"Ha… Ahaha… Is he angry, then? That his precious daughter, next in line to lead the clan, has betrayed him?"

"I told you, he doesn't know."

"You're kidding. But you tell him. Tell him I didn't want to betray him, but that my mean old big brother was so jealous, I was forced to. Tell him how you chased me away."

"…"

Kureto narrowed his eyes a fraction of an inch.

"Tell him how you worked with the Brotherhood of a Thousand Nights to sell out the Hiragis. How I'm not really the one who betrayed him at all."

"No one's going to believe your nonsense, Mahiru."

"They won't? I'm pretty sure that Father places much greater trust in me than he does in you, Kureto. It isn't hard to believe that a weak person would be jealous of a strong one. Remind me, Kureto, which one of us is stronger? I hate to break it to you, dear sweet brother, but I've never once felt jealous of you. Do you see what I'm getting at here?"

"Mahiru, shut up."

"By the way, you've just made a serious mistake. You should have hung up on me as soon as I called. Let me guess… You're trying to trace the line? With enough time, I'm sure you'll be able to find me. After all, I'm not even hiding."

A slow grin spread across Kureto's face. "Actually, we've already found you," he said. "Special forces—"

"They're all dead," Mahiru cut him off.

"…"

"Oh, I'm sorry, Kureto. I forgot how it makes your widdle heart sad when our comrades die. But can we really call them that? You're working with the Thousand Nights, remember? Is anyone who serves under you really on the Imperial Demons' side?"

Just then, the door swung open.

A boy dressed in a First Shibuya High School uniform ran in.

"Lord Kureto! Your conversation with Lady Mahiru is being broadcast throughout the school!" he informed breathlessly.

Kureto spun toward the student and glared at him.

Guren turned around and inspected the door. *Fuda* had been pasted onto its corners. They looked like soundproofing charms designed to block noise. Pasted on a surface, they cancelled vibrations coming through the air.

It was a trap. The room had been set up in advance to keep them from hearing such a broadcast.

A trap set by Mahiru.

There was no telling when she'd pasted them. Could she have done it before she had even run away?

She had them all right where she wanted. Their talk of a betrayal didn't even cut it. Mahiru had long since upped her game.

Everyone else was just a puppet dancing in the palm of her monstrous hand.

"It's terrible, isn't it?" resumed Mahiru. "How many Thousand Nights spies do you think are hiding, right now, in the Imperial Demons' ranks?"

"Hang up the phone, Guren," her brother conceded. "We've lost this round."

Mahiru, however, wasn't done. "The same tragedy is going to repeat itself. How many students are going to die this time, Kureto? As long as a traitor like you is student body president…"

Kureto grabbed the phone from Guren's hand. He switched off the speakerphone and put the device to his ears, but to no avail. Mahiru's voice continued to echo over the school's loudspeakers.

"You've lost your mind, Mahiru," accused Kureto. "What you're doing will spread death indiscriminately."

But that was the point.

That was precisely what Mahiru was trying to achieve. If she could spark an internecine war, there was no telling how many more Imperial Demons might die.

"That's very rich coming from a traitor like you, Kureto," she said.

"I won't allow this. I won't allow you to blatantly massacre our followers in this way. I will protect my people."

"Ha. What are you talking about? You brought this on yourself. You tried to rape me. And then when you couldn't have your way with me, your spite drove you out of your mind…"

Kureto sighed in disgust. He raised his voice so loud it drowned out what Mahiru was saying.

"I hereby call a council meeting to discuss executing the traitor, Mahiru Hiragi!"

Kureto hung up.

It suddenly grew quiet.

Glaring at Guren, Kureto said, "Did you know about this?"

"Know about what?" asked Guren.

"That this was going to happen."

"Do you *think* I did?"

Kureto laughed self-deprecatingly.

"No, I don't. I doubt Mahiru would have handed information like this to you or Shinoa. You're the first two I'd suspect. She must have acted on her own. I can't believe she's going up against the Imperial Demons and the Thousand Nights all by herself. It almost sends a chill down my spine."

Guren had to agree with him there. How had she planned all this? And when? How was she always able to see so many steps ahead?

However she had done it, Mahiru was going up against the two largest magical syndicates in Japan.

She was planning to pit them against each other, to uncover their weaknesses, and to destroy them from within.

And she was doing it all on her own.

"What Mahiru said about you assaulting her—"

Kureto cut Guren off with an exasperated sigh. "You didn't believe that, did you?"

"Some people will."

"Yes… You're right, they probably will," Kureto muttered. He didn't seem flustered. Rather, he seemed to be thinking. He remained silent for a moment before he spoke again. "That won't be enough to bring down the Hiragi Clan…"

"…"

"But the Thousand Nights were probably listening in as well. Any sign of internal dispute is a weakness they can exploit. Our followers on the periphery will probably waver. That's where the Thousand Nights will find their opening. People will probably die. Our friends. And in large numbers."

Friends.

Kureto had chosen to use the word.

Guren wondered if he really thought of his people that way, or if it was all a grand show.

Kureto glanced his way. "Guren..."

"What?"

"What are your ambitions in life? What do you hope to accomplish?"

"..."

"Do you want to destroy the Hiragi Clan to get revenge against the Imperial Demons for having oppressed you for so long? By crushing us and placing yourself at the top? How much are you willing to sacrifice to accomplish that goal?"

"..."

"You saved Norito Goshi. You saved Mito Jujo. Just now, you couldn't stand by if Shinoa was about to be killed. Do you really think someone like you shares the same dream as Mahiru?"

Guren wasn't sure he knew the answer to that.

Could he be like Mahiru?

Could he be a monster?

Guren remembered what Shinya had said.

If you were willing to make the same choice that Mahiru made, we wouldn't be trying to save her in the first place...

But Guren's ambition in life wasn't to save Mahiru.

So what should he do? What did he really want?

"What are you getting at?" he asked.

"I have faith in you, Guren. You're not a monster. You're still on the side of humanity. I want you to join me."

"…"

"We can save lives. Together, we can take care of this problem with as few sacrifices as possible."

Kureto extended his hand toward Guren.

It looked like Kureto was in need of friends. Allies he could trust, who weren't tainted by the Thousand Nights. Allies who hadn't been compromised by Mahiru. The kind who weren't willing to sit back while people died. The kind who would be easy to use.

In other words, Kureto's position was crumbling.

His back was up against a wall. So much so that he had to turn to Ichinose scum for help.

"…"

Kureto still had his hand out toward Guren.

Shinoa stared at the outstretched hand dubiously.

"It's not like I can really say no," Guren replied without taking his hand.

Kureto laughed. "Exactly. All right then, we kill Mahiru."

Of course, that was easier said than done. Kureto knew that as well as anyone. Mahiru had already begun sowing distrust in the Imperial Demons' ranks.

And there was still the war with the Thousand Nights.

The date was August 21st.

The world was supposedly going to end at Christmas. That was just four months away.

"Aren't you taking things a little fast, Mahiru?" Guren muttered, too quietly for anyone else to hear.

◆

Guren was released together with Shinoa.

They left the torture room and returned to the gymnasium. Shinya was waiting by the entrance when they got there, leaning his back against the wall.

He glanced at Guren and was about to say something when he noticed Shinoa, covered in blood.

"Uh oh. What happened, did they torture you?"

Shinoa grinned, twisting her hands up like claws and waving them in Shinya's face. "Nope, it's just makeup. I look like a zombie, don't I? Rawwrr!" She pounced at him playfully.

Shinya hunched over in laughter, holding his stomach.

"Zombies don't go 'Rawwrr!'" he said.

"They don't?"

"No, they go 'Gawrr!'"

"Well, it sounds the same to me."

"Haha, they really went to a lot of trouble to make you up like that, though. Was it all to fool Guren and me?"

Shinoa nodded. "Apparently. Well? Were you fooled?"

"Yeah. I would have never known. For a second I could've sworn you were a real zombie."

"Rawwrrr!"

"Not 'Rawwrrr'—Gawrr!"

What a stupid conversation...

Guren ignored them as he exited the gym.

"Hey, don't just walk away," Shinya called out, running after him.

"How are people reacting?"

As far as Guren knew, Mahiru and Kureto's conversation had been broadcast throughout the entire school.

"It was pretty crazy," Shinya told him. "But things are quiet. I don't think people are sure what to believe yet. They're probably all worried about avoiding any fallout."

"What about Mito and Norito?"

Shinya grinned. "Huh, are you worried about your shogi buddies? Not very like you."

Guren rolled his eyes. Shinya just laughed and walked along next to him.

"Kureto said he was going to call you in next. Did he?" Guren

asked.

Shinya shook his head. "And I don't think he will now, do you? I already know that Shinoa's zombie act is just makeup... He probably has bigger fish to fry now."

After they had walked a little while, Guren began to spot other students standing around the schoolyard. No one was smiling. They all seemed to be huddling in groups and speaking to each other in hushed tones.

They were almost certainly discussing what would happen to them.

Most of the student body hadn't even been aware that there was trouble between the Thousand Nights and the Imperial Demons.

Yet a massive war was beginning. No, not beginning. It had long since begun. They just hadn't realized.

On top of that, an internal conflict was also brewing in the Hiragi Clan.

Guren hadn't lifted a finger yet, but shockwaves were already rippling through his nemesis. The world was poised for a change.

"When did the broadcast begin? Did you hear me and Mahiru talking, too?"

Shinya glanced at Guren and said, "You spoke to Mahiru? Apparently, the broadcast didn't begin until Kureto started speaking. What did she say to you?"

"'So you're still alive?'"

"Ha! That does sound like her. I wonder if she meant it."

"My sister always fakes at times like these," Shinoa butted into their conversation. "My guess is she didn't really mean it."

Guren glanced over at her.

She continued, "Her voice was higher than usual, too. I think she was probably happy to speak to you. Because of how much she likes you."

"Woah, woah, woah, hold on a second," Shinya reacted, laughing. "I'm the one who's supposed to be her fiancé. Where does that leave me?"

"Don't ask me. I'm just a kid. All that adult boy-girl stuff is still a mystery to me," Shinoa said, shrugging her shoulders.

Guren stared at her. He couldn't figure out her motivation for saying what she'd just said. During their previous encounter, he'd asked her whose side she was on, and she'd answered that she was on whichever side was most interesting.

She didn't care about the Hiragis, and she wasn't working for the Thousand Nights, either. But supposedly she loved her sister, who had always been kind to her.

"Shinoa?"

"Yeah?"

"Mahiru just abandoned you. She doesn't care anymore whether you live or die."

"I guess she doesn't," Shinoa agreed with a nod.

"Are you still on her side?"

Shinoa furrowed her brow as if she wasn't sure. She stared off into space, thinking. Her voice sounded very matter of fact when she finally replied to him.

"Even after what happened, I think she's still the one person in the world who would be most upset if I were to die. If I wound up dead in some gutter someday, I don't think there's anyone else who would really care."

Guren stared down at Shinoa and said, "I'd care a little."

"You would? That's pretty weird of you."

"I'd care too," Shinya crabbed in. "If you died I'm pretty sure I'd cry. Even if you stuck around as a zombie I think I'd be sad."

"Rawwrr?"

"Gawwrr!"

Despite her quizzical stare, a smile crept across Shinoa's face. Somehow her expression reminded Guren of Mahiru. Glancing up at the two boys, the girl met their gazes.

"Well, that's a shocker! Considering how little we know each other, I would've never thought the two of you would feel sad if I croaked. I guess that goes to show how much you both love my sister. You even care about me just because I'm related to her."

Shinoa seemed to have pretty low self-esteem. Guren guessed that with a sister as talented as Mahiru, it was hard not to rate yourself poorly.

"Unfortunately," said Shinoa, "it looks like my sister is through with all of us—me, you, and Shinya. She made it pretty clear today that she's abandoned us. I don't think she'll make contact again. She's already accomplished whatever it is she wanted to accomplish at this school."

Shinoa was probably right.

The spark that Mahiru had set off today would spread through the entire Order of the Imperial Demons.

The way things stood now, all-out war was certain to erupt between the Thousand Nights and the Imperial Demons before long.

On the bright side, they probably wouldn't be watching Guren and Shinya as closely as before. In a single day, Mahiru had completely flipped the script. Guren and Shinya may have been plotting against the Hiragis, but what Mahiru had done was so major that those schemes suddenly seemed worth overlooking.

More importantly, now that the entire student body knew that the Imperial Demons and the Thousand Nights were at war, the situation was about to take a very drastic turn for the worse.

Both the Order and the Brotherhood had wanted to hide the conflict and to act behind the scenes without their disciples' knowledge. Those plans had just blown up in their faces. Everything was out in the open now.

If Mahiru really had betrayed the Thousand Nights, they were probably equally in a panic over what had just transpired.

On the other hand, it could all be a strategy cooked up by Mahiru and the Thousand Nights together.

"..."

One thing was clear. There was no place for Guren in this story.

The principal actors were Mahiru; the Hiragis; and the Brotherhood of a Thousand Nights.

The Ichinose Clan wasn't on that list. Just like Kureto and Shinoa had said, no one was worried about them anymore.

Guren wasn't a threat.

But why wasn't he?

He remembered what Mahiru had told him.

I'm so much stronger than you that it's almost heartbreaking. I guess that's what makes me the hare. Hurtling headlong toward destruction. I'm still waiting for my tortoise prince, Guren. Try and save me, before it's too late.

Mahiru had already accepted destruction, accepted ruin. Everything she ought to hold on to, she was willing to throw overboard.

Was her choice right or wrong?

"..."

Guren suddenly felt a strange sensation.

A tingling pain had shot up his right arm. The one he'd cut off. The one that had reconnected thanks to the demon's power. Guren gingerly touched the aching spot with his other hand.

"Well, what should we do now, Guren?" asked Shinya.

At this point, though, there really wasn't much they could do.

They just had to stand back and chew on their thumbs while they watched Mahiru speed off into the distance.

A war was brewing.

A massive war.

Where would the Ichinose Clan stand when the time came? What position would yield the best chance of taking advantage of the situation?

And more importantly, was Guren prepared to do whatever it took? Was he truly prepared to crush the Hiragis?

There was no point in destroying them, however, unless he could do it without bowing to the Thousand Nights. Even if it were to crush the Hiragi Clan, if he went crawling to the Thousand Nights instead, the Ichinose Clan would wind up exactly where it'd started.

What was he to do?

They were out of time. It was too late for indecision.

Think, Guren.

Think hard.

What did he want?

What did he really desire?

If he didn't act soon, the war would be over before he even got off his ass to join the fight.

The Imperial Demons or the Thousand Nights would win.

Either that, or they would both be destroyed.

Whatever happened, scores of people were going to die. All senselessly, on account of somebody else's ambition. Choosing to pursue your ambitions at any cost was a path of carnage. It was a road paved atop an endless mound of corpses.

But if a mountain of bodies was going to pile up either way, why keep up the tortoise-and-hare charade? Whether they went a little faster or slower, the destination was the same.

It was a little late now to start getting scrupulous about methods, wasn't it?

Guren froze in his tracks.

"What's wrong?" asked Shinya.

Guren didn't answer.

His arm was throbbing. His right arm, the one that held the demon. Where the cut had been made. There was no scar. The skin had already healed, without a trace, but for some reason the spot was throbbing now in hot bursts of fire.

"Guren?"

"Huh?"

"Are you okay?"

"I'm fine," Guren said, nodding.

"Are you sure?"

"Yeah."

Just then the bell rang. Lunch was over. Shinya and Shinoa glanced upward at the sound.

"I guess fifth period is starting," Shinya remarked.

Shinoa turned toward Guren. She thrust a tiny hand out in his direction.

Guren stared down at her.

"What?" he said.

"Money, please," she requested.

"Huh?"

"Count me out. All you adults with your grumpy faces and your stupid wars are boring me. I'm going home."

"..."

"I was still at home when they kidnapped me. I don't have my wallet, and I'm not even wearing shoes. I need a taxi."

"Hmph. And why should I pay for that?"

"How can you say no to the little sister of your dear, sweet childhood friend?"

"Easy. *No.*"

"Cheapskate!"

Shinoa grinned.

Shinya laughed too. He took out his wallet, pulled out a 10,000-yen note, and gave it to her. "I'll call for a taxi. If you wanna pay me back, next time you see Mahiru, remind her which one of us is her real fiancé!"

Shinoa looked up into Shinya's face. "Do you love my sister?" she asked.

"Hmm...I don't know if I'd say that, exactly."

"Then why do you want me to tell her something like that?"

"I guess I just don't like losing to Guren."

"You mean it's just a game?"

Shinya thought for a moment. "Hmm...I don't know if I'd say that, either," he repeated his line with a laugh.

Shinoa tilted her head at him.

"Which is it?" she demanded.

"What do you think?"

"I don't know. And I really don't care!"

"You really don't, do you? All right, let me call that taxi."

Shinya pulled out his phone and began dialing.

Shinoa stared at her hands, which were drenched in red blood.

"Will the driver take a zombie?" she wondered out loud.

"Since you're such a cute zombie, I'm sure."

"True. No one can argue that I didn't get my sister's good looks."

Guren ignored them and continued walking back toward the school building.

His mind was preoccupied with thoughts of power, and the coming senseless war.

One thing he knew about power was that he didn't have enough of it.

Not if he was ever going to catch up to Mahiru.

What could he do, though? How was he ever going to make any progress? Mahiru was brilliant. She was the proverbial hare. So far ahead, and so reckless that she had sold her own soul to a demon.

How was he ever going to catch up to her and take the lead? That was all he could think about at the moment.

Suddenly, his phone rang.

He took it out of his pocket. The call was coming from the same number as before.

It was Mahiru Hiragi.

Mahiru was calling him.

"..."

Guren wasn't sure if he should answer. Kureto could be listening in. Guren might be executed as a traitor the moment he picked up. Being weak, he found himself in constant danger—buffeted from all sides, forced to make life and death decisions on a daily basis.

"I'm starting to get sick of this..." he muttered.

He waited until he was out of earshot from Shinoa and Shinya to answer the phone.

"What do you want now?" he said.

"…"

Mahiru didn't speak. Guren wasn't even sure if it was really her on the other end.

"Why are you even calling me? You know this phone—"

"It's not bugged," Mahiru finally spoke, her voice traveling over the line.

"That's hard to believe."

"Trust me."

"Well? What did you want?"

"I…just wanted to hear your voice…" she said.

She sounded very weak and exhausted, entirely unlike the Mahiru who'd been threatening Kureto moments ago.

"You wanted to hear my voice?" Guren snicked. "A few minutes ago you were mocking me. 'So you're still alive?' Remember that?"

Mahiru was quiet for a moment. Guren could hear her breathing, faintly.

"That…wasn't me…" she said.

"Then who was it?"

"The demon."

"…"

"It's possessed me…"

"From the cursed gear?"

"…Yes."

"Are you saying the demon is controlling you?"

"…Yes."

Her voice sounded sweet and artless, not like when she had spoken to Kureto. There was something mellifluous, warm and pleading, about it. It sounded like Mahiru's voice. The one he knew from childhood.

But right now that voice from his childhood was telling him that a demon was controlling her.

The demon's curse.

Guren narrowed his eyes. He touched his right arm, which held the phone. The curse had infected his own body as well. His blood was poison now. Mitsuki Iori's arm had been transformed into a monster simply from injecting it.

Such a monster possessed Mahiru and was controlling her. Unless...

"Is there any way you can prove this isn't the demon talking, right now?"

"No."

"Then we shouldn't be talking..."

"W-Wait!" Mahiru cried in a panic. "Don't hang up, Guren. If you hang up now, we might never be able to speak again."

Was she telling the truth, or was this just another trap? Guren knew he should hang up. Kureto had paid the price earlier by not doing so when he should have. Mahiru was smart. Terrifyingly smart. A conversation was all it took for her to manipulate you.

He shouldn't be talking to her.

His finger hovered over the off button.

"..."

Yet he couldn't bring himself to hang up.

He knew he should, but he couldn't do it.

"What could you possibly have to say to me, anyways?" he asked.

She seemed relieved that Guren hadn't hung up.

"There's...something I want you to do..."

"Hmph. So now you're trying to manipulate me, too?"

"No. It's not like that. I wanted... I... N-No... Not yet!"

Mahiru's voice suddenly grew strained. Her breathing became ragged.

Guren had witnessed this before. Several times, when they had met, it had seemed as if Mahiru were suffering from a split personality.

When it had happened before, Mahiru had told Guren to run. Away from the demon. That she was already lost.

It could all just be an act. But if it wasn't...

"Is this…the real Mahiru?" Guren asked.

She sounded like she was in pain as she answered, "Yes… I had to call now…while the demon part of me was still asleep…"

Guren didn't know if she was telling the truth. But what need would she have to pretend? She had already tricked the Imperial Demons and the Thousand Nights all by herself. What could someone like Guren have that she could possibly need?

"What did you want me to do?"

"I want…" Her voice sounded heavy. "I want you to kill me… I'm in control of myself less and less every day. I'm barely here at all anymore. It has to be now, before it's too late… While I can still resist—"

"Don't be ridiculous," Guren interrupted her. "Tell me where you are. I'll find a way to control the demon inside you."

"No, Guren. Don't try anything foolish. The next time you see me, you have to kill me as soon as you have the chance…"

"No, enough! Just tell me where you are…"

"Guren! Please! This is my only chance. I can't hold on much longer. Once I'm gone, no one will be able to kill me."

"You sound pretty sure of yourself. No one will be able to kill you? What do you think you'll become, a god?"

"Guren, I'm begging you! There isn't time!!"

"No. Tell me where you are. I'm going to save you."

"Guren… It's already too late for that…"

"Enough, just tell me—"

"GUREN!!" screamed Mahiru. She sounded on the verge of tears.

In fact, Guren had a feeling she might already be crying. He could hear a faint, wet sniffling as she spoke.

"It's already too late…"

" …"

"It makes me happy that you'd want to save me…but I'm already lost. I'm not human anymore. Please, Guren…"

"You…want me to kill you?"

"There's no one else I can ask."

"You're really asking me to kill you?"

"I'm sorry, Guren. I'm so sorry."

"How…"

How on earth did you let this happen? That was what Guren wanted to say. How had someone as smart as Mahiru managed to make such a mess of things?

Why had she given up her humanity? Why had she gone so far there was no turning back?

Why…

"Why…couldn't you have waited for me?" he said.

The words slipped out of Guren's mouth. It was a capricious, irresponsible thing for him to say. What good would waiting have done her? He still didn't have enough power to influence what the Hiragis did. He wasn't powerful enough to save her.

He was just spouting nonsense. He sounded like a foolish weakling.

It didn't seem to matter to Mahiru, though. She began sobbing over the line, and her voice was shaky.

"G-Guren…"

"…"

"I love you, Guren."

"…"

"Please, let me die while I'm still capable of feeling this…"

"No," Guren said. "I am going to save you."

"Please."

"No."

"Kill me."

"Shut up. Just tell me where you are. We can talk when I get there."

She didn't fight him anymore, and just told him where he could find her. They also chose a time to meet. According to Mahiru, she would be in control of herself then, but the amount of time she could stay that way was getting shorter and shorter every day. He needed to hurry.

If they were going to meet, it had to be today.

By tomorrow, she might already be gone.

This could be his last chance.

Or it could all be a trap.

She might just be acting.

Going to meet her was clearly a bad idea.

Every ounce of reason in Guren's mind was screaming at him not to do it.

"..."

But Guren Ichinose wasn't a demon. He was weak and naïve. He was human.

So he went to meet Mahiru Hiragi.

The location Mahiru specified was about a fifteen-minute walk from Ikejiri Ohashi Station, which was one stop away from Shibuya on the Tokyu Den'en-toshi Line.

It was a five-story apartment building painted white on the outside that housed five units on each floor. Judging from the size of the building, they were probably all one-room apartments.

According to what Mahiru had told him, she was renting Room 501. The corner apartment on the top floor.

Guren walked down the narrow entrance lobby and boarded an elevator just large enough to fit maybe four people. It would be hard for him to draw his sword if he were attacked. He glanced at the bag slung over his shoulder which held his enchanted blade.

Guren didn't think he had been followed, but he'd switched trains so many times on the way, any tails he may have had he'd probably shaken. More importantly, the road leading to the apartment building was completely exposed, making it easy to see if anyone was following. Mahiru had probably chosen the location for that reason.

That is, if she was really living there.

The elevator door opened. Guren began walking toward Room 501. The hallway was very narrow. If multiple enemies attacked, it would be difficult for them to strike all at once.

The time was 5:30 p.m.

It was still light outside.

And the temperature was high.

Guren wondered if Mahiru was really waiting inside.

He stopped in front of Room 501.

"…"

He searched for signs that someone was in, but he couldn't tell.

Should he ring the bell? Or just open the door?

Guren decided on the latter.

The door swung open easily. It hadn't been locked. A tepid breeze floated Guren's way. Was there a window open inside?

A pair of women's shoes had been left in the tiny entrance alcove. On one side of the short, dark hallway leading in was the bathroom door, and what appeared to be the room was at the far end.

Guren left his shoes on as he walked down the hallway toward the room.

It didn't seem like anyone was there, after all.

The chamber at the end of the hallway was neither large nor small. It was a simple room, the only furniture a bed and a desk.

A girl's sailor-suit uniform, from First Shibuya High School, hung on the wall.

There was also a pair of stuffed animals on the bed, a cute hare and a tortoise.

The swift hare, and the slow and bumbling tortoise…

"Hmph. Is she just making a fool of me?" muttered Guren.

But the room smelled lived-in. It smelled like Mahiru. An unobtrusive scent of perfume wafted in the air. Guren didn't mind it.

The room was deserted, however.

The window was open. Light from outside filtered in as the curtain swayed in the breeze.

The clock above the desk read 5:33.

Mahiru had specified 5:30 p.m. for their meeting.

That meant she was already three minutes late.

"..."

Guren stood in front of the desk, silent.

On top of it sat a picture frame and a thick notebook. The frame held a photo of two smiling children.

A girl, about five or six years old, was happily hanging onto the arm of a boy around the same age. The boy seemed embarrassed and was looking away from the camera.

It was a photo of Mahiru and Guren from when they were kids. Guren was amazed she had managed to keep it all these years.

"..."

He opened up the notebook.

The pages inside were covered with lines of handwriting. Guren couldn't tell at a glance if it was Mahiru's.

Meanwhile, the content was all about experiments into the demon's curse.

They had almost all been on human subjects.

Test subject dies. The data.

Test subject dies. The data.

The notebook's creator had scribbled comments in the margins. Why a certain experiment might have failed... How many more minutes another subject was able to withstand the demon... Whether or not the project showed any possibility of success... According to the notebook, they had had trouble producing any practical results.

"..."

One of the comments, partway through, caught Guren's eye:

—*If something like that happened to my body, I'd never be able to show my face to Guren again...*

Apparently, one of the test subjects had been Mahiru, herself.

No, not just Mahiru. Mahiru and Shinoa.

According to the notebook, Mahiru and Shinoa had been conceived when the Hiragi Clan leader's seed was artificially inseminated into a female test subject already exposed to the demon's curse.

In other words, Mahiru and Shinoa had been test subjects from the moment they were born.

Although a great amount of time and money had been spent on the project, apparently Mahiru and Shinoa had been the only viable, functioning humans born from the process.

Yet they were also simply human.

Extremely gifted, but still just human.

As a result, the experiments had been called off for the time being. Practical implementation of the demon's curse just wasn't possible with their current level of technology. Any further money spent on the project would go to waste.

While the researchers may have given up, the project didn't truly end there.

Because one day, Mahiru began having dreams. Those dreams were dark. Very dark. In her dreams a demon spoke to her and queried her from the shadows.

Shinoa was still very young, but apparently she began having the same dreams. Mahiru told her not to tell anyone. Despite her young age, Shinoa underwent training to make sure she would never reveal the truth to anyone. Not even under torture.

If their father—if the Hiragis—ever discovered that the demon was speaking to them, the experiments would begin all over again.

Their lives as normal human beings would be over.

"..."

But regardless of how thoroughly they hid the truth, the demon's voice grew louder and louder with each passing day.

And it always spoke the same words.

—*Kill the humans.*

—*Give in to your desires.*

—Annihilate everything.

As the years passed, and Mahiru's body matured… As her heart and her emotions, her vanity, her sexuality, and her need for recognition grew, the demon's voice, too, grew louder.

If the two appeared to be ordinary humans at first, it was only because the flowers of desire had yet to blossom inside them.

But that couldn't go on forever.

Things had changed.

Mahiru knew what desire meant, now.

She wanted to be with Guren.

She wanted to be with someone she loved.

Wanted to be held and caressed.

And the demon spoke to her:

Destroy, it commanded.

Destroy it all, every last thing.

Mahiru knew that if she didn't do something to control the voice, she would lose her mind. Maybe even cease to be human.

Her only path to life lay in finding a way to subdue its power.

The surge of desire Mahiru was experiencing seemed closely linked to her development of secondary sexual characteristics. Once she had her first period, the demon's influence grew exponentially stronger. She even began having blackouts, during which she completely lost herself to desire. The episodes increased in frequency with each passing day.

Mahiru was running out of time.

She needed to finish what the researchers had started, before Shinoa also hit puberty.

"…"

Mahiru revived the project.

The experiments into the demon's curse.

She went to the Brotherhood of a Thousand Nights for help.

In exchange for giving them information on the Hiragis, they agreed to provide her with the money and knowledge she needed.

Working with the Hiragis had never been an option. Going to

them would reveal the presence of the demon in her sister, who would be subjected to experiments without delay.

Instead, Mahiru used herself as a guinea pig, engaging in a long and lonely fight.

"…"

That was the information Guren gleaned from the first half of the thick notebook. The handwriting in that half still had a hint of childish roundness to it. Lifting his head up, Guren took a break from his crash course.

According to the clock hanging on the wall, it was now past seven.

The room had grown dark, and the sun had already set. Guren was starting to have trouble making out the words on the page.

"How late is she planning to be?" he grumbled. He stood motionless in the darkness of the room.

Mahiru's experiments into the demon curse hadn't been motivated by her own desires, after all. The experiments hadn't been her choice. According to the notebook, she had been driven to such desperate measures.

"…"

Guren suddenly sensed a vague presence behind him. It was behind the floating curtains, on the balcony outside the open window.

A woman's silhouette came into view.

"Mahiru?" Guren said.

"…It's me," she replied.

"Have you been there this whole time?"

"No…I just got here."

"Then you're very late…"

"…"

She didn't reply.

Guren stared at the window. He loosened the drawstring on the bag holding his sword. He was sure that Mahiru had noticed the move.

"Unless…" Guren said, "you don't know that you promised to meet me here in the first place?"

If she didn't, then that wasn't Mahiru on the other side of the curtain.

It was the demon.

The demon that had possessed her.

Guren placed his hand on the hilt of his sword.

He could draw it in a heartbeat, if he needed to.

Mahiru laughed.

"Aha… And what if I don't know? What will you do about it?"

"…"

"Will you try to kill me?"

"You asked me to kill you," Guren reminded her.

"And now you're here to do it? Do you think you even can?"

It was the demon.

The demon was outside that window.

"Where is Mahiru? Is she already gone?"

Mahiru laughed.

"She's here. I'm Mahiru."

"You're not Mahiru."

"Of course I am. Look. This is my hair, these are my breasts, and this is my body. It's all real…"

"You're not Mahiru."

She laughed again. Her voice sounded bright and unconcerned.

"Aha. Ahahaha… You're so cruel. What about you, then? If I'm not Mahiru, what does that make you?"

"…"

"I've been waiting for you all this time. Waiting for you to come and save me. I wanted you to hold me so much. To hold me in your arms, and take me."

"…"

"I even saved my virginity for you. I wanted my first time to be with you. That's what you want, isn't it, Guren?"

"Shut up."

"Hold me, Guren. Take me…"

"I said shut up!" Guren screamed and ripped open the curtain.

Mahiru stood outside, dressed in her sailor-suit school uniform.

But she wasn't laughing.

She wasn't even smiling.

Her eyes were filled with tears.

The moment their eyes met she lost it, and her face crumpled in sobs. Tears began spilling down her cheeks. She took a step back, as if afraid.

She turned, as if to flee.

Guren reached out and grabbed her arm before she could go. If she actually wanted to kill him—if she was an enemy, the demon—then it would be his last move. She could kill him on the spot if she wished.

But Guren didn't care anymore. He grabbed her by the arm and, pulling her inside, held her to his chest.

She was shaking.

Shaking uncontrollably.

"You should have come sooner, Guren…" she said. "I'm not the one, Guren… I'm not the one who was late…"

"I know. I'm sorry…"

He couldn't manage any other reply.

Mahiru tried to pull away, still shaking.

"Let me go…"

"Mahiru, calm down."

"It's too late now…"

"Mahiru."

"I'm not human anymore, Guren… You can't hold me. I've lost that right. I can't be with you any—"

Guren cut her off. "We're together right now! I'm here, with you, right now!" He pulled her closer, attempting to calm her down.

But her shaking wouldn't stop.

He couldn't banish the shadows lurking inside of her.

So he did the only thing he could, there in the moment, and continued to embrace her as tight as he could.

"..."

At long last the tension drained from her body. Holding on to Guren, she buried her face in his chest as if he were truly her salvation. He heard a muffled choking as though she were trying to stem her tears.

There was still nothing Guren could do for her. He wasn't powerful enough to make it all better. He just held her, silently. Her body was soft. It was a woman's body.

Moonlight streamed in between the curtains and fell across the desk, illuminating the photograph of them as children.

The smile on Mahiru's face, in the photo, was happy and carefree. Guren, meanwhile, was looking away, too embarrassed to meet her joy for joy.

Had Mahiru really been harboring this darkness inside her back then? Had she already been running from the demon's?

Guren suddenly remembered Mahiru's voice.

On that day, long ago.

I want to stay with Guren... she had screamed.

But they had been separated.

And ten years had passed since then.

The carefree smile was gone from Mahiru's face. In its place were tears. And bitter smiles of resignation.

Guren tried to think of some way to make things better.

He stroked her hair softly as he spoke.

"For now..." he said, "I don't want you leaving my side. No more talk of things being too late. I'll find a way. I'll save you..."

"You can't," she said sulkily.

Guren shook his head. "I'll find a way."

"You can't."

"I will."

"But you can't!"

Her voice was plaintive, as if she were begging to just be taken care of. It shook with tears.

"I'll find a way," Guren said, one more time.

He cursed his own weakness. Why couldn't he do anything other than make empty promises?

His words were hollow, almost frivolous.

But he just wanted her to know...

"...you're not alone anymore."

Mahiru clung to him even tighter. Little by little, Guren felt her tremors begin to die down.

She lifted up her face. The tears were still streaming down her cheeks. Even so, her beauty was breathtaking.

"Guren..." she whispered. "Do you still love me?"

Guren still wasn't sure; they had been apart for so long.

When he was six he had definitely liked her. There was no question about it. In a way, she had been his whole world. She was the reason he had first started pursuing power. Because he wanted to get her back someday.

But too much time had passed.

Ten years.

Ten years, and in all that time they hadn't met.

Guren had followers of his own, now. He had the lives of everyone in the Order of the Imperial Moon—the sect headed by the Ichinose Clan—resting on his shoulders. One lapse in judgment was all it would take for those lives to be lost.

Guren couldn't act irresponsibly anymore.

But he had already thrown that responsibility out the window today.

By coming to a place he shouldn't have, and by holding in his arms a woman whom he knew he shouldn't be meddling with.

Guren was risking his own life just by being there.

If he died, it would be over.

He wouldn't be able to protect anyone anymore.

He wouldn't be able to save any more people.

All his childhood ambition, all the cards he had stacked into the deck, would end up being for naught.

Mahiru chuckled quietly. There was fear in her face.

"You...don't love me, do you? Of course you don't. It's been ten years, after all."

"..."

"I'm not even human anymore... How could...how could anyone love a vile monster like me?"

"Dammit..." Guren let out a frustrated groan. "Just be quiet. Isn't it obvious how I feel? Look at what I'm doing. You know I shouldn't have come here. You know I shouldn't be touching you. So why do you think I'm doing it?!"

Guren's heart sank. With disappointment, at himself and his own weakness. He was betraying the friends and comrades who'd trusted him for so long.

Was there at least some part of what he was doing that was calculated? Could they wrest some gain from this situation? After all, if they managed to get Mahiru on their side, surely that would be in their best interests. If Guren could just convince himself that he was here for precisely that reason, he could forgive himself...

"Dammit, I really am a fool," he despaired.

Mahiru's face convulsed again, this time with joy. Fresh tears began spilling down her cheek.

"I love you, Guren," she said, clinging tightly to his chest.

Her shaking had finally stopped.

Had Guren finally managed to banish those shadows lurking in her?

The dark room. The moonlight. The gently swaying curtain.

What could he do to draw her further from the darkness?

"Please, Guren..." she said, murmuring into his chest. "I want you to take me."

"..."

"Will you sleep with me? Even if I am a monster?"

"..."

Mahiru had called herself a monster, vile.

Guren could see she was damaged. How could she not be? She was only sixteen, the same age as Guren.

But she was alone.

She had been alone for all this time.

"If I do, will it help you let go of some of that darkness you're holding?" Guren asked Mahiru.

"I don't know... I don't know anything, anymore. I'm just...so tired—"

Before she could finish, Guren touched her cheek, tilted her chin upward, and sealed her lips with his own.

He wasn't sure if it was the right thing to do, but he felt the softness of her mouth against his own. She didn't look like a monster to him. There was nothing vile about her.

Mahiru's eyes widened in surprise. Her pupils grew large. Then, she slowly closed her eyes in ecstasy.

Guren could feel his desire for her rising up in him.

Desires were supposedly what the demons thrived on. Vile, disgusting.

They remained that way for some time, locked in their kiss.

The curtain drifted into the room, caught on the night air. Guren lost track of how long it lasted.

Finally, Mahiru took a step backward.

"Heh...heheh," she laughed shyly. "I didn't expect you to kiss me like that... My heart's beating so fast I think it might explode."

"Do you feel better now?"

Mahiru glanced at him with a hint of sadness in her eyes. "Did you just kiss me to shut me up?"

"No," Guren replied immediately.

Mahiru smiled. Her face blushed.

"You didn't?"

"No."

Mahiru was still blushing as she spoke. "S-So... Do you still want me? Even the way I am now?"

He did want her. There was no question about that. The desire for her coursed through his body.

The intimate room. Mahiru's scent. The moonlight.

The curtain. The breeze. The photo on the desk.

The summer night. Their memories.

Promises. Dreams.

Ambition. Despair.

Hope. The world.

Christmas.

Destruction.

Friendship.

The Hiragis.

The Thousand Nights.

The Ichinoses.

Once he began thinking, there was no end. No end to the things they should be discussing.

But right now, Mahiru was staring into Guren's face with tears in her eyes.

"Guren, I... I..."

She didn't need to say anything more.

Guren grabbed her arm once more and pulled her to him. She clung to him and the tears flowed as if she had been waiting for his touch.

Was it another chapter in their sad love story?

Or just a fleeting interlude of mercy?

Guren didn't know the answer. Was no longer even sure why he cared.

He took Mahiru in his arms, that day, and made love to her.

◆

"..."

It was over, and Mahiru slipped out of bed.

The room had stayed dark the entire time.

Amid the shadows, Mahiru began fixing her disheveled uniform. She made to leave without saying a word to Guren.

He'd suspected that it might turn out this way.

The entire time they had been making love, Mahiru seemed preoccupied with both bliss and melancholy.

It was like she was just trying to forget the darkness. Like she knew the shadows wouldn't disappear but only lift from her mind for a little while. Guren could feel the longing in her skin. It was the same touch he remembered from when they were little. Her smile had once been so bright and sparkling. As long as they were together—Guren had believed it, too—all of their dreams would come true.

"*I love you, Guren! Do you love me too?*"

"..."

"*Guren! Guren, are you listening?*"

"..."

"*Guren, tell me that you love me!*"

"*I don't want to.*"

"*Why? When I love you this much?*"

When they were children, she used to badger him with silly questions. He had always been too embarrassed to answer her.

But now, apparently, it was too late. Guren felt an empty pit in his stomach.

"Are you leaving?" he asked.

Mahiru nodded.

"Isn't there anything I can do to save you?"

"It's all right. This helped."

"Don't go, Mahiru. I..."

"You can't protect me. Not yet. You know that, don't you?"

"..."

"Besides, you already have people to protect. People other than me."

"…"

"I'll tell you what, if you can give me some proof, then I'll come with you. If you really love me, and want to be with me…then kill your friends. Kill all of them."

Mahiru turned to face Guren. There was a sad smile on her face. She looked like she was about to cry.

"You can't do it, can you?" she said.

"…"

"It's because you're kind. So kind that you were willing to sleep with me when I seemed lost and sad, just to make me feel better. You're so different from me. All I ever think about is myself."

Guren glanced up at Mahiru. Bathed in the moonlight, her face was exquisite.

"Is wanting to protect your friends really that foolish?" he asked.

Mahiru shook her head. "No… I think it's chivalrous. You're very chivalrous, Guren. But that's not how you become stronger."

"You've been trying to protect your sister, though, haven't you?"

"Yes, I have. I ate Shinoa's demon. I was so desperate to save her that I swallowed it up whole. But that turned out to be my downfall. Once I had two demons inside me, I couldn't hold myself together any longer. Still…" Mahiru stared at Guren. "I might be broken, but I don't think I'll forget what we did today. I love you, Guren. And I thank you. You finally gave me what I wanted."

She spread both her arms out wide.

"Thanks to this…the last bit of weakness left in my heart has finally died. Mahiru, the pathetic little six-year-old girl who called you on the phone to cry about how much she loved you, has let go of her attachment to this world and passed away."

Guren glared at Mahiru. "That's what you wanted? You were using me…"

"Exactly."

157

"You wanted to kill off your remaining weakness? Is Mahiru really gone? Are you just the demon now?"

"That's right."

"Don't fucking lie to me. How am I supposed to believe what you say, when you look like you're about to burst into tears while you're saying it?"

Mahiru stared back at him. Her face looked sad.

And human. Still the face of a weak little human girl.

"I'll leave the research log with the data on the cursed gear," she said. Her voice sounded lonely. "If you really want to save me, then come find me again after you've killed the others."

"Mahiru, just tell me what you're fighting against."

"..."

"If you swallowed Shinoa's demon, then she's not in danger anymore, is she? What are you worried about, then? The demons inside of you? If that's the case, then you should just come with me to our research lab—"

"Is that the extent of your ambition?" interrupted Mahiru.

"..."

"Once you have me, would I be enough to make you happy? There are so many other people you have to protect. Could you really toss them all aside just to run away with me?"

"..."

"I didn't think so."

Mahiru smiled. But she still looked ready to cry.

"And your ambition?" Guren said, staring back at her. "Why are you doing all this? What are you trying to achieve? Are you just trying to destroy the Hiragis?"

Mahiru didn't answer. She pushed off one foot and leapt into the air, sailing backward. As though weightless, her body traveled across the room toward the window. Guren couldn't catch up to her. He couldn't stop her. He was too weak. She was untouchable.

"I'm sorry for getting you wrapped up in all of this, though,

Guren…"

"What do you mean?"

"I managed to get the demon out of Shinoa, but in the end I wound up splitting it with you. Now you're going to become a demon, too. I guess I still wanted to depend on you a little…"

"Then stay here. We can fight this thing together."

Mahiru shook her head. "There's no time left."

What was she talking about?

Time she had left as a human?

Or time until the world came to an end?

"What in the hell is going to happen at Christmas, Mahiru?"

"I already told you, the world is going to come to an end. It's exactly what it sounds like. The adults will be destroyed first, because they're the most tainted and filled with desire. When it happens, everyone in the world over the age of thirteen will die."

"What?"

"God is angry. At us, for our greed. At mankind's vile nature and insatiable desire. At the unspeakable research we've been pursuing.

"The land will rot.

"Monsters will roam the Earth.

"Poison will rain from the sky.

"The Seraph of the End will blow its trumpet, and this world will fall.

"Mankind won't be able to survive in the new world. Not the weak, at least."

Mahiru's words reminded Guren of everything he had learned.

Christmas. Destruction. A virus.

"Is it going to be an act of terrorism? Is the Thousand Nights planning to release a virus?"

Mahiru just smiled in response, poignantly, and enigmatically.

The curtain behind her suddenly billowed outward. It wasn't blown by the wind this time, though. A black silhouette appeared, and the curtain was torn to shreds.

The silhouette came leaping into the room. It was the figure Guren had seen the night before, in the park.

She was beautiful.

And her mouth was open wide.

In a gaping maw of fangs.

She was a vampire.

An opponent so strong no human could dare to face her.

"I finally found you, Mahiru Hiragi..." the vampire said.

"Mahiru!" shouted Guren.

The smile remained on Mahiru's face.

"Come, Ashuramaru..." she said.

It was a name Guren had never heard before. An obsidian blade appeared in Mahiru's right hand in response to her call.

Was it another cursed weapon? Mahiru swung the sword. Guren couldn't even see her arm move, her strike had been so fast. Much faster than even the vampire could dodge.

"Ah..."

The vampire's body was sliced clean in two. A look of surprise crossed her face, but then it was over. Both halves of her disintegrated into thin air.

Guren hadn't even been able to budge. All he'd managed before it was over was to shout Mahiru's name.

Mahiru glanced over her shoulder at him. She was still holding the cursed sword in her hand. She looked sad.

"Were you scared, Guren?" she asked. "When the vampire was chasing you yesterday?"

"So you were behind that?"

"Behind killing everyone from the Thousand Nights? I concocted a rumor that the Hiragis did that. Today, the Thousand Nights are going to get their revenge. And then the Hiragis will get revenge against the Thousand Nights. And then the Thousand Nights will—"

Mahiru's words were cut off by the sound of an explosion in the distance.

Bam! B-B-Bam! Kabam!

A staccato roar filled the air. It almost sounded like a war movie.

Moments later, the sound of police sirens and fire engines reached Guren's ears.

The noises were coming from the direction of Shibuya.

Mahiru smiled. She smiled at him.

"It looks like it's started. Until yesterday I was the only hare in the race...but things are going to change today. Everyone will need to become a hare. Everyone in the world. Make haste, make haste."

Guren stared at her. He glanced past her shoulder out the window.

The sounds continued.

Explosions even began to ring out near their current location, which was at least two miles from Shibuya.

"Aha. Let me guess, you're worried about your friends. What about little Shigure and Sayuri, whom you care so much about? Do you think they're already dead?"

Guren glared at her.

"Don't look at me like that. I thought you loved me? Enough to sleep with me, remember?"

"What are you trying to accomplish?"

"The same thing you are!"

"Don't mess with me."

"I'm not messing with you."

"I said don't mess with me!"

"I'm trying to be with you, Guren," Mahiru assured him with a smile. "To live with you, even if it's in the next world. Even if it's in a world where mankind can no longer survive. But for that to happen, we're going to have to be demons."

"I'm not going there with you..."

"Oh? Weren't you just telling me to always stay by your side?"

"You'll come with me. I won't let you give up your humanity."

A sad expression appeared again on Mahiru's face.

Then the sound of another barrage rang out. It came from behind

Mahiru, out the window. Something exploded. Guren could hear screaming, as well. And angry shouts.

—*Kill these Thousand Nights scum!*

The battle was growing heated.

Mahiru moved further away from Guren, toward the window.

"Haha. Look at how vile humans are. Give them the slightest reason to doubt, and they tear each other's throats out. Is that the side you want me to join?"

"Mahiru."

But she wasn't listening. She was still drifting away from him.

"There's one thing I know though, Guren. You're strong. Very strong. That's why I love you. Kureto can't hold a candle to you. If you ever get serious, the whole world will tremble at your feet. Because human strength lies in naïveté, weakness, and vileness. A demon's favorite things."

"Mahiru, wait!"

But she didn't wait. She turned her back to him. Before leaping from the window, however, she turned around one last time. As if she had just remembered something.

"Oh, by the way, Guren, how old are we now?"

And then she was gone.

All that she left behind was the darkness and her scent.

How old were they?

Guren had just turned sixteen in August.

According to Mahiru, however, the virus was going to kill off everyone over the age of thirteen. It was hard to believe.

A world where mankind could no longer survive.

Or at least, not the weak amongst them.

Guren's phone, which was lying on the bed, began to ring. He picked it up and answered. It was Sayuri.

"Sayuri, are you all right?"

"Master Guren!" she shouted. "You have to ru... ... ousand Nigh..."

And then the line went dead. Guren tried calling back immediately. No one answered.

He tried Shigure next, but she didn't pick up, either.

"Dammit!"

Buttoning up his shirt with one hand, Guren reached down to grab his sword from the floor.

Outside, the sound of another explosion filled the air.

Just then, Guren's phone rang again. He picked up immediately.

"Sayuri?"

It wasn't her, though. It was Mito, and Guren could hear that she was crying.

"G-Guren… You're alive! Wh-Where are you?"

"Where are *you?*"

"At school, in the audiovisual room. I barricaded myself inside with some of the other students."

"I'm on my way."

"No, don't come. If you come you'll be killed."

"Then why are you calling? You wanted help, didn't you? So just shut up and tell me what I need to know—"

"No, Guren," Mito cut him off. "That's not why I'm calling… I just…wanted to thank you…"

Guren grabbed the notebook off the desk and dashed out of the room.

Mito was still talking. "The truth is…yesterday was the first time I'd ever been to a friend's house, let alone a boy's…"

The elevator was on the first floor. There was no time to wait. Guren took the stairs.

"Everyone was always so uptight around me growing up, treating me like some princess because I was from the Jujo Clan. I couldn't talk to anyone about how I really felt…"

Guren reached the first floor and raced out into the street. An explosion rang out nearby, but there were still no signs of fighting in sight.

"But you treated me like no one else did. The first time we met, you told me I talked too much, and that I got on your nerves... At first I thought you were just rude. But..."

Mito's voice shook. It sounded like she was crying.

"I think I was also glad. It was the first time anyone had ever addressed me like a normal girl. Not a Jujo princess, just a normal girl... That's why..."

"Why what? Just be quiet and listen to what I say. Tell me what's happening there. Who are you with, and what's your status..."

"Guren, please, listen..."

"No, you listen to me..."

She didn't, though.

"I think...I'm going to die today. B-But it occurred to me... I'd never even been to a friend's house until yesterday...never fallen in love... What kind of life is that?"

"Be quiet. You're not going to die. Just listen to what I say..."

Mito kept talking. "But I liked you, Guren. I think, maybe, you might be my first love..."

"Don't 'maybe' me! Come out of this alive and you can figure out how you feel later. Love won't mean shit if you die!"

"..."

"Mito!"

"..."

"Mito, are you listening?!"

"I'm scared, Guren... I'm scared... The bleeding, it won't stop..."

"..."

"We're surrounded by enemies..."

"..."

"Norito, Sayuri, and Shigure, they protected me... It's my fault..."

"..."

"The door's not going to hold much longer..."

"Calm down, Mito. I'm coming, just wait for me. Everything will be fine. I'm coming and I'll save you. Don't give up, just hold out until I get there..."

"Please, Guren, don't come. If you came as well—"

"Forget about me. Just hold the audiovisual room with everything you've got until I get there."

"Guren..."

"What?"

"Please..."

Just then, an explosion rang out on Mito's end and the phone went dead.

"Dammit..." muttered Guren. Then he shouted, not caring if anyone heard. "Dammit! Fucking dammit!!"

He was going to save her? He was powerless. Who did he think he was? He could talk big, but when it came down to it, he didn't have the power or the guts to back up what he said.

If he wanted to be able to protect people, really help them, he should have started making progress sooner.

What had he been doing all this time? What in all hell...

"..."

Something strange that he spotted out of the corner of his eye interrupted his train of thought. Something miraculous.

It was waiting at the end of the dark road.

A motorcycle, engine running, with no one straddling it.

And next to the motorcycle...

A single sword, thrust into the earth.

It was jet black. It shone with heartless beauty beneath the pale dark moon.

"..."

It was the sword that Mahiru had once wielded.

The sword she'd used to infect Guren with the demon's poison.

It was cursed gear.

Guren's jaw dropped.

The sword was waiting for him.

The demon's curse was a power too dangerous for human hands. As Guren stared at the blade, it all became clear.

How foolish and pathetic was he going to become—how far was he going to play into Mahiru's hand—before he was satisfied?

Guren began chuckling.

"Ha… Haha… Ahahaha… Okay, Mahiru, I get it. I give up. I'll become a hare, too. A demon. But I won't be like you. I won't give up everything. I won't stop being human."

Guren dialed Kureto's number on his phone.

Picking up on the first ring, Kureto said, "What is it?"

"Are you safe?"

"Huh? You're not actually worried about me, are you? Where are you, now?"

Guren told him his current address. He knew it without checking. After Mahiru had given him her location, he had looked up the surrounding neighborhood and memorized all the streets.

"Ikejiri?" asked Kureto. "Why are you in Ikejiri?"

"I was meeting with Mahiru Hiragi."

Kureto's voice suddenly grew cold. "I see…"

"She was the one who killed the men from the Thousand Nights."

"And? What does it matter? It's too late to stop the war now."

"I know."

"So what's your point?"

"Mahiru was researching demonic curses. I'm about to let the curse into my own body. I'm going to use that power to try and save the others at school."

"…"

"But if I lose control of myself and become a rampaging monster, I want you to kill me. I'm going to leave Mahiru's research log here in the alley, at the address I just gave you. If anyone could use it to figure out a way to kill me, it'd probably be you."

"What in the hell are you talking about? Who put you up to this?"

"No one. I'm just a pathetic Ichinose mongrel. I don't even have anyone I can turn to now other than you. You're my only choice."

"And what makes you think you can trust me?"

"The fact that *you* trusted *me*," answered Guren.

"..."

Kureto didn't answer right away. It wasn't important. Guren had said all that he needed to. Whatever happened later was up to fate.

"Understood..." Kureto said. "We'll drive out these Thousand Nights scum together."

With that, Guren hung up.

He had one more number to dial. Shinya picked up the phone immediately, just as Guren expected.

"Guren? You're still alive?"

"Yeah. We need to talk."

"You're not kidding. I can't believe what's happening..."

"I slept with Mahiru," Guren said.

Shinya was silent for a moment. "Are you calling to brag?" he finally asked.

"You're angry, aren't you?"

"I don't know... I always knew Mahiru was in love with you. Still...I guess I am. I just don't like losing to you. Why do you suppose that is?"

"How should I know?"

"Haha. So after all these years, you got your wish. How was it?"

"Terrible. Everything's turned out a mess."

"You're telling me... I just need to take a look around to figure that out. And what are you going to do now?"

"Wield cursed gear, and become a demon."

"What?! Why?"

"Sayuri, Shigure, Mito, and Norito are all at the school. They're under attack from the Thousand Nights."

"Yeah?"

"I'm going to save them."

Shinya let out an exasperated sigh and said, "You really are an idiot, aren't you?"

Guren remained silent. He couldn't argue.

"So," Shinya wanted to know, "why are you calling me?"

"If I die, I want you to take care of Mahiru."

"Are you asking me to marry her? Or to kill her?"

Guren hung up without answering. There was nothing more for him to say.

The cursed sword was still thrust into the ground. Guren stared down at it. The last time he had touched this sword, the demon inside had tried to possess his body, and Guren had been almost entirely powerless to resist it.

The same thing would probably happen this time, too.

Once he touched the sword, he would cease to be human. But right now he needed its power.

Desperately. There was no time to hesitate.

Guren remembered what Mahiru had said moments ago.

How old are we again?

Guren was sixteen.

That was the age at which he was giving up his humanity.

But the time for hesitation—the time for second-guessing—was past.

Mongrel or not, if Guren was going to save anyone... If he was going to save his friends... Then he had to take this plunge and move forward. He spoke quietly to himself as he stared down at the blade thrust into the earth.

"I'm going to save Mito. I'm going to save Norito. I'm going to save Sayuri. And I'm going to save Shigure.

"I'm not like Mahiru. This is my humanity... I'm doing this to save my friends..."

Guren gripped the sword.

The moment his fingers touched the pommel, his world turned black.

Dark.

Obsidian.

Soaked pitch black—

That was the moment when it began.

Guren Ichinose: catastrophe at sixteen.

Seraph of the End, the novel: Book Three!

I know a lot of shocking things happened this time, but what did you think?

We saw characters get caught up in the storm as their world moved closer to destruction.

What will happen to Guren, Kureto, Shinya, Mahiru, Shinoa, and all the others at First Shibuya High School?

And how does everything that's happening relate to the world after the fall, as depicted in the manga?

You're gonna have to keep reading to find out!

By the way, they originally asked me to write three pages this time for the afterword, but then I got a call from the editor. It went like so:

Editor: Hello, Mr. Kagami? Have you written your next afterword yet??

Me: No, I haven't! Many, many apologies! I'm sorry I'm always late!

Editor: No, no, that actually works out great this time. Mr. Yamamoto was saying that there's another scene he wants to draw. He asked if he could illustrate an extra page this time...

Me: I *see!* So there will be eleven drawings this time? That's great! What scene will it be?

And so that's why there is one extra B&W illustration in this volume.

I wish I could tell you which scene it is… But you're going to have to guess!

By the way, it seems like Mr. Yamamoto's schedule has been pretty hectic.

My schedule has been pretty hectic, too.

But we both love *Seraph of the End*. So we promise to work extra hard on it next year too!

Until then, thanks for your support!

Takaya Kagami
Website:
"Healthy Living with Takaya Kagami"
http://www.kagamitakaya.com

Book Four

A voice.

It is soft and gentle and bright, like the voice of an angel.

It asks a question.

Q. At some point in your life it becomes clear that your dreams will never come true. What do you do?

Please choose one of the following:

1. Give up.
2. Try harder, even though you know doing so is pointless.
3. Force your dreams to come true, even if it involves violating certain rules—for instance, you might murder someone, betray your friends, or sell your soul to a demon.

Guren Ichinose chose answer number three.

Guren thought about all the coarse desires he harbored inside him.

He wanted to be with a woman.

He wanted freedom.

He wanted to be important.

He wanted to have power over others.

These were the kind of ordinary, run-of-the-mill desires any sixteen-year-old boy might have.

" ... "

He wanted to show off.

He wanted to be stronger.

He wanted praise.

He wanted people to tell him how amazing he was.

" ... "

He wanted to dry the tears from his childhood girlfriend's face.

He wanted to end his family's humiliation.

He wanted to save the lives of his friends and followers.

These desires swirled like a tornado inside his head.

" ... "

But when you realize that nothing you want will come to pass, what should you do?

When you realize that every last one of your dreams will fail, what should you do?

" ... "

Guren began to think.

He had so many desires in his head.

His mind seemed to overflow with the need to make those hopeless dreams come true.

But the more he wanted, the deeper his disappointment and loneliness grew.

None of his dreams would come true.

He was incapable of protecting anyone.

Whenever it mattered most, he was never strong enough.

Mahiru was damaged. He had watched her cry.

His father had been tortured and he hadn't even been able to complain about it.

And now, Mito was about to be killed by soldiers from the Brotherhood of a Thousand Nights.

For all Guren knew, Sayuri, Shigure, and Norito might already be dead.

What in hell had he been doing all this time?

What gave him the right to be so foolish and weak?

Mahiru had known how weak he was. It was like she had said.

Why don't you grab me in your arms and make me listen to you? That's right. Because you can't yet, can you? I'm so much stronger than you that it's almost heartbreaking. I guess that's what makes me the hare. Hurtling headlong toward destruction. I'm still waiting for my tortoise prince, Guren. Try and save me before it's too late.

But Guren hadn't been able to save her.

He had failed miserably.

And she had cried.

It was too late, now. She was past the point of no return. And she had cried.

He was the tortoise, after all.

Just the tortoise in the end.

Slow and bumbling and on a race to nowhere. A worthless, stupid tortoise who had failed to keep his promise.

"…"

But not anymore, not after today.

He was ready to change.

Guren had had enough.

Enough of being weak. Enough of not being able to protect anyone.

"..."

He had reached out to something foul, a power no human hands were meant to touch.

He had more than enough excuses for doing so.

To justify giving up life as a tortoise, violating the rules, and becoming a hare.

"I'm going to save Mito. I'm going to save Norito. I'm going to save Sayuri. And I'm going to save Shigure," he whispered to himself.

They were his excuses.

It was late at night.

He was still close to the apartment building where he had slept with Mahiru.

In a small alley, leading to her building.

The sword that had infected him with the demon's poison was thrust into the earth before him. It pulsed with a sinister blackness beneath the moonlight.

It was demon cursed.

One touch...

One touch, and it would all be over.

If he touched that sword he would cease to be human. The demon's curse couldn't be controlled. The research was still unfinished.

Guren had just come from seeing Mahiru. He had seen how the curse had broken her completely.

The same would almost certainly happen to him.

Don't.

Guren's sense of reason cried out to him.

Don't touch it.
Don't step off the path…

If he touched the sword he would become a demon.

He would cease to be human. He would lose control of his desires and turn into a demon.

That was running away.

It was a coward's choice. To give up the fight, and run away out of fear. Fear of the difficult, of despair, of the dark. It was tantamount to suicide.

But it was the only choice left.

Mahiru had manipulated him into a corner.

"…"

To tell the truth, though, Guren was really just sick of it.

Sick of being the tortoise.

He stared down at the cursed sword thrust into the ground. The expressions on his face vacillated between determination, disgust, and tears.

"I'm not like Mahiru. I'm doing this to save my friends, humanity…"

Guren gripped the sword.

The moment his fingers touched the pommel, his world turned black.

Dark.

Obsidian.

Soaked pitch black—

From deep in his soul, Guren screamed.

"I'm giving up my humanity so that nothing else will be lost!"

In that brief moment, Guren could have sworn he heard a sound.

It was faint, like the sound of a gear grinding one notch forward.

Closer to destruction.

Closer to the end.

Closer to apocalypse.

Like the trumpet of an angel sitting in cold judgment upon man's greed.

◆

Q. An insurmountable darkness appears before you. You cannot proceed further in human form. What do you do?

Please choose one of the following:

1. Give up being human.
2. Give up being human.
3. Give up being human.

A voice spoke in the darkness.

"Hello, Guren."

" … "

"Guren?"

" … "

"Answer me, Guren."

"Ngh?"

Guren Ichinose's eyes cracked open. He found himself in a very strange place.

Everything around him was blank and white.

He had never seen anywhere like it.

"Where am I?" Guren muttered, glancing around.

"We're inside your mind…" a voice came from behind him.

"Huh? Who's there?"

Guren spun around. A young boy stood in the middle of the blank white space.

He was very beautiful.

He looked to be around twelve.

With milk-white skin.

Scarlet eyes.

And scarlet hair.

Two horns peeked out from atop his head.

" … "

A demon.

The boy was a demon.

There were horns growing out of his head, just like a demon in a fairytale.

Guren finally remembered how he had gotten here.

He had touched the sword.

The cursed sword, which Mahiru had left waiting for him.

And it had brought him here. Into his own mind.

Guren stared down at the demon and spoke.

"Of course… Are you here to hijack my thoughts, demon?"

Surrounded by empty white space, the beautiful demon boy laughed.

"'Hijack' makes it sound like I'm doing something wrong. I'm here because you wanted me, Guren."

"…"

The demon grinned. He was right. Guren had wanted him. He had broken a taboo, done something he knew he wasn't supposed to do.

"It makes me very happy that you want me," the demon said, smiling. "You desire power, don't you? You couldn't have chosen better than me ♪ Once we get inside each other, you'll be stronger than you could have ever imagined."

The demon took a step forward. Inky blackness spread beneath his foot.

"…"

As the blackness spread, Guren had the sense that something precious in him had disappeared.

It felt as if something that was important to hold onto—some part of his warmth or humanity—had just decreased slightly.

He finally pieced together what was happening. He was locked in a battle with the demon for dominance. With every step the demon took, Guren would lose another piece of whatever it was that made him human.

If the demon won, Guren would probably lose control of himself.

He would go mad.

And turn into a fiend.

He would lose all grasp of reason, just like Mahiru. The demon would take over his mind and his body.

"Stay back, demon," Guren said.

The demon grinned.

"♪ Aha? But I don't want to stay back. I'd rather come closer!"

The demon took another step.

A piece of Guren's sanity was shorn off.

"I won't lose to you."

"I'm not your enemy, Guren. You called me. You wanted power. 'Give it to me, I want it so bad,' you said."

The demon stepped closer.

Another piece of Guren's sanity was shorn off.

"Stop speaking my name," he commanded, glaring at the demon.

"Oh? But we're going to be so close. We're going to be together for the rest of our lives. You should say my name, too. It's Noya. Go on, say it. Speak my name, and I'll give you a night of overwhelming carnal pleasure."

The demon stepped closer.

A piece of Guren's sanity was shorn off.

Suddenly, he realized that the empty white space had already turned pitch black.

Darkness. Above, below, inside.

Guren's heart began beating so fast he thought he might throw up.

Arousal and fear played leapfrog inside him.

Desire. Desire began swelling up from deep inside.

Noya was standing right in front of him. He was so close—just another inch and their bodies would touch.

His head at Guren's waist level, he stared up with excitement on his face.

Just another inch.

A single hair's breadth.

But Noya stopped there.

"Guren," he said. "Look at me. Look at how close I am. But I want the last inch to come from you, Guren."

"…"

"Want me, Guren. Hold me. Give your mind and body over to me. Then…"

"…"

"…you'll be able to protect them all." The demon smiled sardonically.

Guren felt the words' seductive pull.

"You've never been able to protect Mahiru. Never been able to protect your parents, your followers, or even your own pride. But now, for the first time in your life, Guren, you'll be able to protect someone."

Guren stared down at Noya, who was still smiling.

Everything around them was dark.

Guren's world had turned pitch black.

He didn't have the strength in him to discover any remaining light in that darkness.

And he was out of time.

If he was going to save his friends and followers, he couldn't waver.

Noya laughed. He knew that Guren was out of time.

"Well? Are you just going to run away again? Say that you're not prepared to make your move yet? That the timing isn't right? I like humans who're like that, too. The kind who can run away shamelessly when it's their own skin on the line. But you're different, aren't you, Guren? I already heard that you were different."

"From whom?" asked Guren.

"From Mahiru," the demon answered. "She said she knew you would wind up here, because of how kind, and good, and human, and endearing you are. She was right. I thought you were adorable the minute I laid eyes on you ♪"

"…"

"You're just so lost, and gentle, and weak, that it's hard not to love you. Once we join together, our strength will be unstoppable!"

"..."

"There's no need for us to hurry, though. It will happen sooner or later. You'll become a demon. Even if you don't touch me today, you'll reach out for me eventually."

"..."

"They'll all be killed, because you weren't able to protect them... And then you'll turn into a demon out of absolute despair. That suits me fine. Either way, it's too late to stop. You can't help but turn into a demon. We're already intertwined."

"..."

"But what will you do today? Will you move forward? Or continue to stand still? You're running out of time, you know. The only reason Mito and the others are still alive at all is because Mahiru has been protecting them. Another ten seconds of hesitation and you'll be too late. If you don't want that to happen, you need to take what's yours. Caress me, take my power. Ten seconds, Guren. I'll count them."

10...
9...
8...

The demon began counting.
His voice was a singsong chant.
Guren stared down at him.
This was all going according to Mahiru's plan.
According to the plans of the dark, shadowy world.
There was nothing Guren could do about it. He couldn't fight fate.

7...
6...
5...

Five seconds left.

If Guren touched the demon, he would give up his humanity.

On the other hand, if he did nothing in the next five seconds—if he ran away—what then?

If he chose to abandon Mito, Norito, Sayuri, and Shigure, what humanity would he have left?

Whether he moved forward or stepped back, the outcome was the same. He would be giving up his humanity.

The demon—Noya—knew this.

It was what filled his voice with glee as he counted.

4...
3...
2...

"If the outcome is the same either way, then I choose to move forward."

Noya tilted his head up. The expression on his face was ecstatic. He spread his arms wide.

"One. Come to me then, Guren. Give up your humanity."

Guren reached out for Noya and grabbed him by the throat.

"Aha, Guren!" Noya shouted in rapture. "Wrong choice ♪ You'd think it would be obvious, but humans should never give up their humanity? You really didn't know that? You're so adorable!"

Guren's eyes widened in surprise.

But it was too late.

Blackness.

Everything went dark.

And relentless power surged into his soul.

Guren opened his eyes. He was back. In reality.

"..."

He was holding a sword in his hand.

It was the sword containing the demon, Noya.

A motorcycle was waiting next to him, with its engine still running. Mahiru had left it there for him.

Sounds suddenly filled the air.

Thud. Da-da-da. Boom.

It was the sound of a battle unfolding nearby.

The sound of the Brotherhood of a Thousand Nights and the Order of Imperial Demons fighting each other tooth and nail.

Guren was in Ikejiri—a neighborhood in the Shibuya Ward of downtown Tokyo. There was no way the two groups could hide a war going on in such a place.

Nonetheless, it was on.

The war had begun.

But Guren was no longer bothered very much by that fact. It was probably because he had joined with the demon. It had already become an irrevocable part of his own being.

Guren could sense the difference.

He wasn't bothered very much, anymore, by the thought of humans dying.

He wasn't bothered very much, anymore, by the thought of human suffering.

Because he wasn't human anymore.

Instead, he was filled with an immeasurable desire to kill. Somebody. Anybody. It was a little…

"…too much… I need to be able to sheathe all these desires with the blade."

Muttering such things, Guren hoisted himself onto the bike.

Meanwhile:

Shinya Hiragi killed a man. He was in the middle of a busy neighborhood when he did it.

Someone—an ordinary citizen—saw what he did and began screaming.

"Eeeeek!"

They were standing in front of the statue of Hachiko, of all places, in Shibuya, Tokyo—one of the busiest nightlife areas in all of Japan. Tens of thousands of potential witnesses surrounded him.

There were so many people packed there that it was hard to believe they were actually outdoors. Maneuvering through the crowd was almost impossible.

There were office workers hurrying home.

Scantily clad women, eager to usher in Shibuya's nightlife.

Young men out on the prowl for women just like them.

Some of the people were waiting for boyfriends, girlfriends, friends. Others were just killing time. But this was a place where people came to meet.

It was August.

Summer.

Another long night of debauchery was about to begin.

That was exactly why Shinya had chosen that spot to slip into the crowd and hide. He figured not even the Thousand Nights would attack in the heart of Shibuya. If they tried to fight in a place like this, they would never be able to cover it up.

But Shinya had figured wrong.

The Thousand Nights had attacked him.

And Shinya had just killed one of them.

He'd killed the man quietly. The only one who seemed to notice, out of that whole throng of people, was a girl in a flower-print one-piece dress. She stared at Shinya with a panic-stricken expression and began screaming.

The crowd all turned their eyes toward her.

If Shinya was going to run, he had to do it now. This was his chance...

Just then, another man in a black suit burst free from the crowd and came at Shinya. He was an assassin from the Thousand Nights.

"Shit!"

Grabbing the arm of the blacksuit, who was holding a knife, Shinya wrestled it from him and thrust it into his neck—not the best spot to have stabbed him. A fountain of blood erupted at once, spouting high into the air. Shinya was drenched, his vision stained red. Unfortunately, the difference in strength between them had been too slight for Shinya to be able to kill the man stealthily.

The men after him were strong.

Just like you would expect from the biggest syndicate in Japan.

People began turning their attention in Shinya's direction.

Their eyes opened wide in confusion, still trying to figure out what had occurred. Once enough people realized what was happening, full-on pandemonium would erupt for sure. Shinya couldn't afford to get swept up in that chaos.

He took quick stock of his surroundings and spotted an escape route. There were no enemies that way.

He was surrounded by a sea of faces.

Face. After face.

After face.

"What's this supposed to be?" one guy said. "Some kind of performance art?"

The guy had bleach-blond hair and the kind of face that made you want to punch it—always sneering at everyone else. He was chewing loudly on a piece of gum.

His girlfriend stood next to him. She had bleached hair as well.

"Forget about that, Shin baby," she said. "You promised you'd take me to a love hotel."

Nearby, an office worker was talking on his cell phone.

"Daddy will be home soon, Yumi," he said. "Real soon. Can you put mommy on the phone?"

And behind him was a blacksuit.

And another.

And another.

There were three of them altogether.

They were coming from the direction of Shibuya Station.

"Oh man, give me a break already," Shinya moaned and stepped backward.

Toward the screaming girl. The one in the flower-print dress who had seen him kill the first man.

She was the reason panic still hadn't broken out. Thanks to her screaming, everyone was still looking at her instead of Shinya.

Only a few of them had seen the spray of blood.

If she hadn't been there, they would have all seen him kill the second man.

It was just a matter of seconds, though. Soon people would spot the body. And then pandemonium would ensue.

But if it was going to happen either way...

"...maybe I oughta just speed things up!"

He grabbed the screaming girl by her neck.

"N-No!" she shouted.

Shinya shoved her in the direction of the fresh corpse.

"Aiiiiiiiiieeeeeeeeeeeeee!"

She started screaming even louder than before. Like a siren. With two dead bodies lying at her feet. The crowd—there were so many people nearby that most of them couldn't see her, but the people closest—turned their attention to the girl.

A chain reaction swept through Hachiko Plaza.

One person spotted the bodies.

And then two.

And then four.

And then eight.

They began to scream. And then their screams spread like lightning to the thousands of people nearby.

"Agggghhhhhh!!"

Soon nearly everyone was screaming. A stampede broke out. The ground seemed to shake beneath their feet.

But Shinya had been prepared for that. In the flash of an eye he worked a spell. He did it so fast that not even the handful of people standing directly behind him noticed.

He was directing the chaos in the opposite direction, away from himself and towards the blacksuits from the Thousand Nights, so that the stampede would swallow them up.

But would it be enough to facilitate his escape?

He turned on his heel and fled.

He headed for the Shibuya Scramble intersection, threading himself like a needle through the gaps in between people. The blacksuits weren't following, but there was no telling when they would find him and attack again. Shinya already knew that the room he was renting nearby was unsafe. He had fled to Shibuya Station because he had been attacked there.

Which meant...

"...the enemy has already gathered plenty of intelligence on us. I wonder how the Imperial Demons are doing."

Shinya pulled out his phone as he continued to make his way.

He dialed the number for the president of the student council.

196

Kureto Hiragi.

The call went through.

"Hey."

"Shinya? What's all that noise in the background? Where are you?"

"Shibuya Scramble. They attacked me here. Can you believe it? Does this mean the war is already out in the open?"

"What's the situation there?"

"I'm afraid Shibuya is in danger of partying all night long."

Kureto didn't laugh. Some people just had no sense of humor.

"Can you make your way to the school?" the student council president asked.

"Is the school being attacked too? Are you assembling troops?"

"Yes. I want you to take command of them."

"Me? Hmph. How are things elsewhere?"

"There are casualties on both sides. The numbers are still unclear. We don't know what they're after or how far they're willing to go. Father is getting ready to go negotiate."

Shinya narrowed his eyes.

Father. He meant Tenri Hiragi, the supreme ruler of the Order of the Imperial Demons.

Kureto's father.

Mahiru's father.

Shinoa's father.

Seishiro's father.

And, of course, Shinya's adoptive father.

Shinya, however, had never met the man. Not even once...

"Father?"

"Yes. But until he's back, it's up to us to defend Shibuya."

"The enemy, though, is clearly..."

"I know. The ones who attacked you were tough, weren't they? Higher-ups? The same thing happened here. But we have information on some of the Thousand Nights' most dangerous combatants. We've set up counterattacks and have already taken out many of their best."

"But they've killed many of ours, too?"

"Yes. Right now, though, we have to protect the school. A lot of the kids there are from the great clans. This is the second time the school's been attacked. If we keep letting their sons and daughters get slaughtered like this, it will destabilize the order."

"I thought you great and venerable Hiragis were above such worries," Shinya said with a smirk.

Kureto laughed a little. "You're part of the Hiragi Clan, too. Or have you forgotten that?"

"I'm just adopted. And after what happened with my bride-to-be, I'm guessing I don't hold much value for the clan anymore."

"Then stand by our side now, and prove yourself through service on the battlefield."

Shinya was silent.

If there was an opportunity for him to prove himself in such a way, that must mean that the battle wasn't going well.

The corollary also crossed his mind: this was an opportunity for him to betray the clan.

If Shinya wanted to crush the Hiragis, now might be an interesting time to switch sides, but that was no longer his ambition.

It didn't really matter to him anymore whether the Hiragi Clan stood or fell.

Nothing about the world would change, either way. If the Hiragis fell, then the Thousand Nights would simply step in to rule the magic-using world undisputed.

The world would continue to turn, as dark and desolate as before.

Mahiru—his former bride-to-be—had already been swallowed whole by that darkness.

"..."

Even now, Shinya realized, there was still a part of him that wanted to save her.

It wasn't because he loved her or had special feelings for her. It was just a natural inclination for someone who'd never been given any other reason for living.

Mahiru had broken free from the Hiragis and made her way to the outside world. Shinya had just been trying to follow her.

Sometimes, he wondered if he had any unique self.

He seemed to be incapable of finding his own reason for living, just like some spoiled rich brat who coasted through life on the path his parents had set out for him.

To top things off, his supposed fiancée had been stolen from him. She had cheated on him by sleeping with Guren.

"Ha...hahaha..." he chuckled.

Holding the phone to his ear in the middle of busy Shibuya traffic, Shinya was laughing at his sorry self.

"What's so funny?" said Kureto.

"It's nothing... Can I ask you something, though?"

"What is it?"

"What's your reason for living, Kureto?"

"Huh?"

"Do you have some purpose in life?"

"What the hell are you talking about?"

"Nothing, never mind," Shinya said with a self-deprecating laugh. "It was just a joke."

After a moment of silence, however, Kureto answered.

"I have one goal in everything I do. My role is to secure all profit and interest in any given situation for the Hiragi Clan, and the Order of the Imperial Demons."

"Haha. So you're just carrying out your assigned role, too. That's what you were raised to do ever since you were a child, huh?"

"That's right."

"But it's not really what you want in life."

In the end, Kureto was also just coasting along the path set out for him. It couldn't be something he had chosen for himself.

But that didn't seem to trouble Kureto.

"No, it's what I want," he said. "It's what I'm here for. In the end, people are blank slates. Hollow. Like an empty box. They're formed by their environment. They become a person in the process of fulfilling the role assigned to them."

"…"

"Don't waste time worrying about something like that right now, Shinya," Kureto said. "I will grant you your new role in life. As long as you follow me, you will find new purpose. I am your one true leader."

Chuckling, Shinya said, "You're not trying to brainwash me, are you?"

Kureto laughed. "Hahaha. Of course I am. Did you forget what we are?"

"A sinister cult?"

"Exactly. Trust in me and your faith will be rewarded."

"You're starting to scare me."

"Die in my name, and your soul will tremble in ecstasy."

"Heheh…"

"All right, talk over," Kureto cut back to the matter at hand. "Go to the school. Your first goal is to save your team."

"You mean Mito and the others? They're still alive? I haven't been able to reach them by phone."

"Maybe they are, maybe they aren't. But I'm sending troops that way now. Take command of them and head toward the school."

"Got it. What will you be doing?"

"I have something else to take care of."

"What?" asked Shinya.

But Kureto hung up. Apparently he had nothing else to say to his adopted brother.

Shinya glanced at the phone dubiously before turning his eyes upward to the sky.

The moon shone bright in a patch of night visible between the buildings. Alas, Shibuya gave off so much light that not a single star could be seen even when the sky was clear.

Screams. More screams. Shinya heard screaming coming from

behind him. It was soon followed by the sound of fighting. It seemed that there were other members of the Imperial Demons nearby.

Shinya stopped to think. What should he do now? What did he want to happen?

Guren had called him earlier.

He'd told Shinya that he had slept with Mahiru.

And that everything had turned out a mess. Shinya suspected the whole situation right now was actually Mahiru's doing. It was just the kind of thing she was capable of. She had been possessed by a demon. It was impossible, at this point, for any ordinary person to anticipate what she might do.

She had pushed Guren into a corner. And it seemed as though he'd responded by choosing to move forward.

To wield cursed gear and become a demon.

Obviously, it was the wrong choice.

Nothing in this world was worth a trade with your humanity.

Regardless, at least he was moving forward.

Because he had desires.

Ambition.

Purpose…

"Unlike with me…" Shinya muttered, laughing derisively at himself again.

"I guess that's why Mahiru chose him over me. Not that I can blame her. There's just something about him."

He recalled his conversation with Guren on the phone. His classmate had been saying some pretty ridiculous stuff.

Sayuri, Shigure, Mito, and Norito are under attack from the Thousand Nights. I'm going to save them.

That was why he was giving up his humanity.

To save his friends.

To save Mahiru.

Fighting for truth and justice, like some blockhead in an American comic book.

"Talk about a superhero complex…" Shinya muttered.

As he spoke, though, he realized that he actually idolized Guren a little.

Shinya had killed countless people in order to ensure his own survival. Guren, though, was trying to live for someone else's sake now. He dazzled so hard in Shinya's eyes that it was almost blinding.

"So in order to save Mito, Norito, Sayuri, and Shigure…in order to save other people…he's going to give up his own humanity. Haha! It all sounds pretty crazy to me."

Yet Shinya was on his own way to save Guren.

"I guess I must be as crazy as he is."

He reached the other side of the intersection.

He walked along the sidewalk a little ways before hopping over the guardrail. There was a guy driving a motor scooter along the curb. Shinya slowly extended his hand.

The guy had a slack-jawed expression on his face. He had long hair and was wearing shorts. His helmet was also hanging halfway off his head—which seemed to defeat the purpose of wearing one. Shinya snagged the helmet as he drove past, clothes-lining the man.

"Agghh!"

The guy shouted in surprise. His scooter tipped over and he went skidding onto the ground. He stared up at Shinya in disbelief, and Shinya stared back.

"See, that's exactly what happens. Didn't they teach you to wear your helmet properly in driving school?"

"H-Hey, what in the—"

"I'm gonna borrow your ride for a bit. Hope you don't mind!"

Shinya pushed the scooter upright and hoisted himself onto it. He gave the engine a good throttle.

"Get the hell off my bike," the guy shouted, but Shinya ignored him.

Doubting he would get pulled over, Shinya didn't bother putting on the helmet. With everything going on in Shibuya right now, the police hardly had time to go around arresting people for driving without one.

Behind him, a siren blared in the distance. The cars on the street had all stopped in a massive traffic jam. Those blacksuits probably wouldn't be able to follow him through this.

Ka-boom.

Ka-boom.

The sounds of battle filled the air around him. He wasn't sure where the actual fighting was going down, but he was clearly in the middle of a battlefield.

People were going to die.

Many, many people.

The stoplight up ahead flickered several times.

And then it went out.

The power grid was down.

Shinya's surroundings suddenly grew dark.

The only source of illumination that remained was from the car headlights, but these weren't enough to brighten the streets. Overhead, the stars were still invisible. They were in Shibuya, after all.

Screaming.

Howling.

There were so many people in Shibuya...

"Maybe it wouldn't hurt if a few of them bit the dust."

Just moments ago, Shinya had been surrounded by people for as far as the eye could see. Once he got past Tokyu Department Store, however, he suddenly found himself in a peaceful residential district. The streets here were quiet and lined on both sides by detached family houses.

He could still hear the screaming, though. Tendrils of flame had shot up in several locations, but it didn't seem like there were any firefighters on the way.

They probably couldn't reach the flames. There were too many roadblocks along the way.

In other words...

"...this is the center of the war, ground zero."

Shinya pulled on the throttle.

He was heading toward one of the Imperial Demons' largest training centers—toward First Shibuya High School.

Still meanwhile:

Mito Jujo was using every ounce of strength she had to hold the door shut. Her face was on the verge of tears.

"Dammit, dammit!"

She had wrapped a chain around the door and plastered it with *fuda*—paper charms inscribed with spells—to create a magical barrier.

Enemies pounded on the door from outside. If she let her strength slip for even a moment and let her magic falter, they were certain to get through.

And once they got through the door, everyone would be killed.

Mito, and all the others.

She was in First Shibuya High School's audiovisual room. Several of her classmates had barricaded themselves inside with her.

She had been separated from Norito and Guren's two bodyguards—Sayuri Hanayori and Shigure Yukimi—on her way there.

The last Mito had seen of them, they had been fighting off their attackers, giving Mito and the other students a chance to escape.

"Dammit, dammit!"

Mito continued to push against the door.

She could feel her concentration slipping, and with it, the barrier keeping the door shut.

Earlier, Mito had been caught in the middle of an explosion. A piece of wooden debris had caught her in the leg and stabbed through her right thigh. As she glanced down now, there was blood gushing down her leg from beneath her skirt. It wouldn't stop. But she didn't have the supplies, or the time, to take care of it.

—*Mito! Mito!*

The students behind her called out her name.

They were in the same class as her. Their voices sounded scared.

It seemed like they had already lost their will to fight. It was hard to believe they were the Imperial Demons' elite students, personally chosen by the Hiragi Clan. Mito couldn't blame them, though.

She was so scared herself, she was almost ready to cry.

She had even called Guren earlier to tell him how afraid she was and how she was going to miss him.

In the face of death, she had lost her courage. She had turned to Guren as to a light in the storm.

"Heh…I bet that really caught him off guard…" she muttered, recalling their conversation.

Mito's anxiety eased for a moment. But then the door bulged inward like it was about to burst open, and her fear came rushing back in full force.

She pushed back hard. Her hands were shaking.

"Ahhh… I-I don't want to die, not when I've never been in love," she whispered.

It had been lonely.

So very lonely.

Always having to grow stronger.

The Jujo Clan's only objective was to earn more recognition in the eyes of the Hiragi Clan. Mito's life had been dedicated to constant training.

But now, she was finally realizing…

No matter how hard she trained…

No matter how strong she got…

In the end, when her time came, her life could be snuffed out in a heartbeat.

And if that were the case…

What was the point in trying so hard?

What had she been doing with her life all of this time?

Instead of falling in love?

Instead of having fun?

She had always scolded her classmates for being lazy.

Had constantly pushed herself, like a fool, to become stronger. And now, this was all it had gotten her.

"Ah...haha..."

If the world she had known could crumble down so easily, why hadn't she been a little more honest about what she wanted? Indulged herself a little more often?

Why hadn't she eaten that piece of cake?

Or hung out with friends to have fun?

Why hadn't she let herself fall in love?

"..."

Like the other day, when she had gone to Guren's house after school. She had skipped training in order to hang out and have fun.

She had eaten junk food, even though she knew she shouldn't.

Played shogi.

Laughed with her friends.

It was the first time she had even been to a boy's house.

Her first time doing all sorts of things that she'd never let herself before. And it had been so much fun, it almost brought tears to her eyes.

"..."

Maybe this was all some sort of punishment. For her moment of weakness.

For having given in to desire.

It had to be. She knew it.

After all, she had a feeling she'd never be able to go back to the way she was before. Back to the strict, disciplined life she used to lead.

Even if she somehow managed to survive today, she wouldn't be able to return to that.

Because she had fallen in love.

Fallen in love with Guren.

No…that wasn't true. She was just trying to run away. To the idea of love, to escape from abject terror.

" … "

Now that she was confronted with death, Mito finally accepted her desires. Her weaknesses.

Now that death was staring her in the face, she finally understood that her position, in the Jujo Clan and the Order of Imperial Demons, had little to do with her own happiness in life.

All sorts of ugly feelings began welling up inside her.

She didn't care if anyone else survived—she just wanted to live. Then she could have as much fun as she wanted. Spend the rest of her life eating junk food and falling in love…

—*Mito!*

—*Mito, what should we do?!*

Her classmates weren't helping her fight. They were just crying. Why risk so much, why work so hard, to protect them? What a fool she was. If she had run away on her own, she might have had a chance of surviving.

—*Mito!*

—*Mito, help us, please!*

Her face contorted with tears. She couldn't hold the door on her own any longer. The bleeding wouldn't stop.

Her head was spinning.

She felt like throwing up.

She just wanted to run.

Away from all this responsibility.

Her hands began to shake.

She felt the barrier slipping.

"Keep it together, Mito…" she whispered to herself. "You just need to stay calm and think of a way out of this…"

But the words were barely out of her mouth when the door was slammed hard from the other side.

"Ah!"

The barrier broke and the door sprung open. It happened so suddenly in the end that she didn't even see it coming. Several armed men came rushing into the room.

They were Thousand Nights soldiers, and they began attacking as soon as they were through the door.

—*Aiiieeee!!*

Mito could hear the screaming from behind her.

—*Agggghhh!!*

So much screaming.

But she couldn't turn around to look.

She tried to swing at one of the soldiers in front of her, but was too slow. He dodged her easily.

"Your red hair…" the man said. "You must be the Jujo girl. We have orders to capture you alive."

He reached out and grabbed her arm.

Mito's eyes widened in shock.

She was going to be used as a hostage. Either that or they wanted to run experiments on her and the Crimson Halo—a special kind of magic she had that could only be used by people with Jujo blood.

The right thing to do in this situation was to kill herself. It was her duty. If they took her alive, there was no telling what kind of problems it might cause the Hiragi Clan.

But…

" … "

She couldn't do it.

She didn't want to die.

She was scared.

"Ah…ahh… Dammit!"

She tried to hit the man once more, but he was too fast. And strong. He punched her in the face and then kneed her in the stomach.

"N-Ngh…"

Mito felt the wind get knocked out of her. She couldn't move. The man picked her up like she was a sack of feathers.

At last, she caught a glimpse of her classmates.

They had all been killed.

She'd tried so hard to protect them, but in the end they were dead.

The soldiers from the Thousand Nights laughed.

"I thought the Jujos were supposed to be hot shit or something. That was barely a fight. These Imperial Demons are a joke!"

The man kicked one of the bodies. They all laughed.

Mito was helpless.

And afraid. So very afraid.

Help. Somebody, help me, she thought.

But who could help her now? Who was left to save her?

"Help," she whispered shakily. "Help me, Guren..."

But her voice was overshadowed by the laughter of the men.

Still meanwhile:

In the girls' bathroom, three floors above the audiovisual room.

"Ahh..."

Norito Goshi sat in one of the stalls, perched on the toilet seat. He was trying to think.

What was he gonna do now?

What was his next move?

During the initial attack, he had used his illusions to help Mito, Sayuri, and Shigure get away.

"But how am I gonna get out of this mess?" he groaned.

The window in the girls' bathroom was too small to slip through. He couldn't escape that way.

Norito had lit several *fuda* on fire.

He stuffed them into a small incense pipe resting in the palm of his hand. The burner let off an odorless, invisible smoke that would make his opponents see things that weren't there. He was using it to hide the entrance to the bathroom from sight.

"I bet it won't be long before somebody notices, though…"

For all he knew, in fact, they might have seen through it already.

After all, it was the Thousand Nights he was dealing with, an organization so powerful it could attack the Imperial Demons head on. There were sure to be a few people in their ranks who could see through an illusion like his without difficulty.

If he'd managed to give himself some breathing space, it was only because…

"…the fighting elsewhere is too heated. That must be how I slipped under the radar. Maybe I should try to make a break for it instead of waiting."

Norito blew another strong puff of smoke through the incense pipe, strengthening the illusion's effect.

An onlooker might mistake him for a teenage boy hiding out in the girls' bathroom to sneak a cigarette.

"Which would make me both a pervert and a delinquent…" remarked Norito, chuckling to himself.

This was no time for laughter, though. Several students had already been killed before his very eyes. And he was injured, too. Plus, he had no idea if Mito and the others had gotten away safely.

"Should I try to hold tight until the Imperial Demon Army gets here? Or is this too much for even them to handle?"

If the Army couldn't help, then he should probably surrender at the first chance.

Because if they were going to lose the war, then what point was there in holding out?

After all…

"…it's not like I feel much loyalty toward them, in the first place."

Norito had been born into the great Goshi Clan. Because of that he had been forced to work hard, against his will, and had somehow managed to get accepted into First Shibuya along with all the other elite boys and girls.

"But I never meant to risk my life like this…" he muttered. He had never been very keen on trying hard.

After all, no one seemed to expect much from him anyways. His relatives—especially his parents—were only interested in his little brother. Even though Norito was born first, his brother seemed to be better at everything.

Norito was pretty sure his brother was going to be the one to inherit the clan.

So why even bother?

Because he was the eldest?

Because the Goshi men were all expected to be strong?

If they all thought he was a loser who was never going to inherit the clan anyways, then they could save all that bullshit for someone who actually cared.

Norito wasn't interested in trying hard.

Or in taking on responsibility.

Could he really be expected to feel any sense of duty toward that lot?

"You gotta be kidding," he said, smirking.

Of course, things had started to change lately.

He had been chosen by Kureto Hiragi as part of a special squad—along with Guren Ichinose, Shinya Hiragi, and Mito Jujo.

His family was beginning to look at him in a new light and to make a fuss over him. It was gratifying, in its own way.

But at the end of the day…

"…I still hate putting in an effort."

Norito stared up at the ceiling of the girls' bathroom.

A deafening roar filled the air. The entire building seemed to shake.

The sound of gunfire.

Explosions.

And magical detonations.

Norito had cast an illusion as soon as the first strike hit in order to help his friends escape.

"I wonder if Mito and the others managed to get away from the school…"

To be honest, Norito was starting to wonder if he had made a mistake. Sacrificing himself in order to save his friends…

"I usually don't try to play the hero like that," he muttered.

The sound of explosions drew near.

Each blast was closer than the last.

It wouldn't be long, now, before someone discovered the bathroom.

There was nowhere left for him to run. But unlike his goody two-shoes brother, Norito hadn't spent his time working hard, studying and training. He wasn't strong enough to step outside and fight them.

Norito sighed.

"This is what I get for showing off…"

Screaming.

And more gunfire.

"Man, it's really those three girls' fault. For being such hotties. I may not be loyal to the Hiragis, but I'm still a slave to love."

Norito laughed.

Just then, a man's voice came from outside the door.

"Over here! Be careful, someone's cast an illusion!"

It looked like the jig was up.

Norito glanced at the door out of the corner of his eye.

"This is the girls' bathroom," he yelled, "no boys allowed!"

It didn't work.

Norito heard a crash as they burst through the door.

"Kill everyone inside!" one of the men shouted.

"Kill them!"

"Kill the Imperial Demons!"

With all that shouting, thought Norito, their blood pressure was probably through the roof.

He put away his incense pipe. They had already seen through his illusion. There was no reason to keep up the spell.

"Okay, guys, you got me, let's just talk about this," he said, standing up from the toilet seat. "There's no reason to get violent, I'm willing to betray the Imperial Demons…"

In response, the door to the stall swung open. Several armed men were standing outside. One of them threw a punch at Norito.

"Shit!"

Norito caught the soldier's fist in mid-air and twisted it, breaking the man's arm.

"Agghh!"

Norito slipped past him, stepping free from the stall.

"I told you, I surre—"

Another man standing outside swung at him. This one was faster than Norito.

A punch hit the eldest Goshi son square in the jaw.

"Ngh!"

Norito fell to the floor.

As soon as he was on the ground, the soldiers swarmed on top of him, grabbing hold of both his arms and his legs.

"Hey, this one's from the Goshi Clan," one of the men said.

"Should we take him captive then?"

"Nope," the first man said with a shake of his head. "Apparently some other Goshi Clan brat already surrendered. We don't need this one."

"Let's kill him, then."

Some other Goshi Clan brat. They were probably referring to Norito's brother.

Apparently, despite what the rest of the family thought, and despite the way he always looked down on Norito, Little Mr. Perfect had already managed to get himself captured.

As far as Norito knew, his brother was in Kichijoji at his junior high school, which was also run by the Imperial Demons. Had Kichijoji been attacked as well? Or had the Goshi Clan been attacked directly, at their home?

Either way, the conflict had spread much further than Norito had imagined. This was full-blown war.

The Thousand Nights were trying to wipe the Imperial Demons off the face of the map. Someone on the peripheries of the organization, like Norito, was already out of his league in this fight.

One of the men pulled out a knife.

Norito stared at it, perfectly resigned.

But the man stayed the knife in mid-swing.

"Hold on," he said. "A minute ago you said you'd surrender, didn't you, kid? Tell you what. You tell us where your friends are—all the other important kids from the major clans—and we'll take you prisoner instead of killing you."

It was a tough offer to refuse.

If Norito valued his own skin at all, it was obviously in his best interests to take the man up on his offer.

Instead, with a tired face, Norito chuckled again.

"You already took my little brother captive, didn't you?" he said.

"That's right," the man confirmed.

"I don't know if you know this, but he's the one who's good at everything in our family. Everyone in the clan has big hopes for him."

"What's your point?"

"He already betrayed the Hiragis and surrendered, right? If I do the same, what will people start saying about the Goshi Clan? It'd look bad. All lopsided. We'd be known as the family of traitors. So instead of ratting out my friends…"

Norito suddenly twisted his right arm loose and took a swing at the man.

"…how about I don't?!" he yelled.

The fight was over as soon as it began.

They easily re-pinned him.

They were just too strong. His brother, Little Mr. Perfect, must have been helpless too.

It was probably why he had surrendered.

He was smart, after all. Capable. Everyone expected great things from him.

In comparison…

"You're pretty stupid, you know that, kid?" one of the men said.

Norito shrugged and grinned.

"You got me there. But I guess even disappointing older brothers have their pride."

"Time to die."

"No thanks."

"It's over."

"Oh, come on…"

The man swung his arm downward, and Norito stared at the knife as it descended.

"What I get for trying," he bitched.

A little earlier:

School building. The rooftop.

"Aiiieeeeee!!"

The sound of Sayuri Hanayori's screams reached Shigure Yukimi's ears.

There was a group of men assaulting Sayuri. They were trying to rape her. Sayuri was doing her best to resist, but it was only a matter of time until the men managed to rip her clothes off.

"…"

Shigure watched. There was a deadpan expression on her face, and her eyes were as cold as ice.

Another soldier was holding Shigure's arms behind her back, keeping her captive.

"What's with that face?" he said. "Your friend over there is about to get raped. Try to look a little more afraid, eh?"

Shigure didn't reply.

What reason did she have to be afraid?

She had been prepared all along for something like this.

First Shibuya High School was controlled by the Hiragi Clan. Shigure, meanwhile, was a servant of the Ichinose Clan, which was despised by the Hiragis. She knew she could be killed, raped, or subjected to any other degradation their enemies could think up, at a moment's notice. She had been prepared for it since day one.

Sayuri had probably been prepared for something like this as well.

The girl sometimes let her feelings for their master, Guren Ichinose, show too much, but she always had her act together when there was work to be done.

Her scream, a moment ago, had probably been fake. It couldn't be otherwise. If things really did become hopeless, Sayuri wouldn't hesitate to kill herself. Shigure doubted her fellow bodyguard would have made a sound under normal circumstances even if she were already being raped.

But right now Sayuri was fighting with all her strength, doing her best to resist the men. She was even jerking back and forth to draw their attention to her breasts, which were large and plump enough to be noticeable through her uniform.

She was trying to distract them in order to create an opening.

Shigure was waiting for their chance.

Carefully watching.

One of the men suddenly spoke. He was dressed in a black suit and seemed to be their leader.

"My, but this is quite the picture. Guren is a lucky fellow to have such well-trained guards."

Sayuri's screams suddenly stopped.

Shigure turned her eyes toward the man in the black suit.

He knew their master. He knew who Guren was, and he had come after them specifically because they were Guren's retainers.

This wasn't good. None of the other Thousand Nights soldiers had tried to violate any of the girls.

They had just killed them, instead.

These men were different.

For some reason, the soldiers on the rooftop had decided to rape Sayuri. The man in the suit was the one who had put them up to it.

"Look at how big this one's tits are. She's hot, isn't she? Why don't we fuck her?" he'd said.

But as it turned out, he knew who Guren was.

That meant his real objective was...

"Sayuri!" shouted Shigure.

Sayuri nodded.

They had to kill themselves. It was their only choice.

They didn't care if they were ravished or murdered, but there was no way they were going to let themselves be used as hostages against Guren.

The two girls kept poison capsules hidden inside their mouths at all times. They made to swallow them now.

Before they could do so, however...

"Not so fast, ladies," the man in the black suit said.

He raised both of his arms in the air. Chains suddenly came flying from his hands. They shot into the two girls' mouths and snatched the capsules straight from their tongues.

It all happened in the blink of an eye.

They hadn't been able to stop him. They hadn't even been able to resist.

He was strong. The other soldiers didn't even begin to compare.

"You can try to chew through your tongues if you like," he said. "I'm pretty sure you both know how difficult it is to kill yourselves that way. The worse for wear you both wind up, the more Guren will be affected and the more powerful he will be."

Shigure wasn't sure what he was talking about, but she knew he had already begun using them against her master.

"Who are you?" she said.

"I don't really have a name," the man in the black suit replied. "But Guren refers to me as Saito."

"What are you trying to accomplish?"

Saito laughed. "I'm trying to rape you, obviously. Okay, everyone, we're running out of time. You better get started on this shorty as well."

Soldiers began pawing at Shigure's clothing.

"Ngh... Get off me..."

Her skirt was torn.

And her sailor-suit school uniform was ripped open.

The assassin's weapons she kept hidden inside her clothing at all times fell to the ground with a clatter. She was powerless to fight back. The soldiers began to get rough, but she couldn't stop them. They were stronger. And they were going to rape her.

"..."

But it wasn't herself that Shigure was worried about.

She was more focused on Saito, who wasn't looking at them. Instead he was staring outward, past the rooftop and away from the school.

"Uh oh, it looks like the demon's already here," he said. "Guren gave in sooner than I thought."

Shigure followed his gaze.

There was still fighting taking place in the schoolyard, and it was bathed in blood.

Just then, a motorcycle rolled in through the gate and into the throng of Thousand Nights soldiers lurking inside.

The bike came straight toward the school building, not bothering to stop. A boy was on the motorcycle.

He had black hair and piercing eyes.

It was Guren Ichinose.

As soon as she saw him, Shigure felt the cold steel inside her melt and grow hot.

Her agitation got the better of her.

At the sight of Master Guren riding toward her, weakness took ahold of Shigure for the first time in her life.

"N-No! Master Guren!" she screamed. "Don't come!"

Sayuri also realized what was happening.

They had already stripped her down to her underwear. She began screaming as well.

"Don't come!" she yelled. "If you come, they'll kill you!"

Moments earlier they had been cool and collected. Now, their voices cracked with fear.

Guren had to stay away.

It was clear that Saito was attacking the two girls in order to lure him there.

"Haha. Here he comes," he congratulated himself. Then he shouted, "All right, everybody! Get on with it. Hurry up and have your fun with the girls!"

He himself, however, began moving away from the group. He ran far back almost like he was fleeing.

Guren suddenly raised his head.

Shigure's eyes met with her master's.

He drew his sword.

Its blade was black.

So dark.

So very, very dark.

He took one step forward.

And then two.

On the third step, he vanished.

Then, in the blink of an eye...

"..."

...he was leaping through the air and onto the roof. When his foot touched, he was already slashing at the soldiers.

With a single stroke he killed three of them.

Only then did the soldiers finally notice him.

"A-An enemy..."

That was as far as the man got before he was skewered through his open mouth. Guren slid past him and moved in a beeline toward Sayuri and the soldiers who were trying to violate her.

There were five men surrounding her.

Soon there were none.

Guren's blade danced through their gut and hacked them into gory pieces.

The way he moved wasn't like the Guren that Shigure remembered.

The way he moved wasn't even human.

The soldiers had been killed before they even realized what was happening. The ones holding Shigure captive were rooted in place trying to process what they'd witnessed.

Sayuri looked up at Guren in surprise.

"M-Master Guren…" she whispered.

Guren stared at her for a moment, not uttering a word.

And then he turned toward Shigure.

That was when she finally noticed.

Guren's eyes were black. The whites had turned pitch black.

The expression on his face was hollow.

"I-I-I've got a hostage…" warned one of the men holding Shigure.

Guren sprang into action.

His sword spun in an arc, and one of the men fell over dead.

"Ah…agghhhh!"

Another of the men tried to point his gun at Guren. The arm, chopped clean off, sailed through the air.

His head soon followed.

The last man tried to run, but Guren stabbed him through the back and pinned him down like some specimen.

"Ngh… H-Help me," it croaked.

Guren grabbed Shigure by her arm and pulled her to him. His touch was surprisingly gentle.

"Ah," a gasp escaped from her lips.

Guren continued to stare at the man on the ground.

"Keep your filthy hands off my woman…" he spat before finally killing the man.

My woman.

"..."

Guren had called her that. Shigure couldn't think of anything to say.

Clearly, Guren was acting strange. Something was wrong. Still...

"M-My woman, he just called me..."

As ridiculous as it sounded, Shigure's heart began to flutter in her chest.

Was it because she had already resigned herself to death? To being raped?

Or was it because she hadn't expected to set eyes on Master Guren again in this lifetime?

Either way, Shigure couldn't seem to gather her usual poise.

If Sayuri had overheard what Guren had just said, there was no telling what might have happened. A pandemonium of sorts, no doubt. Shigure would have never heard the end of it.

But she had been the only one to hear.

Guren was obviously acting strange...

"..."

...but he had called her: my woman.

"Ah..."

Shigure blushed. Suppressing her embarrassment—she was standing in front of Guren half-naked—she pulled herself together and said, "Master Guren, the situation—"

"Be quiet, I don't need to know," he cut her off. "I'm going to kill all of them anyways."

Guren swung his sword to the side, flicking off the blood that had collected on its surface.

Sayuri sat up. She was half-naked too. And crimson red, covered from head to toe in the dead men's blood.

"M-Master Guren!" she cried.

Guren glanced at her and put a hand to his forehead.

"Dammit..." he groaned. "I can't believe this body is even turned on by blood..."

"M-Master Guren?"

"Don't come near me," Guren said. "I don't know what I might do to you."

"B-But..."

"Just stay back!" he shouted.

The girls froze in place.

Saito began clapping, slowly.

Clap.

Clap.

Clap.

"Impressive, impressive... It's made you stronger than I expected. Much, much stronger. How do you like the demon's curse? How does it feel to give up being human? Does it feel good?"

Shigure felt a shiver run down her spine.

The demon's curse. It was forbidden magic. Supposedly impossible to perfect, and definitely too dangerous to meddle with.

Had Master Guren turned to a demonic curse?

What for? Why take such a step?

If Guren needed guinea pigs to experiment on, surely there were plenty of other candidates. Even Sayuri or herself. The Order of the Imperial Moon was full of people whose lives weren't as important as his. Many would gladly sacrifice themselves for the sake of Guren Ichinose.

So why had he taken it upon himself?

"..."

The answer that occurred to Shigure almost made her sick. It was the worst possible thing she could think of.

"You...did this to save us, didn't you?" she murmured.

How?

How could he?

Guren turned toward her. His eyes weren't black anymore. She could see reason and kindness in them. And a self-deprecating sort of sorrow.

222

"Ha. Don't get so full of yourself, Shigure. You're just a sacrificial pawn…"

He was lying. If he really thought that, he wouldn't have come protect her. Shigure hated herself for being so weak she needed protecting. She hated it so much she could cry.

Because of her uselessness, something terrible had happened to Master Guren.

Saito spoke.

"By the way, how long are you able to stay in control of yourself? How many minutes are you human and how many minutes do you go berserk?"

Guren glared at him and said, "You're working with Mahiru, aren't you?"

"Not at all. I'm with the Thousand Nights. Remember?"

"Don't lie to me. Not that it matters. I'll just torture the truth out of you."

Guren brandished his sword.

Saito just spread his arms wide, still smiling.

"We didn't make it to the final act, unfortunately, but what did you think of our little performance? That forbidden power feels better than you ever imagined, no? You were able to save your two followers from being terribly abused. The truth is I was hoping to injure these two lovely girls beyond repair. So that I could drive you even further into despair and teach you the sweet, sweet joy of revenge."

Guren suddenly kicked off the ground, leaping forward into the air. In the next instant he had sliced Saito's body in two.

The upper half of Saito's body went floating off—his smile still intact.

"So strong! So strong, indeed! I've never seen anyone move so fast. I bet it won't be long until you can take on even a vampire."

Saito's body began to fade away as he spoke and to disperse into mist.

It was an illusion.

An apparition.

Guren grinned as he watched the body slowly fade away, and his smile was ghoulish. Shigure could see two fangs peeking out from his open mouth.

They were almost like a vampire's.

Or a demon's.

A dark and beautiful demon.

Shigure felt her heart sink with despair.

"You won't get away so easy," challenged Guren. "I'll sniff you out."

He reversed his blade, thrusting it into Saito's still dissipating body.

But Saito just continued to smile.

"Do you really have time for this? There are many more desires you need to fulfill. More people you want to impress. You have to show everyone how strong you've gotten and make them bask in your glory.

"Remember, you're strong now.

"So very, very strong.

"And it feels good.

"That's why you gave up your humanity. Just to feel this pleasure. To fulfill your desires. That's how you grow more powerful. Stronger, and stronger, and stronger."

"…"

Saito's body finally vanished from sight.

His voice, however, continued to fill their ears.

"Saving your friends was just an excuse, wasn't it? You told yourself you were giving up your humanity in order to protect others. But I know the truth. You needed an excuse to justify taking the next step forward. But it was a lie. Just an excuse. The truth is you couldn't resist your desires. In any case, you've given up your humanity, and it's time you enjoyed yourself. Go while you may. You don't have any to waste on me."

"…"

"This is your chance. Save young Norito first, in the fifth-floor girls' bathroom, and then Mito in the audiovisual room. If you go in that order you'll be able to protect them both. Once you do, you'll understand just how incredible this power really is. It will consume you. You won't be able to turn back, to shake how good it feels. Yesterday you were pondscum. Today you are a god. You're their savior. Once you see how good that feels, you won't be able to resist becoming a real demon."

Shigure didn't know what Saito was talking about, but she was sure of one thing. Whatever Saito was trying to get Guren to do, he had better not do it.

"Who are you really?" Guren asked.

This time Saito's voice came from further away. "I told you, I'm from the Thousand Nights." He was perched in the distance, atop the school's fence.

Standing next to him was a beautiful young girl dressed in a First Shibuya High School sailor-suit uniform.

She had long ashen hair that seemed to sparkle in the moonlight.

A commanding smile, bewitching and clear.

And soft pink lips.

She was Guren's childhood girlfriend, Mahiru Hiragi.

The smile on her face seemed to radiate delight. She seemed to be enjoying herself. She stared at Guren with affection in her eyes.

There was a katana strapped to her waist. Its blade was black.

Shigure glared at her.

At the succubus trying to tempt Guren into darkness.

Mahiru noticed her and stared back, a gleeful smile on her face. Then she spoke.

"You don't have much time, Guren... If you don't hurry, you're going to be too late. Mito Jujo is waiting for you in the audiovisual room. She's on the brink of death, and she's hungry for you. She needs it so much. You should take her, Guren. Just like earlier, when you took me."

Just like earlier.

Just like earlier.

"What did you people do to Master Guren?!" Sayuri shouted, almost in tears.

Shigure could hear the rage in her voice, and she felt the same.

"We just did to him what you two wish he would do to you," Mahiru said, still smiling. "If you're jealous, maybe you should ask nicely. He might give you some, too."

"You bitch!" shouted Sayuri.

But Mahiru didn't seem ruffled.

"Aha…haha…ahaha… You two are so pathetic. You spend every day of your lives just thinking about how much you want him, don't you?" mocked Mahiru, gazing at Sayuri and Shigure like they were two ants crawling in the mud.

Shigure's face crumpled up in anger. She felt bile rise in her throat. It felt like some part of her deep inside—a part that she didn't want anyone to see—had suddenly been exposed, raw and naked, to the world. It was only then that she finally realized what was happening.

An illusion had been cast.

Someone was using magic, on the rooftop, to manipulate their thoughts and emotions.

"Sayuri! Close off your mind!" she shouted in a panic.

But it was already too late.

Mahiru was suddenly next to Sayuri. Shigure had no idea how she had gotten there.

"It's okay," Mahiru whispered into Sayuri's ear. "It's only natural for humans to feel lust. But you'll never be able to get what you want. Not in this world. You just aren't strong enough. I'm the one that Guren loves. Not you. He'll never love you."

"N-No…"

Sayuri's eyes trembled.

The spell was affecting her.

"What will you do?" continued Mahiru. "If you can't have what your heart desires as things are now, then what will you do? Kill me? Kill me and take Guren back? But you're not strong enough. You just aren't. You don't have enough power to make your enemies feel your wrath. But…what if you had this? Look. This is the power you so desperately want. And it's here, just waiting for you to touch it."

Mahiru pulled out a long dagger and flashed it in front of Sayuri's eyes.

Its blade was black.

Obsidian. Dark as night.

It was dangerous stuff.

But Sayuri stared at it and swallowed hard.

"..."

The illusion was overpowering, so lucid and irresistible. At some point, without their realizing it, several *fuda* had been placed in spots across the rooftop.

Shigure had never seen *fuda* like them before. They all seemed to be under Mahiru's command.

"Strong" wasn't the word. Mahiru was on a whole different level.

Fear.

Overwhelming fear gripped at Shigure's heart.

She had to get him away.

It was too late for Sayuri. They had to abandon her. That was what Sayuri, herself, would want.

All that mattered now was Master Guren. She had to find some way of getting him out of there...

"..."

But it was too late. Guren was already charging toward them.

"No!" Shigure shouted, but her voice didn't seem to reach him.

A bewitching smile played across Mahiru's face.

As Guren swung his sword at her, she drew hers from her waist and blocked the strike. A shrill metallic ring filled the air. Mahiru's slender left leg sunk into the roof with a crunch.

"I'll kill you!" Guren screamed.

"Ahahahahaha!!"

Mahiru suddenly threw the obsidian dagger. It was aimed straight at Sayuri.

Guren reacted instinctively. He reached out with his left hand, caught the dagger in flight, and grunted. The blade had cut his palm open, and his blood sprayed into the air. It was black.

Mahiru laughed.

"Ahaha. I love how you try to protect these humans, Guren. I love how greedy you are. How you try to have it all, and in the end wind up with nothing. I love you so much, I want you to have even more of the demonic poison!"

Guren's hand, where he had caught the dagger, began to turn jet black.

"Ngg… Aggggghhhhhh!!" he screamed in agony.

"Master Guren!" cried Shigure.

It was happening again. They had gotten in his way. They were there to guard Guren, but instead he was suffering because of them.

Why?

"Why am I always so weak?" she muttered to herself.

Mahiru glanced at her, almost as if she had overheard.

"Because you're a fool," she said. "You're the slow and steady tortoise, still waiting to catch the hare napping. But you don't realize how frantically the hare is sprinting… If you really love him and want to protect him, then let the darkness touch your soul as well. If you don't…the world may well end before you ever reach the starting line."

Shigure tried to respond but never got the chance.

Before she could, Guren fell to one knee, clawing painfully at his chest. A single horn had sprouted from his head.

Mahiru pointed at Sayuri.

"Does it hurt? If you're in pain, then kill her. Kill her, and some of your pain will go away."

Guren stared at Sayuri. His eyes had turned pitch black again.

The situation was out of control. Shigure wasn't sure what to do.

But she did know one thing. Every instinct in her body was telling her to get Master Guren away from that woman. Away from Mahiru.

She had to lure him away even if it cost her her life.

"Master Guren!" she shouted. "Don't listen to what that woman says! If you want to kill someone, kill me! Come over here and kill me!"

Guren turned his eyes toward Shigure.

He took a step toward her.

"N-No, don't!" interceded Sayuri. "If you're going to kill someone, kill me!"

Guren froze in place. He lifted his sword into the air...and swung it straight at Mahiru!

Parrying the blow, she leapt backward.

"My, my," she said. "Even with all that poison in your system, you're able to hold onto reason. I'm impressed. You really are amazing... Amazing, and sad."

Mahiru still seemed to be enjoying herself more than anything.

"Give up...Mahiru," Guren hissed in pain. "I won't let you...have your way—"

"No, I won't have my way," Mahiru cut him off. "It's your way I want things to go, not mine. And I've given you the power to make that happen. Use that power. Enjoy it. Revel in it. Exercising that power will make you feel so good that soon you won't be able to turn back."

Mahiru was on her perch atop the fence again.

And then, in the next instant, she was gone.

"Well then..." said Saito, now that Mahiru had made her exit. "If you do manage to hold on to your sanity, I look forward to meeting you again."

And then Saito disappeared just as suddenly as Mahiru had.

The fight, too, was over as quickly as it had started.

"Huff...huff...huff...huff..."

Guren's breath was ragged. His shoulders heaved. He turned his eyes slowly toward the door that led from the roof into the school.

Given what Saito had said, Guren was probably planning on going to save Mito and Norito now. It was the wrong choice. If he went, something even worse was bound to happen.

It seemed the demon's curse poison consuming Guren from within was designed to work its way deeper into his body each time he helped another person or fulfilled another desire. If that was true, they had to keep him from going inside.

"Master Guren, we have to go to Aichi," Shigure called to him. "We have to go back home. You can't stay here!"

Sayuri, who was apparently thinking the same thing, begged, "Please calm down, Master Guren. Listen to what we're saying!" She reached out and grabbed his arm.

Shigure rushed toward them.

Whatever else happened, they had to get him away. He could not stay.

Guren, however, brushed Sayuri's hand aside. The simple movement was enough to send her flying a dozen feet backward.

"Ack!" she screamed in shock, sprawling on the ground.

Ignoring her, Shigure swooped her weapons up along with several *fuda* and threw them in the air to try to ensnare Guren.

Even if she injured him slightly, at this point it was better than the alternative.

Right now, the only thing that mattered was to keep him from going inside the school…

Unfortunately, Shigure's magic barely seemed to hit him. He didn't even look her way.

Guren stood up straight. The movement was enough to rip through Shigure's barrier.

"Shi…gure…" he said.

"Master Guren, please, don't go in there…"

"I'm going to…lose control…again… Take S-Sayuri…"

"Don't worry about us! Please, Master Guren!"

"Rrrraaaaaaa… Hahahahaha… Blood… Give me blood… I'll kill them all! I'll kill everyone who gets in my way!!"

The horn sprouting from his head grew even longer. He brandished his sword and dashed away.

Faster than any human could move.

There was no way they could keep up with him.

Shigure just stared at him from behind.

At her master, who had become a demon.

And she remembered what Mahiru had said.

Because you're a fool...

The words echoed in Shigure's head.

The present (again).

As events continued to unfold moments after Guren dashed from the roof:

" ... "

The knife was descending.

Another second and Norito's life would be over. This is it, he thought, as he watched the blade fall.

When all was said and done, he couldn't help but think that it hadn't been much of a life.

Not that he was looking forward to it ending, just yet.

There were lots of things he still wanted to do. Lots of hot girls he still hadn't met. And he wouldn't mind getting his motorcycle license. Maybe even traveling overseas.

But who was he kidding? Stuff like traveling and motorcycles sounded nice, but it didn't exactly rise to the level of regret.

So what was actually holding him back?

What made him feel like he wasn't ready to die?

" ... "

There were only a handful of things he could think of.

Like the shogi game he, Shinya, Mito, and Guren had played recently.

He had lost quickly.

That was embarrassing. But it was also fun. He wanted to do it one more time. Now that he was about to die, he couldn't help wishing he had learned a little more about shogi. Maybe even won a match, to hear the others say, "Not bad, Norito!"

"…"

Or putting shogi aside…

He wouldn't have minded a little more appreciation from his family. Being the strong, smart brother—the one that everyone admired—for a change.

It stung a little, dying without ever having beaten his brother.

Not at sparring.

Or at spell duels.

The whole family had seen him lose to his little brother.

For some reason, when push came to shove, he could never quite bring himself to try his best against his brother. He knew that if he won sometimes, his parents' opinion of him would rise. His other relatives would praise him. But what was the point of taking family matters so seriously?

"…"

To be honest, he had to admit that was an excuse.

The truth was that his brother was just better than him. He worked hard at everything. Norito could see that. He was even proud of his brother in his own way. Norito, after all, was just the black-sheep older brother. Defective goods. A supporting actor huddling in the shadow of his perfect brother. If life was a game, Norito was an NPC.

He knew the truth.

Even so…he couldn't help but wish he'd beaten his brother at something, just once.

Now that he was staring death in its face, Norito realized for the first time that he felt that way, and that it was the most central, defining feeling in him.

He actually wanted to beat his brother.

He actually really wanted to beat his brother.

That conceited brat, always looking down on his older brother. Just once Norito wanted to hear him say, "I'm no match for you. I guess you really are the older brother."

Was this really what he was thinking about before he died?

"Aha…haha… I'm so lame…"

Norito had to laugh.

His face, though, was on the verge of tears.

Deep inside, he was screaming that he didn't want to die.

In that moment, more than anything, he didn't want to die having never beaten his brother.

There was nothing he could do about that now, though.

It was already too late.

His heart was beating like a jackhammer.

There wasn't enough oxygen. It hurt to breathe.

He even wanted to kill him, he thought.

He wanted to kill his brother.

It was a strange thought. It made Norito suddenly realize that something was amiss.

"…"

He glanced around, out of the corners of his eyes.

He was still in the cramped girls' bathroom.

He was being held down by soldiers from the Thousand Nights and about to be stabbed to death. His opponents were strong. Too strong for him to resist on his own.

But there was something else he noticed, despite the danger he was in.

It seemed to be an illusion.

Some sort of brainwashing spell.

It was faint.

Very faint.

It was just the faintest trace, yet enough for Norito to pick up on it. Illusion magic was his specialty, after all. It was the one area where he gave his brother a run for his money.

Someone else had been burning *fuda*.

There was no odor.

And no color.

But a sinister, illusory pall had been placed over the entire school.

Was the attack just some sort of experiment?

Somebody's complicated idea of a game?

Countless people had already died.

The soldiers from the Thousand Nights and the students at the school were fighting each other to the death. The halls were littered with their bodies.

Why? What was the point behind it all…

"I guess that's someone else's problem now, though, since I'm about to die…"

The time for thinking was over now.

The knife was about to land. It was aimed straight for his heart. If Norito just held still, he would probably die instantly. That would be the easiest way to go. Since he couldn't escape anyway, he might as well just get it over with instead of getting stabbed painfully, over and over, while he tried to delay the inevitable.

It was pointless to fight.

To try to dodge.

If he could just sit back and watch as the knife entered his chest…

"…Shit!"

He couldn't do it.

Norito flinched like a coward, dodging the blow.

The knife struck him in the chest but missed his heart.

"Agkk!"

Blood welled up in his lungs and spewed out of his mouth.

"Don't fight it, kid," the soldier said.

He grabbed Norito by the hair and tried to push the knife into his throat.

But Norito continued to struggle.

"I-I don't want to die!" he said, terrified. "Not like this!"

All he could think about was how much he wanted to live. He wrestled his arms free from the soldier's grasp and clawed at his face, trying to dig his finger into the man's eyes. But his killer moved out of the way.

The knife came down again.

This time at his neck.

Norito dodged it.

It sank into the tiled floor.

"Hold him," the man bellowed.

Two of the soldiers grabbed Norito and pinned his arms again.

"Dammit! Dammit!"

He couldn't move. He thrashed as hard as he could, trying to break free.

But he was stuck.

"Dammit!"

He tried to piece a spell together in his head so he could activate the *fuda* hidden in his uniform pocket, but he couldn't seem to think straight.

"Dammit!"

The knife began to descend once more.

It was terrifying.

Death was terrifying.

Norito's eyes welled up, unexpectedly, from fear.

And then suddenly…

—*Aiiiiiieeeeeeeee!*

Norito heard screaming coming from the hallway behind the soldiers.

The knife stopped in mid-swing.

—*Aggghhhhhhh!*

—*It's a monster!!*

—*Help, oh god, help! Don't kill me!*

The screams seemed to grow nearer.

The soldiers all turned around.

Even the two pinning Norito's arms turned to look.

The screaming had stopped right outside the bathroom door.

Suddenly, it burst into two, mangled apart by some force. The hallway came into sight through the shattered door.

The walls, floor, and ceiling were all crimson.

A spray of blood filled the air.

It was everywhere. It looked like someone had knocked over several buckets of red paint.

In the midst of all that blood stood a single boy.

Someone whom Norito knew very well.

"G-Guren?" he whispered.

Guren turned his eyes toward them.

His body was scarlet from head to foot.

Surrounded by a sea of red, he grinned.

Norito could see fangs protruding from his mouth.

One of the soldiers who had been attacking Norito spoke.

"What in—"

That was as far as he got.

Guren lunged into the bathroom and swung his sword. One strike, and the soldiers inside were all reduced to chunks of flesh.

A spray of blood fountained into the air.

Guren's hair, his skin, and even his clothes were soaked. Only the sword he was wielding remained spotless, clean and free of nicks. It gave off a spectral black light that made Norito's skin crawl.

He stared at it.

At the black gleam that had saved his life.

"…"

Somehow, he had survived. And he owed his life, once again, to Guren Ichinose.

His classmate had saved him again.

"Heh, you've gotta be kidding me," Norito said, still slumped over on the ground. "I thought I was a goner for sure."

Norito barely had the strength to move. As soon as he started to relax, he felt all the tension drain from his body. He stared up at Guren, who was drenched in blood.

"Hey, Guren…" he said.

Guren didn't answer.

"If you keep saving me like this, I might fall in love," Norito joked.

Guren still didn't respond.

He was staring down at Norito, but his eyes were black. Or rather, they were shifting back and forth, from black to white to black again.

"Huff…huff…huff…"

And he was breathing heavily.

The expression on his face alternated between pain and ecstasy.

"Guren?"

"…"

"Guren?!"

"Blood…" When Guren finally spoke, his voice was hoarse with pain and glee. "Bring me more blood…"

Something was wrong, he was acting strange.

"Guren, what hap—"

Suddenly turning in Norito's direction, Guren opened his eyes wide and smiled ghoulishly, as if he'd just spotted prey. He raised his sword into the air.

"I'll kill you, too! I'll… Ngh… Run, you idiot! I… Ah… Ahaha-hahahah… …rrrgg…."

His face contorted, in pain one moment.

And overcome with bliss the next.

He kept vacillating between the two.

Something clearly wasn't right.

He was acting crazy.

"Geez, what happened to you, man?" Norito said. "Whatever happened, it looks pretty grim…"

Guren's face twisted up in convulsions. He clutched at his chest, spun around, and bolted from the bathroom.

"Guren, wait!"

Norito tried to run after him, but his body wasn't cooperating. He had just been stabbed in the chest, after all. He may have avoided a fatal injury when he flinched, but still…

"…this fucking hurts."

Norito held his hand to his chest. Blood was welling up in his throat. He had a feeling his lung might have been punctured.

But at least it hurt.

The pain was agonizing, but it was also proof that he was alive.

His life had been saved, again.

For the third time.

And now, the person he owed that life to—his classmate and friend—was in trouble. Norito had seen it in his face.

If Norito ran away now…

"…I really would be a black sheep."

He staggered free from the bathroom, gritting his teeth in pain.

Once he was outside, he realized just how grim things had really gotten.

The hallway was drenched in blood.

And there were bodies as far as the eye could see.

Corpse…

…after corpse…

… …after corpse…

Men and women, boys and girls, they were all dead.

Enemies.

And friends.

All that remained was death, and the black horned demon who was spreading it in his wake.

Norito heard screams coming from down the hallway.

—*A demon!!*

—*It's a monster!!*

And then the screamers were dead too.

Dead by Guren's sword.

This was nothing Norito needed to get mixed up in.

He could gather that much from Guren's receding form. The smartest thing to do now was to keep his distance.

Maybe Norito was a dyed-in-the-wool coward. An NPC. A supporting actor. And maybe he harbored an inferiority complex toward his brother. But one thing he did have in spades was an instinct for saving his skin.

Right now, that instinct was telling him not to be a hero.

If he went any further down that hallway, the shit was going to hit the fan.

That instinct had spoken to him earlier, too. In fact, he had thought of a way of escaping. If he hadn't used his illusions to get Mito and the others to safety, he probably could have made his way outside on his own.

Back in the bathroom, the soldiers might have let him live if he'd told them where his friends were hiding.

Norito had a knack for getting by, by skirting attention and staying out of the spotlight.

That skill was on red alert right now.

Every cell in Norito's body was ringing an alarm and telling him to stay away from the demon.

Instead, however, he continued to drag himself down the blood-stained hallway.

Because, as bad luck would have it, that demon was his friend.

And his friend needed help. It looked like he couldn't control his power.

"Dammit, what did I do to get wrapped up in all of this…" Norito groaned.

He continued to stagger down the hallway, after Guren.

"…"

Guren could feel his power grow each time the sword drank blood.

He killed someone. And felt pleasure.

He killed someone. And felt joy.

The demon inside him, meanwhile, continued to grow in power. Its influence over Guren was intensifying.

Desires swirled in his head.

—*More, more.*

And the demon spoke inside his mind.

—*Doesn't it feel good? You're strong. Doesn't it feel good to prove how strong you are to everyone?*

Noya's voice filled his mind.

—*You saved Sayuri! Isn't that great* ♪

"Shut up!"

—*You saved Shigure! Isn't that great* ♪

"Shut up!"

—*You saved Norito! Isn't that great* ♪

"Be quiet, demon!"

—*But you saved everyone! You did it! It's because you chose strength. You were able to save everyone because you let me in. But now you need to save more people. There are so many people to save. Let's save so many that there's no turning back! You'll be their savior, Guren* ♪ *Want it. Want the power. Want me, Guren. More, and more, and more!*

The demon—Noya—was purring in his mind.

The entire school seemed to be under the effect of some sort of illusion. It had been cast by Mahiru to magnify people's desires. Guren had noticed it as soon as he arrived. And it felt incredible. The spell made it feel amazing just to admit that you wanted the things you wanted.

"…"

And every time he saved somebody…

Every time he killed another enemy…

The demon inside gobbled up more of his humanity.

This is bad, Guren thought.

Everything was going just as Mahiru desired.

Just as Noya desired.

If this kept on much longer, pretty soon Guren wouldn't have any humanity left to cling to.

He'd become a demon.

Inside and out.

He needed to stop.

No matter how good it felt to kill these people.

No matter how much pleasure it gave him each time to save a friend. If he had any shred of reason left, he needed to stop.

But he couldn't.

He still had his excuses.

He couldn't stop until all of his friends were saved...

—*Next, let's save Mito,* Noya said. *What will you do if they've raped her? I bet it would feel good to punish the rapists? How about if she's been killed? I bet it would feel good to avenge her. There's so much fun to be had in the human world! I can't wait until you and I are one, and I can finally be set loose!*

For now, Guren just continued to kill.

To kill his enemies.

The audiovisual room was located on the second floor.

How many enemies had he killed on his way there?

And how many First Shibuya High School students had he saved?

Guren had lost count. Why was he even killing the Thousand Nights soldiers to begin with? He couldn't remember. It was all starting to become a blur.

It wasn't like the First Shibuya students were his allies.

Or the Hiragis.

Why was he protecting people who weren't his allies and killing people who he wasn't even sure were his enemies?

None of it really made any sense...

Wouldn't it feel better if he just killed them all?

Then he wouldn't have to worry about why, would he?

Or bow his head to anyone...

Submit to anyone...

Follow anyone...

Worry about anyone...

Stand with anyone…

Not if he killed them all.

Or conquered them.

If he did that, there would be nothing left for him to worry about. Would there?

That would just solve all his problems. Wouldn't it?

—*That's right,* said Noya.

" …"

—*It's true, Guren.*

" …"

—*It was smart of you to notice. You're very clever, Guren.*

" …"

—*As long as you never love anyone, you'll never be hurt.*

" …"

—*As long as nothing is precious, you'll never need to follow anyone.*

" …"

—*You'll never need to worry whether someone's more powerful than you, or if you should bide your time for now…*

" …"

—*Maybe you've been keeping your nose to the ground so far. Telling yourself to wait. That someday your time will come. Those in power will change their mind. Or your luck might…*

" …"

—*But that won't happen. There is no someday, Guren. Someday is an illusion. Humans are so sad, forever letting others hold them back! Accidents of affection. Obligations, family, friends, lovers. People are always groveling like submissive pigs. And then afterwards, they make excuses and tell themselves it's just the way life is.*

" …"

—*You're done with all that now though, aren't you, Guren? You've moved on. You did it, Guren! You've gotten rid of your humanity.*

"No…"

—*What do you mean, no? Just a little further. You're almost there. You just need to say it. Say that you'll make them submit. Say that you won't be bound by anyone, not any longer. Look, Guren. Your life is all laid out before you like a carefully set table. Just baubles and lies. Pick it up and turn it over. Everything will change.*

"…"

—Kill everything you set eyes on, say that you've given up your humanity, and everything will change. You'll become stronger than in your wildest dreams.

"That's just running away," Guren dissented.

—It's strength.

"It's running."

—You're wrong. Power is what you've been running from. You can become stronger. So much stronger. That's what you want, isn't it? You finally found a shortcut through life. You chose to let me in. It's too late now to start talking about humanity. It really is easy, Guren, to flip that table over. See for yourself. It all looks so precious at first. But it really isn't. It's just useless obligations. Flip it over. It's right there before your eyes. Just flip it over.

By this point, Guren was already down the stairs and past the hallway. He had arrived at the audiovisual room.

Soldiers from the Thousand Nights were waiting inside.

One of them was holding Mito by her shoulders. She was crying.

The man looked stronger than the others encountered so far. Sizing him up at a glance, Guren saw that Mito had almost certainly been powerless against him.

"…"

But he wasn't a threat to Guren. Not now.

Because Guren was no longer human.

"Who the hell are you?" the man said, turning toward Guren and narrowing his eyes. "Stand guard," he ordered his troops. "Don't let him in here!"

They rushed toward Guren and attacked.

Mito jerked her head up and spotted Guren. Tears were streaming down her face.

"Guren?!" she cried.

Her face lit up like salvation. Like she had just seen her prince come riding on a white horse, or as if a superhero had flown down from the clouds.

—*Go ahead, flip the table over,* Noya said. *All those pretty baubles are just a sham. The prettier the table, the better it will feel to upend it.*

" . . . "

—*If you don't want to kill her, then rape her instead. Do something you would never do, something that isn't like you... Something you can't return from...*

" . . . "

The soldiers from the Thousand Nights pounced.

Guren swung his sword at them.

Human lives were nothing to him. He could snuff them out like insects.

Strong.

He was so strong.

One strike. Two strikes. Three.

And now eight men were dead.

Who was he kidding, Guren thought, the way he was slaughtering these men? He didn't want to give up his humanity?

The man holding Mito drew a *fuda* from his pocket. It was an explosion spell. He tossed it at Guren.

He hacked straight through it with his sword. The moment his blade struck, the *fuda* exploded. Guren was unfazed. A normal human's arm would have been blown clean off, but Guren's new body wasn't even scratched.

Bam!

Bam! Bam! Bam!

Guren sliced through four more *fuda* the man tossed.

"What in hell's name are you?!" the man shouted.

He threw another handful of *fuda* onto the floor and began casting some sort of complicated spell. Guren never got to learn what it was.

Because he stepped forward before the man finished and thrust his sword.

Straight through the man's neck.

It was over, just like that.

The enemies in the AV room were all dead.

Mito swayed for a moment, then collapsed to her knees.

She latched onto Guren's arm and clung to him desperately.

As she stared up at him, tears welled up in her eyes.

"You... You came for me..." she said.

Her cheeks flushed red. Guren could smell the sex on her. Her gratitude. His lust kicked into overdrive.

The demon boy whispered in his mind.

—*Kill her.*

"Y-You saved me...again..." Mito said.

—*Destroy her.*

"I thought it was over... I thought it was all over. I'd given up hope..."

—*Rape her.*

Guren's hand seemed to move of its own accord. He reached out toward her breast and grabbed the neckline of her uniform.

"Ah?"

Mito's eyes widened.

Guren ignored the shock on her face. With one pull, he tore her shirt open.

"S-Stop! What are you—"

He planted his mouth over hers, silencing her.

"Ngh...mff... Mmm..."

At first she resisted, but Guren forced his tongue between her lips. Once his tongue was past them, she relented.

"Ahh..."

Mito's body melted into his, accepting him, her lips parted.

Tears still shone in her eyes. She looked almost spellbound.

"Ngh... Guren..." she said. "As long as it's you..."

She was quick to give in. She was probably under the effect of the illusion as well. Mahiru was taking advantage of all the blood, deaths, and danger to make their passions run wild.

It was a wicked illusion, and she'd cast it over the entire school.

Just then...

"..."

Guren's own consciousness managed to struggle to the surface.

Every few minutes he was able to snap out of it.

To win out over the demon and assume control.

Guren saw what he was about to do. He was about to violate Mito, in order to cut ties with her, to sunder any bond that had come to exist between them.

"Get away from me!" he yelled, pushing her away.

"Ngh!"

Mito went sprawling. Her sailor-suit school uniform was already torn open, and her chest was exposed.

He'd done that, Guren realized. He had torn her shirt open.

He clutched at his own chest. He was trying to fend off the lust bubbling up in him. His base, selfish desire for a fleeting moment of grotesque pleasure.

"Don't...don't come near me!!"

Mito looked surprised. She stared at Guren with a frightened expression and said, "What's going on..."

She suddenly noticed Guren's face. And his mouth. The horn, and the fangs.

Her expression changed instantly, the surprise replaced by concern.

Guren cringed. He no longer deserved her concern. He wasn't a person anymore.

Blinded by temptation, he had gone down a forbidden path.

He moved back, away from Mito. He needed to put some distance between them, to run away. But she kept moving closer.

"What's going on? Please, tell me what happened!"

"I told you, stay away!"

"How can I? Not when you—"

Just then, Guren's gaze landed on Mito's thigh. She was injured. Blood was trickling down her leg.

Hot blood, dripping down her white skin.

Thick and red.

As soon as Guren saw it, he was overcome with lust.

"Ngk...agghhhhhh!!"

—*Kill her! Kill her! Kill her!*

"Shut up!"

—*Kill her! Kill her! Kill her!*

"I said shut up!"

He felt his consciousness slipping.

His sanity fading.

He punched his own face with his left hand to stop himself from giving in.

"Ngh!"

His head snapped sideways on his neck, and his brain shook in his skull. For a moment the voice stopped.

But he had already reached his limit and couldn't resist anymore, couldn't resist the temptation of giving up his humanity.

"Guren!" cried Mito.

Please, just stay away, Guren thought. No one ever coming near him again was all he wanted.

Because any time anybody got close, his desires took over.

If Mito didn't leave him alone, he would probably ravish her, mutilate her, and kill her.

And of course, the instant he was done, he would forget about her.

All he was interested in now was blood, and destruction, and proving his own might.

Mito took a step closer.

"Stay back!" Guren howled.

He stepped backward, trying to think of anything but his need to kill.

But Mito—his sacrifice, his prey—continued to move closer.

"I want to help… I want to help you, Guren!"

Help him? She didn't know what she was talking about. She was a weakling, a nobody. How could she help?

It was *her* fault.

Her fault that I…

"I don't know what's happening to you, Guren, but if you're in pain, I want to help!"

Why wasn't she shutting up?

You're nothing, thought Guren, you're just a human. How could you help me?

That was why he had given up being human. Because as a human, he was too weak to save anyone.

Guren stared at her.

"Enough… E-Enough… Just do what I say…"

"No, I'm here for you…"

"It's too late…for me… I already gave up my humanity… I can't be saved…"

"I want to help you!"

"Shut up! Stay away from me! You can't save me!"

His scream was so loud it shook the room. Because of the demon, his throat sent off vibrations that were louder than any human vocalization.

Mito froze in her tracks.

She was crying again. Her cheeks were red, and she was crying.

"There's got to be something I can do…"

" … "

"You've saved me again and again… I want to repay you."

" … "

"Isn't there something I can do?"

Guren mustered every ounce of clarity he had left to formulate an answer.

"You disgust me… I hate you. I can't stand the sight of you. Stay away from me. I don't ever want to see your ugly mug again…"

Mito's face twisted up in pain, and tears spilled down her cheeks.

"If…that's what you really want… But can I ask you one last thing?"

"What."

"Did this happen because of me? Did you do this to yourself because you wanted to save me?"

Conceited bitch. Get lost. I just want you out of my sight…

That was what he tried to say.

Keeping her away from him, for her own good, was all that mattered now.

But the demon was waking up again. Noya. The boy demon.

He began laughing inside Guren's skull.

"That's right," the demon spoke. "I gave up my humanity in order to save you."

The words had come out of Guren's own mouth.

Mito's eyes opened wide in shock, and the demon continued: "I don't regret it, though. I've always liked you. I did this to myself so…"

"Ahhh! Mito, don't listen! It's the demon speaking! I can't hold out any longer. I'm begging you, please, just go aw—

"No, no. I'm sorry, Mito. Forget what I just said. It's me, Guren. Come and save me. You know, I was just thinking that I wanted a woman. Why don't you take your clothes off and get on your knees? It's your fault that I gave up my humanity, so it's only right for you to take responsibility and service me."

All of those words had issued from Guren's mouth. But they weren't his thoughts.

Or were they? Was that what he was really thinking deep down?

He couldn't tell anymore; it was all getting mixed up.

He couldn't tell where he ended and where the demon began.

Mito stared at him. Her eyes glistened with fear.

"I-I guess…" she said. "If it's my fault…if it's my fault that you got this way…"

Mito lowered herself down onto her knees. Guren felt his hunger to dominate grow at the sight.

It was horrible. But he couldn't stop.

His body was in thrall to the demon. To desire.

He wanted to rape her. He wanted to break her. He wanted to kill her.

That would make him feel so much better. Another one of the bonds holding him back would be sundered.

He took a step forward.

Mito didn't move.

Another step forward.

She still didn't move.

Run! Why won't you run? I can't control myself a second longer.

He tried to shout at her, but his voice failed him.

He raised his sword into the air.

Mito stared at it blankly.

"If we did this," she said, "would it...would it take away some of your pain?"

"Absolutely," assured Guren.

"Then... If it'll help you...even a little... I'm okay with it."

She smiled at him, weakly.

Guren was lost. Mito's expression was so arousing that he lost all hope. It would feel so good to slash that smile to pieces.

He suddenly felt something stick to his back.

It was a *fuda*.

It exploded. The skin along his back burned, but there was no real damage.

When he spun around, the door to the AV room seemed to shimmer and bend. He couldn't focus on it.

It was an illusion.

Someone had cast an illusion. It didn't matter, though. Illusion or not, Guren would simply slay whatever tried to attack him.

"..."

But no attack came.

He suddenly realized that Mito was gone. She should have still been right in front of him, but she'd disappeared in a flash. He glanced around and spotted a figure carrying her away.

"…"

It was Norito.

Norito Goshi.

Blood pouring from his chest and mouth, he trudged across the room with Mito in his arms.

Once they were farther away, Guren felt some of the pressure lift. His desires seemed to quiet down ever so slightly.

"N-Norito?!"

"We've gotta run, Mito!"

"L-Let me go!" she yelled, trying to push free. "I have to stay here… I have to help Guren…"

"What are you, nuts? How do you think it's gonna help Guren to get yourself killed?"

"B-But…it's because of me that Guren…"

Norito stared down at her face and said, "I know how you feel. He saved me too. It's my fault that Guren did that to himself!"

Mito stopped resisting. She stared up at Norito.

"But I'm not gonna go and get myself killed just because it's my fault!" the Goshi scion protested. "Maybe I'm putting words into his mouth, but I don't think that's what Guren wants. So I'll take a rain-check on that front! If he wanted his friends dead, he wouldn't have risked his life to save us. That would be crazy! Listen to me, Mito. We have to run. We have to leave him behind, and run."

"But…"

"We'll come back for him. If we die now, then who will be left to save him? You've gotta snap out of it!"

The expression on Mito's face suddenly shifted. It seemed like she was finally free of the illusion Mahiru had cast over the school.

Norito was good at that sort of thing. He had a natural talent when it came to illusion magic. Unfortunately, illusion magic was about his only forte. At the speed he was moving, they didn't stand much of a chance of getting away.

Guren brandished his sword.

"You'll come back for me?" he said. "I don't think so. You'd have to get out of here alive, first."

Norito kicked out the glass in the AV room's window and stumbled out onto the balcony. Once he was outside, he turned around.

"Guren, please, let us go," he entreated.

Guren ran toward them.

"Die!"

"We'll come back for you. Next time we'll be the ones to save you, I promise."

"Die! Die! Die! Die!"

Guren's sword was aimed at Norito's face. He was about to kill his friend.

But Norito didn't flinch. He grinned, half smiling and half embarrassed.

"Guren!" he shouted. "We're friends... You're a nice guy...and I believe in you! Stop! We'll get through this together!"

A nice guy.

A nice guy?

Was he a moron?

What good was a nice guy? Could a nice guy ever save people?

Nice guys were weak. Nice guys were losers.

Nice guys couldn't save their childhood friends.

Or their families.

Or their comrades.

Or their followers.

Nice guys couldn't even save their own nice little worlds.

Nice guys were pathetic. Useless, useless, useless! Nice guys were just a waste of skin.

"..."

And yet…

Norito's words struck an irrational chord deep inside of Guren.

—*Don't try to resist, Guren,* the demon sighed, exasperated. *Just kill him already.*

But Guren did resist.

"Be quiet, demon."

His sword halted for just the briefest of moments.

The edge had already burrowed into Norito's cheek a fraction of an inch. When Norito smiled and his cheek lifted upward, the blade pierced another fraction of an inch into his face. But Norito didn't seem to care.

"We'll be back, I promise," he said. "Wait and see."

"Just stay away, you fool," Guren spat.

As he spoke, though, he could feel the demon taking control once more. The strength returned to his arm. He was still going to do it. He was going to kill Norito.

—*Ha. I told you not to bother resisting.*

"Fire!"

A shot rang out before Guren could deal the fatal blow.

He turned his eyes in the voice's direction. It had come from the schoolyard.

Shinya was standing in the middle of the premises and staring up at Guren. A sea of Imperial Demon soldiers surrounded the adopted Hiragi son. Apparently the Thousand Nights had already retreated.

Was that because Guren had killed so many of them? Or was it the main phalanx of the Imperial Demon Army arriving on the scene?

Either way, the soldiers under Shinya's command weren't fighting the Thousand Nights. Instead, their attention was focused on Guren.

Scattered among the soldiers were several armaments that looked like giant cannons. A large boom filled the air, and flames spouted from the mouth of one of the cannons.

A cannonball was launched into the air.

It was headed straight toward Guren.

Guren halved it easily, but a cloud of *fuda* burst free from inside the shell. He considered slicing through them as well but decided against it, unsure what they might do. Cutting them could make things worse.

Instead he took a step backward, retreating out of their way.

In the meantime, however, Norito continued to get away, along with Mito. The two leaped from the balcony to the schoolyard below.

They had escaped. Guren had lost his chance to kill them.

Cannonballs kept flying, one after another.

Blam. Blam. Blam. Blam.

Each shell contained a massive cloud of *fuda*. When one cannonball hit the balcony, the concrete was blown to bits, but the *fuda* worked like some sort of adhesive and stuck in place, forming a lid over the missing piece of walkway.

Guren realized immediately that he couldn't let those *fuda* touch him. The magic they held was clearly very strong.

If the *fuda* hit him, he would be incapacitated for a moment. His newfound strength would allow him to break free, so a single shot wouldn't suffice to hold him, but that split second would be all the opening that Shinya needed.

More shots would follow, and a whole barrage of cannon fire might just be enough to immobilize him.

"..."

Guren retreated back into the AV room.

It was dark inside. He didn't sense anyone else in the building.

That was only natural. He had already killed everyone. The stench of blood filled his nostrils.

The room was full of shadows, and outside, the cannons still roared.

Shots splattered against the window. *Fuda* clung to the balcony and the walls.

They were plastering over the entire school.

The building was being sealed.

Still the cannon fire didn't cease.

They were going to trap Guren—and the demon—inside.

"…"

Finally…

The last rays of light disappeared, and Guren was sealed into darkness.

"…I'm saved," he murmured.

He had already reached his limit.

Had resisted as long as he could.

He was turning into a demon.

First his consciousness would be consumed, and then he would turn.

But the Imperial Demon Army would find a way to deal with him.

Kureto had probably recovered Mahiru's research data by now, and that meant they already had all the information they needed.

"They'll be able to kill me…"

For the first time since it all started, Guren let down his guard.

As soon as he did, the demon's curse surged through his body.

A little earlier:

"Let's see, then. What should our next move be?"

Shinya Hiragi had just finished positioning his troops throughout the schoolyard of First Shibuya High School.

By the time he and the others arrived, the fighting was nearly over.

Guren had killed most of their enemies.

All Shinya had done on his way there was rescue some fleeing Imperial Demon students and capture a few dozen Thousand Nights soldiers.

The school building, itself, was nearly deserted inside.

They were using thermal sensors to spy on what was happening in there. Only a few people were left.

Three people inside.

And two on the roof.

If the sensors could be trusted, then there were only those five.

He had no idea whether Mito, Norito, Sayuri, and Shigure were dead or alive. He couldn't worry about that right now.

Guren had said he was going there to protect their friends. It was the reason he had given up his humanity.

Shinya's job lay elsewhere.

Besides the school, the Imperial Demons seemed to be winning most of the battles throughout Shibuya. The district may have been a cesspool, but it was still the Imperial Demons' headquarters.

"If they had managed to beat us so easily on our home turf, everyone would want to join the Thousand Nights, I suppose."

Shinya didn't know if things were going as well across the rest of the country, though. If the fighting had reached this level even in Shibuya, then they were already in the middle of a full-scale war.

Something this big couldn't be covered up.

Branch churches throughout Japan were doing battle against each other.

The Thousand Nights would probably win some of those fights, and the Imperial Demons would probably win others.

But Shinya suspected that overall they were losing.

After all, the Thousand Nights were larger. They had more believers. Both groups secretly fed money into the Japan government, but the Thousand Nights' bribes were probably larger.

If the war stretched on, the government and even foreign nations would start to get involved. That boded to be more of an advantage for the Thousand Nights than the Imperial Demons.

Even then, the war wouldn't end immediately.

Both organizations were gigantic. Just because the Thousand Nights was stronger overall didn't mean the fighting would be decided overnight.

It would be a vicious war, protracted, bloody.

To make matters worse, it would be one between two enormous religious syndicates, each with a countless army of fanatics swelling their ranks.

Once zealots got involved, it didn't really matter who was right or who was stronger.

The blood would just keep flowing.

"If both sides are smart, I'm sure they'll make peace before things get that far..."

Of course, it wouldn't be the first prolonged religious war in history, so there was no telling what might happen.

Shinya glanced up at the sky.

The time was around 11:00 p.m. That left just one hour before the day was over.

"I doubt any of this will be finished today, though…"

If the war continued, magical syndicates from other countries were also bound to get involved. The Thousand Nights and the Imperial Demons were both based in Japan, but they were also internationally powerful. There were many overseas entities that would love to take them down a notch or two.

"Not that there's anything I can do about it. That stuff's for the big boys to worry about."

Shinya turned his eyes from the sky back down to the schoolyard.

There was a monster inside the school. A monster that had single-handedly slaughtered the Thousand Nights' entire attacking force.

Shinya was getting ready to seal that demon inside the building. He had tracked down some large-scale immobilizing cannons—the largest of such magic weapons they had—and brought them with him. They were directed toward the building. The same magic in the cannons had previously been used to successfully hold a vampire.

The time it took to get the magic ready meant that Shinya had been a little late to arrive, but in the end it looked like he had made the right decision.

The fighting at the school was already over.

Shinya's job now was…

"…to hunt a demon," he muttered.

He was there to save his friend. His friend who had become a demon.

Shinya glanced at the thermal screen that lay at his feet. The heat sources the sensors were picking up inside the school building were coming from the audiovisual room.

One of the creatures there was giving off an amazing amount of body heat, far too hot to be from a human.

That was probably the demon.

It was probably Guren.

"Aim three of the cannons at the audiovisual room, on the second floor," Shinya ordered the soldiers who were preparing the cannons.

The troops began working immediately. They were all superior operatives, Kureto's men.

According to their official rank, they were First Class Special Force Spellcasters. Each and every one of them was strong without exception. In fact, many were as good as Shinya, himself—perhaps even better.

And there were five hundred of them.

They had sworn absolute allegiance to the Hiragi Clan. Not one of them would hesitate to lay down their lives at a word from Kureto.

"Lord Shinya," one of the men said. "The cannons are in place."

Three had been directed toward the audiovisual room.

The other cannons had already been aimed toward the building's other windows, without Shinya needing to give the order. The troops clearly knew what they were doing.

These first-class soldiers were currently all following Shinya. They did it without hesitation, because that was what they were trained to do.

A slight chill ran down Shinya's spine at the thought.

Their presence was testament to just how much power the Hiragi Clan wielded. Individual strength was irrelevant. Even if an individual was strong—so strong that he became a demon—in the end, nothing changed.

No matter how much power one person held, individually he was still powerless.

Mahiru must have understood that, too. She was smart. She had been born in the heart of the Hiragi Clan—the very lion's den.

What did it mean to be an organization?

What did it mean to be an individual?

Mahiru had learned that for herself, growing up.

Just becoming a demon wouldn't be enough for Mahiru to get her hands on the things she desired. So what was she actually trying to accomplish?

"Scary," Shinya muttered. "I almost wish I could just wash my hands of this whole mess."

He turned his eyes back toward the AV room.

Mahiru had probably instigated the entire war. She had manipulated both the Thousand Nights and the Imperial Demons into fighting.

But what was she trying to achieve by doing so?

What was her goal?

Shinya couldn't begin to guess. She was out of his league. There was no telling what sort of shadows lurked in Mahiru Hiragi's heart.

By comparison, Guren's reason for becoming a demon was much simpler. Endearing, even.

He wanted to save his companions. He wanted to save his friends.

Guren had told him as much. Before turning into a demon.

"..."

Any way you cut it, it was a dumb thing to do. It was so stupid you almost had to feel sorry for the guy.

On the other hand, with so much darkness in the world...

"...he's precisely the kind of person we need. Someone worth saving."

Shinya checked the thermal sensors one last time. There were three people in the AV room, just like he originally thought.

What appeared to be Guren's heat blob still hadn't rubbed out the other two. He could have done so easily, but hadn't.

That meant that the two people inside with him...

"...must be his friends."

Either Norito, Mito, Sayuri, or Shigure.

Then Shinya couldn't seal the school just yet.

One of the blobs inside suddenly moved. It looked like one of the blobs had rescued another. Now they were trying to make a break for it.

Shinya raised his hand into the air.

If the two turned out to be Thousand Nights soldiers, they could begin firing immediately. It would be safer to seal the school up right away with their enemies still inside.

But Shinya had been right. It was one of their own who kicked out the window and emerged onto the balcony.

Norito. He stumbled through the window carrying Mito in his arms.

Guren came after them, waving a sword. He looked like he was out of control. He was trying to kill Norito and Mito.

"Shit…" Shinya spat.

He watched, waiting for the right time to shoot.

If they fired now, Norito and Mito would get sealed inside the school along with Guren. If that happened, they would both be killed. He had to let them out first.

But if he didn't give the order now, Guren might get out as well. That would ruin their whole plan.

If they didn't seal Guren, the whole world would be in danger.

How many more people would he kill? And not just from the Thousand Nights and the Imperial Demons, either. Countless others would die.

Guren would slaughter one person after another after another. Until finally he was slain in turn.

Humans weren't as weak as they seemed.

As terrifying as Guren might seem, he was still just one demon. As long as he was just one demon, humans could find a way to slay him if they set their minds to it.

History had already proven that to be the case. Archival documents described how people had been taken over by demons, and how others had risked their lives to banish them. There were even several instances, supposedly, of people successfully slaying the overwhelming powerful creatures known as vampires.

Eventually, Guren was certain to be killed as well.

Once the Thousand Nights and the Imperial Demons put their minds to it.

Maybe they would suffer a lot of casualties in the process, but the two groups would manage to kill Guren and Mahiru in the end.

That was why it was so important that Shinya seal him inside while he had the chance.

He had played all his cards to stop Guren, to protect his friend. Before coming here, he had revealed everything he knew to the Imperial Demons.

Just like Guren, who had given up his humanity, Shinya had abandoned his own ambitions.

All their sacrifices couldn't be worthless in the end...

"Come on Guren, cut it out..." he muttered. "Snap out of it. You became a demon just to save your friends. If anyone can do it, I know it's you..."

Shinya wanted to believe.

"Lord Shinya, what are you orders?" one of the soldiers asked.

The implication was clear. They needed to fire. No one had to explain that to Shinya.

The soldier was hinting that now wasn't the time to be prioritizing Norito and Mito's wellbeing. Plenty of lives had already been lost. They couldn't start valuing one life over another.

Mito and Norito were worth very little to the world, at the moment.

Regardless, Shinya stared at the window and continued to wait, ignoring the soldier.

"You'll come to your senses, Guren... I know you will. If you don't, I'd have come in vain."

Norito was shouting something.

Guren! We're friends... You're a nice guy...and I believe in you! Stop! We'll get through this together!

It was such a naïve thing to say it was almost cringe-worthy.

Friends?

A nice guy?

Get through this together?

If that was all it took to stop him, Guren really was a doofus.

"..."

But he did. He stopped.

Just for a moment.

You had to feel sorry for the dope.

"All right," nodded Shinya. He fixed his eyes on Guren…

…and lowered his arm.

"Fire!" he yelled.

Norito and Mito were already out of the way.

Guren turned in Shinya's direction at the sound of his voice.

Shinya stared back.

"…"

For a split second, their eyes met.

Something in Guren's seemed to be crying out for help. He was begging Shinya to kill him—maybe that was just subjective, merely what Shinya wanted to believe Guren was thinking.

But he did get that feeling.

"No way, Guren. You're not gonna sleep with my fiancée and get off the hook so easy," he said. "I'm gonna save you whether you like it or not. I'll make sure no one else kills you, either. If I messed this up, too, my whole life would be just one big failure."

Guren hacked his way through the first cannonball. The *fuda* inside burst free. If they hit Guren, there was a chance they might immobilize him then and there. Unfortunately, Guren seemed to sense that something was amiss and retreated out of the way.

Back into the school, and out of sight.

Shinya didn't let up on his assault, however.

He was going to seal every window, every opening, every wall with *fuda*. They were going to create a barrier several layers thick to trap the demon inside the school.

Before long the entire building was covered. They had gotten everything ready in advance, and the barrier activated immediately. Now no one could get out. It stretched pretty far into the sky as well. Provided that Guren couldn't fly, there would be no escape.

The thermal sensors still showed the two heat blobs on the roof.

Shinya narrowed his eyes.

"Well, can't make an omelet without cracking a few eggs..." he mumbled.

Those two would have to fend for themselves. They were going to seal the roof later, as well, but that would require aerial fire.

Chances were the two on the roof were Sayuri and Shigure.

"Hey, they're your bodyguards, Guren. You look after them," Shinya said, laughing.

He turned toward the soldier closest to him.

"The two kids who escaped are from the Jujo and Goshi Clans. Go help them."

"Sir!"

The man began moving immediately. They truly were perfect soldiers. Give them a specific task, and they executed it to perfection.

Shinya's phone rang.

"Hey. So I finally got ahold of you," Shinya said, answering the call.

The voice on the other line belonged to an elderly man.

It was Sakae Ichinose. He was the head of the Ichinose Clan and the leader of the Order of the Imperial Moon.

He was also Guren's father.

"Is this phone being tapped?" Sakae asked suspiciously.

"Left, right, and sideways," replied Shinya. "Does that really matter at this point?"

"..."

"It can't be helped, can it? Your son's in a bit of trouble, here. I'm guessing you've already discussed which is more important, your organization or your son's life. Am I right? After all, you wouldn't be calling me if you hadn't."

Sakae was silent for a moment before he answered, "How is he?"

Shinya glanced toward the school. He was remembering how Guren had looked when he had tried to attack Norito and Mito moments ago.

"Pretty bad. He's turned into a demon, and he's on a rampage."

"According to what you say...my son was meddling with cursed gear."

"That's right."

"If that gets out we…the Order of the Imperial Moon…are finished. We'll be annihilated."

"Maybe. And?"

"I don't understand what you get out of this if that happens. In your message, you said you wanted me to hand over any information I had so that you could use it to save Guren… But why are you doing this? I know your name is Hiragi, but you're adopted. If you get involved in this affair, you'll probably be killed as well."

"Maybe."

"So then…why do you want to save Guren?"

"Because he's my friend?"

"…"

"I know, just kidding. I understand that it's hard for you to trust me. You're worried this could be a ruse. But we don't have time for that right now. Things have taken a pretty big turn for the worst here. Me and your son were fighting over the same girl, and we were carrying out a bunch of research to try and save her… But we slipped up. We both pretended to be unpopular loners, but in the end we were the ones who were getting played. You know, pops, you probably should have taught your son how to deal with girls a little better."

"…"

Sakae didn't respond, but Shinya didn't mind. He just kept talking.

"To be honest, this girl is pretty dangerous…"

"You're talking about Mahiru Hiragi, aren't you?" Sakae said, his voice trembling.

Shinya could hear hatred in the man's voice. From Sakae's perspective, Mahiru was probably a spoiled Hiragi girl who had toyed with his precious son's heart and nearly gotten him killed.

Shinya had heard the story from Mahiru. As children, Guren and Mahiru had been close, and Guren had been beaten up for it by a group of adults.

Shinya recalled the expression on Mahiru's face when she'd told him about the incident. The expression on her face, in fact, anytime she talked about Guren. Since she was usually so cold with Shinya, he couldn't help but wonder what kind of guy could make her smile in such a way. Sometimes Guren was all he thought about.

"I think this war might be her doing as well. She's managed to trigger a full-scale war between the Thousand Nights and the Imperial Demons, all by herself. Hey, you people listening in? You hear me? The villain behind this is Miss Mahiru Hiragi. You're all being manipulated by her. If you don't hurry up and end this stupid war, she's going to make complete fools out of all of you. Is that really what you want?"

Of course, nobody answered.

Shinya continued speaking.

"Anyway, that's why I changed my strategy. I want to release the research me and Guren were hiding, from when we were trying to save Mahiru. We did everything we could to keep it secret in order to protect her, but we can't do that anymore. Me and Guren are in over our heads with her. It's time to let the higher-ups in the Imperial Demons handle this. Mr. Ichinose, I'm asking you to share any data you have on the research Guren was carrying out at your compound."

Almost everything Shinya said was a lie.

Guren and Shinya had never carried out any research to save Mahiru.

They had both simply wanted power. That was all. Enough power to turn the tables.

It wasn't a total lie, though. They'd wanted that power partly so that they could save Mahiru. For Guren, it would bring closure to his childhood romance. Shinya would be able to show the fiancée who never took him seriously how wrong she'd been about him.

"..."

But they hadn't really been prepared for it. Not by a long shot. Mahiru had started miles ahead.

She'd thrown her own life away. Thrown away the world she knew.

She had already become a demon. In order to catch up with her, they needed to be as equally ready to cast off what they held dear.

In any case, Sakae seemed to have grasped the situation.

"I'll give you the information... And I'll suffer the consequences for allowing research into forbidden magic. Just save my son—"

"I will," Shinya cut him off. "Okay then, send the data to the email address I gave you. I'll use it to save Guren."

Shinya hung up. As soon as he did, his phone rang again. He glanced at the screen before answering.

"Yes?"

"Are you stupid? The Thousand Nights are tapping your email account too."

It was Kureto.

"Ah, big brother," Shinya replied, grinning. "You shouldn't listen in on people's phone calls."

"If you think for one moment I'm going to let you leak data on cursed gear to the Thousand Nights—"

Shinya interrupted him. "They already have it. Or if they don't, I'm sure Mahiru will give it to them. After all, she was working with them, too. My guess is that she's been feeding the data to both sides in order to speed up development. Eventually, she probably meant to bring matters to a head so we'd destroy each other."

Kureto was smart. He had obviously already figured the situation out for himself.

They were in an arms race over who would be able to utilize the demon's curse first. It was a scramble Mahiru had maneuvered them into.

She had fed her data in small doses to both sides to ensure a power rivalry and mutual slaughter.

As long as the organizations were at war with each other and engaged with a clear and present enemy, the research would barrel forward at lightning speed. Before, the researchers had been hesitant to conduct human experiments. But in a time of crisis, their morals would grow considerably more lax.

And then the forbidden magic, which everyone had said was impossible to perfect, would show record progress.

Because the side that stalled even for a second would lose. Falling behind in developing cursed gear spelled total defeat.

Of course, they could also try forming a pact. Both sides could agree not to develop any cursed gear.

"Unless you think there might be a peaceful way?" ventured Shinya.

"Not possible," Kureto shut him down immediately.

"Well, in that case..."

"You have a point. Our real enemy isn't the Thousand Nights. Even if we tried to keep the information from them, Mahiru would just leak it in the end."

"Right."

"That means our only option is to surpass Mahiru in developing such gear."

"Exactly."

Kureto didn't need to hash out everything with Shinya like this, but was nevertheless laying out the details. It was obviously directed at somebody listening in on their call, not at Shinya himself.

Maybe the Thousand Nights. Maybe even Mahiru Hiragi.

"I'll say this once, just in case," said Kureto, "but the individual can only win against the group at first, while she's got the element of surprise. You made a mistake giving us this information. We're going to win this fight. A demon might be strong, but it's still just one against many."

So he was talking to Mahiru.

"Can you hear me, Mahiru? You're alone now. You're just one creature. It's we humans who will perfect cursed gear. We'll leverage the information you so carelessly gave us and make peace with the Thousand Nights."

Those were big claims. Shinya didn't know if Kureto was serious about them. But if he was, it might just be what they needed to steal the lead from Mahiru.

"Don't underestimate us humans. Together, as a group, we can develop magic far more powerful than anything you can muster."

Mahiru didn't answer. Someone as powerful as her was more than capable of hacking into their line, but there was no reply. Maybe she wasn't even listening; maybe this was all a part of her plan.

"Shinya, I'm heading to Aichi Prefecture," Kureto continued. "Apparently there are several mutant-demon samples at the Ichinose research lab. They were created by injecting Guren's blood into test subjects. I'm going to go retrieve them."

He was referring to the research Guren himself had initiated. Sakae had been worried that the Hiragis might discover what the Ichinose-led Imperial Moon was up to and proceed to squash the order. But apparently Kureto already knew all about the research.

"Should I keep Guren sealed inside until you get back?" Shinya asked.

"Yes, I'm relying on you," replied Kureto.

I'm relying on you. The great and powerful Kureto Hiragi had just said that he was relying on Shinya.

Before hanging up.

As soon as the call was disconnected, a car came rolling in through the school gate.

It was a top-of-the-line luxury vehicle with a V12 engine from one of the biggest car manufacturers in Japan, a special edition, the kind of affair that wasn't made available to the general public.

It entered the schoolyard and stopped behind Shinya. The back driver's side door opened and someone stepped out. It was the very person Shinya had just been talking to on the phone.

Shinya smirked when he saw his brother.

"Hey, I thought you were going to Aichi Prefecture."

"Since when have I ever needed to rely on you for anything?" Kureto said with a cold stare.

"So that was just a lie."

In other words… It had all been a lie.

Making peace with the Thousand Nights had been a lie.

Going to Aichi Prefecture for the test subjects had been a lie.

And putting Shinya in command, in order to protect the school, had also been a lie.

Kureto smiled. "This is the epicenter, Shinya. Where everything is happening. I'm not talking about some huge battle across Japan. That's child's play. The sort of thing that could happen at any given time, on any given day. What's happening here..."

Kureto turned his eyes upward, toward the school. Where the demon was.

"...might very well be the evolution of the human race. If the cursed gear is perfected, and we can regulate it as an organization, everything will change. Japan, the world... It will all belong to the Order of the Imperial Demons. My job is to make sure that happens."

"I didn't know you were so power hungry," Shinya accused with an exasperated sigh. "You're playing right into Mahiru's hands."

"No, I meant it when I said we would share information with the Thousand Nights and make peace. We need to get the drop on Mahiru. Besides, the information is trivial now that we've got something better..."

"You mean Guren?"

"Exactly. We have an actual demon. Mahiru was always infatuated with him. Which means that thing in there, the demon, represents the forefront of her research. If we can tame him, it will give us our first step in the lead."

More cars rolled into the schoolyard behind them. Several people dressed like scientists got out.

"Mahiru is probably watching all of this as well..." said Shinya, eyeing the cars.

"What's your point?"

"The fact that she hasn't attacked must mean that everything is still going according to her plan. She wants the demon's curse research to proceed."

"I imagine she does. But we're going to leave her expectations in the dust. The lead will be ours before long."

"What if the only thing waiting in the lead is catastrophe?"

Kureto laughed. "Catastrophe? Why would you think that? Because it will be too much power for humans to wield?"

"I guess."

"If mankind needed to be punished for seeking power, then the world would have come to an end long ago."

Kureto had a point.

Man had learned to use fire, and the world still was.

Man had learned to use oil, and the world still was.

Man had learned to use the atom, but the world still was.

Time and time again, mankind had played with forces that were beyond their control, and was rewarded with incredible progress each time. Perhaps, no matter how much power humans sought, no matter what forbidden arcana they pursued, the world would never come to an end so long as they learned to harness it.

None of that really mattered for Shinya, though.

"All I care about," he said, "is getting Guren back alive and restoring him to his senses."

"What?" Kureto glanced at him dubiously.

Shinya grinned in reply. "I lent him a bunch of porn mags and he still hasn't given them back."

"..."

Kureto ignored him. He began issuing orders to the troops gathered behind him.

—*Lord Guren! Lord Guren!*

This shouting also came from behind, from a woman. She was dressed in a white lab coat and was missing one arm. Apparently she was one of the Ichinose Clan's researchers.

Kureto already had the Imperial Moon scientists in his custody.

Had he been working behind the scenes when Shinya first contacted the Imperial Moon to speak to Sakae Ichinose? If not earlier?

Either way, everything was working out the way Shinya had hoped.

If he was going to save Guren, then human intelligence needed to be consolidated. All of the data needed to be collected in one place for now, under the Hiragis' control.

So far everything had gone according to plan. Kureto had acted, and the Imperial Moon research materials had been culled.

But that also meant that Shinya's own ambitions for power would never be realized. He would never get the chance to grow stronger on his own. Now that the Hiragis were controlling this new power, the world would remain the same.

Shinya would continue to be the same disposable adopted trash that the Hiragi Clan had groomed him to be.

"Seriously…" muttered Shinya, chuckling. "What the hell am I doing?"

He turned his eyes toward the school.

Mito and Norito were limping toward him, each leaning on a soldier's shoulder. As they got closer they noticed Shinya.

"Shinya!" Norito exclaimed.

Mito's clothing was torn at the chest. Shinya frowned and turned to one of the nearest soldiers.

"Get Ms. Jujo something to cover up with."

The soldier left immediately.

Norito and Mito were both injured from head to toe.

"Lord Shinya…" said Mito. "Guren… He saved me…"

She was crying.

Norito glanced at all the soldiers and vehicles surrounding them.

"Lord Shinya…they're not going to kill Guren—"

"No, this is a rescue squad," Shinya interrupted.

The relief on their faces was obvious. They both wanted to save Guren just as much as Shinya did. Even though they were supposedly on the Hiragi Clan's side, they were worried for that demon trapped inside the school.

Shinya had to admit, there was just something about Guren.

Yes, he was rude and surly. But he was also forthright and steadfast. The kind of doofus who went so far as to become a demon to save his friends. He was human in a way that few others seemed to manage.

Shinya could understand why Mahiru—Mahiru, who had also become a demon—had chosen him.

Shinya continued speaking, this time in a voice loud enough for Kureto, and the troops, to hear.

"Of course we're going to save Guren. Our clan would never abandon someone as loyal as Guren. He just risked his own life to single-handedly drive off the Brotherhood of a Thousand Nights."

Shinya turned around to glance at his brother, who stared back at him.

"Our clan?" questioned Kureto.

Shinya smiled. "The last time I checked, my name was still Hiragi."

"Fine, but you're going to have to take responsibility then. I'm putting you in command of the squad to capture Guren—"

"You mean rescue, not capture," Shinya corrected him.

" . . . "

Kureto narrowed his eyes.

"Don't get presumptuous," he hissed.

His voice was very quiet, but in a heartbeat the air around them was bristling.

If Kureto wanted, he could kill Shinya on the spot. In a one-on-one fight, Kureto would easily come out the winner. Plus, the soldiers in the schoolyard were all his men.

Norito and Mito also tensed up.

But Shinya just grinned pleasantly.

"I wasn't being presumptuous at all, big brother. I know how terrible you can be when you get mad. And how terrible the Hiragi Clan can be. My loyalty, now, is absolute. I'm going to spend my entire life in your service. I accept that."

"In that case—"

Shinya interrupted him again. "But as my last act, let me save my friend. To the clan I'm just a worthless stepchild. My fiancée went and ran off on me. And now, I've given up on whatever ambitions I had left… If I betray my friend on top of all that, what will I have left?"

"Won't service to me bring enough glory and meaning to your life?"

Shinya wasn't sure if Kureto was being serious, and just shrugged his shoulders in reply.

Kureto walked toward him slowly. Was it to kill Shinya?

Reaching for him and grabbing him by his collar, Kureto yanked him close and whispered into his ear, "If you value your life, you'd better stop challenging me in front of my men. I plan on saving Guren, too. It was the last thing he asked me to do."

Shinya glanced up at Kureto. "He did? You mean he called you, too, before he turned into a demon?"

Kureto pulled his face back slightly and laughed. "Did you think you were the only one? I guess getting used by Mahiru wasn't enough for you, now you're getting used by Guren as well."

"Couldn't I say the same about you, though?"

Kureto smiled. "It doesn't matter how we get there. In the end I still come out the winner."

Kureto turned around and began giving orders to his troops once more.

The woman with one arm—the one who appeared to be a scientist from the Ichinose Clan—was suddenly injected with a syringe from behind.

A look of shock appeared on her face.

"I-I don't care what happens to me. Just help Master Gur…"

Before she could finish speaking she collapsed, unconscious.

A group of Imperial Demon researchers immediately lifted her up and swooped her into a van.

"What was that about?" Shinya asked, watching them go.

"Our guinea pig," Kureto enlightened him. "Don't worry about that. I want you to wait here on standby for four hours. Afterward we'll be able to solve this issue."

"Heh. That's a pretty specific time frame. Don't tell me the Hiragi Clan has already been researching the demon's curse…"

Kureto laughed. "The Hiragi Clan are the ones who started what Mahiru has been up to. You thought Mahiru was the one researching forbidden magic? Wrong. It started with us. And now our work has finally produced results."

"You mean…with Guren and Mahiru both turning into demons?"

Kureto nodded. "Exactly. We're reopening the project, as of now. Our first step is to rescue Guren Ichinose."

Kureto used the word "rescue" this time, but did he have any real interest in saving Guren? Shinya didn't buy it for one minute.

All Kureto wanted was power. All any of them wanted was power.

And they were willing to trade in any amount of humanity to get it.

Shinya began to suspect they were all the same deep down.

Eager to play into Mahiru's hand.

Shinya stared at Kureto as he walked away…

"…"

…then turned his eyes toward the school again.

A dark classroom.

Guren sat alone.

He was in his own classroom, at his own desk.

The only illumination in the room came from the emergency lights. Guren stared vacantly at the blackboard.

" … "

He had finally calmed down a little, now that he had killed everyone there was to kill. Or maybe he was just growing used to the demon.

"Ah…"

Guren sighed softly.

The demon was sleeping at the moment.

It spent much more time asleep now. Guren wasn't sure if this was because he was reclaiming some of his humanity, or if it was just a sign that he and the demon were becoming one.

He glanced toward the window.

It was entirely encased in *fuda*.

Shinya had sealed him.

Guren had tried cutting through the barrier with his sword, but the blade was unable to pierce the seal. His helplessness was what finally quenched some of the fire burning in him, what allowed him to quiet the demon for a little while and dampen his constant cravings for blood and destruction.

But maybe he was just growing used to it. Mahiru had always appeared more or less sane. The original Mahiru was gone, but the new

Mahiru wasn't constantly slaughtering others, either. Perhaps, with enough time, you were better able to manage the destructive impulses.

"But how much time?" Guren muttered.

He glanced up at the clock on the wall.

It was 2:40 a.m.

Several hours had already passed since the building had been sealed, but he'd only been back in control of himself for the past hour or so. He had a feeling he'd been slashing at the wall constantly up until then.

The demon had tried to hack through the *fuda*-sealed wall for hours, laughing maniacally the entire time.

All Guren had been able to think about during that time was how much he wanted to kill everyone.

Kill. Them. All.

It seemed to be the demon's main impulse.

To destroy anything and everything he came across in this world.

As time went by, however, little by little the demon and Guren seemed to merge. His desires grew more complex and nuanced.

He began to want to use the demon's power to fulfill subtler goals, instead of just base primordial urges.

And then, all of a sudden, the demon had gone to sleep.

It was a deep slumber.

Guren was back in control of himself.

But…

"…this must just be part of the process of turning into a demon."

Mentally, Guren felt drained, but his body continued to pulse with strength.

He reached over and grabbed Shinya's desk. He lifted it up with one arm and threw it.

It went sailing through the air like a ballistic missile, landing half embedded into the blackboard.

His strength was inhuman.

"…"

He bent back in his chair and stared up at the ceiling. He rocked back and forth, and his chair creaked in time.

Obviously it was no time for sitting around. But what else could he do?

The next time the demon woke up, he hoped to control it and make it do his bidding. But he knew he was just kidding himself. The cursed gear research was clearly incomplete. No sane person would ever try to use it.

But Guren had been in a bind. So he had resorted to it. He didn't regret doing so. He had accomplished what he had set out to do. He had saved Sayuri, Shigure, Norito, and Mito. Now, however, he was all out of options.

No amount of self-control was going to get him out of this.

If willpower was all it took to control the demon…

"…Mahiru would have done it long ago."

Mahiru, Guren muttered her name.

She was strong. A genius.

Always stronger than him, ahead of the curve, light-years in the lead.

Everything that had happened had gone exactly according to her plan.

The war between the Imperial Demons and the Thousand Nights.

Guren's cursed gear experiments.

It had all turned out just as she wanted.

As long as she dangled power before their eyes like a carrot on a string, the Imperial Demons and the Thousand Nights would put everything they had behind researching cursed gear.

If, at any point, Mahiru were to make contact again claiming to have produced further results, both sides would probably begin fighting over her, all over again.

She was the main actor in this drama. But until she showed up on stage…

"…I guess the role of understudy falls to me."

Shaking his head, Guren chuckled.

For the time being, all the world's mystical and magical syndicates would be directing their attention toward Shibuya, at this school.

Mahiru had taken all the time she needed to attract that attention.

She had instigated a war between the Imperial Demons and the Thousand Nights and brought slaughter to their school, all in order to catch the world's eye.

It was exactly as she had said.

This war would be enough to transform the world from a clutch of tortoises into a pack of hares.

Groups worldwide would fight to be the first to master cursed gear. It wouldn't be long before they began killing each other. Once that happened, it might even bring the world to an end.

Mahiru had said something to that effect as well.

That the world was going to end.

Not just end, but end this year at Christmas.

Guren remembered what she had said. It had sounded almost like fuel for some sort of doomsday prophecy. Like what a false preacher might bray to lead a congregation woefully astray.

The adults will be destroyed first, because they're the most tainted and filled with desires. When it happens, everyone in the world over the age of thirteen will die.

If so, it seemed like the rampaging, desire-fueled demon Guren had awoken would be one of the first to die. However, Mahiru had said more.

God is angry. At us, for our greed. At mankind's vile nature and insatiable desires. Angry at the unspeakable research we've been pursuing.

The land will rot.

Monsters will roam the Earth.

Poison will rain from the sky.

The Seraph of the End will blow its trumpet, and this world will fall.

Mankind won't be able to survive in the new world. Not the weak, at least.

Did that mean that Mahiru was trying to turn them into demons to ensure they could survive in the new world?

But she said that God was going to punish mankind for their greedy desires. Wouldn't that punishment apply to greedy, selfish demons as well?

Or were all these religious terms just a metaphor? Was he letting himself get distracted by them?

"..."

Yet somehow Guren, too, felt that a catastrophe loomed.

The moment he had joined with the demon, he could have sworn he detected the faint roar of ruin in the distance.

He wasn't quite sure why...

But it was as if he could hear the world ending.

It was already August.

If the world was going to end at Christmas, then it would be over in just a matter of four months.

"I guess my own life is going to end today, though..."

The phone in Guren's pocket suddenly began vibrating.

"Hm?"

He pulled it out. The screen said "Mahiru Hiragi."

As far as Guren knew, her name wasn't registered in his contact list, but it was showing up on his screen as plain as day.

Mahiru must have added it herself. Guren wasn't sure when. Maybe when they were sleeping together in her bed? Subterfuge came easily to her.

Guren stared at the phone.

"..."

But he didn't answer. Talking to Mahiru right now probably wasn't a good idea.

Eventually the vibrations stopped.

And then an email arrived.

It was from Mahiru, just as Guren expected. It read:

—Answer your phone.

The phone rang again.

"…"

Guren didn't answer. Answering was a bad idea. Mahiru was dangerous. Beautiful and terrifying.

The phone stopped ringing.

Another email came.

—Next time, if you don't answer my call after the first ring, I'm going to kill all of your precious human friends.

The phone rang again.

Guren pressed the talk button and placed the phone to his ear.

"I'm getting tired of this, Mahiru," he said in a low voice.

"Do you hate me now?"

"I do."

"I love you, Guren."

"And I hate you."

"You're a terrible liar. I'm the only one who understands you now. We should at least try to get along."

"…"

"I am impressed, though. It sounds like you've already gotten your senses under control. That's much faster than it took me. You really are—"

"Can this power actually be controlled?" Guren cut her off, not caring a whit what she had to say.

"I think so… Just a little patience."

"How close is your research to being complete?"

"About 70 percent? I don't think I need to continue it any further, though. The humans will take care of the rest," replied Mahiru, seemingly excluding herself from the subject of her last sentence.

"Aren't you human anymore? How much of you has been assimilated by the demon? Is your reason still intact?"

"That doesn't matter," she skirted Guren's question. "What's important now is that my brother, Kureto, is about to bring the cursed gear project to nearly 90 percent completion. He's going to create an antidote to save you. People will be able to use it to wield cursed gear while still holding onto their sanity... But greatness requires more. Any plan put together by a rational person like my brother will always include a large margin of safety. An approach like that will never aim high enough."

Guren was ready to hang up.

Apparently, in that short amount of time, Kureto had already succeeded in fulfilling Guren's request. He had used Mahiru's data—to which Guren had pointed him—to manage a breakthrough.

The best course of action now was to sit and wait for Kureto to send in a rescue squad.

He tried to hang up, but Mahiru spoke before he could. Her voice sounded amused.

"Hang up on me now and I'll make sure you regret it for the rest of your life," she said.

Guren froze. He couldn't defy her now. If Mahiru said she would make him regret it, she meant it.

"And what happens if I stay on the line?" Guren said. "As long as I'm dealing with you, I'm sure there'll be plenty of other things for me to regret anyway."

"Ahaha..."

"What have you been trying to accomplish?"

"I wanted information the Hiragi Clan had that I couldn't access, on the demon's curse."

She probably did have access now. It was exactly what Guren had requested. He had handed Mahiru's data over to Kureto and asked him to continue the project.

In short...

"You anticipated my every move, didn't you?"

"It was easy. You're so kind," Mahiru said.

"By kind, you mean stupid and easy to manipulate, don't you?"

"No. You're kind and you're weak. That's how I know you'll be the strongest in the end."

"I don't want to talk to you anymore."

"Oh, Guren. You can't just screw a girl and run."

"Mahiru."

"What?"

"Mahiru…" Guren called her name, ignoring what she'd just said. "Mahiru, can you hear me? Are you there? Don't let the demon beat you. Control it. Listen to my voice."

He was speaking to the real Mahiru. He knew she was still in there, somewhere. Some part of her, at least.

Guren knew she was joined to the demon.

The demon couldn't thrive on its own. It was only able to exist and prosper by feeding on human desires.

Of course, once it devoured a soul entirely, maybe there wasn't anything of the original person left. Still…

"Mahiru. You're still in there, aren't you? Answer me."

"Ahaha. Are you still hanging on to that ridiculous notion? Fine. If that's what makes you happy, I'll pretend to be the Mahiru you desire…"

Guren continued to ignore her words. "Mahiru! Don't give up! We'll control the demon. We're going to find a way to control it. Just don't give up, snap out of it!"

"Ahahaha. That was a very touching speech. But it's hopeless…"

"Mahiru! We can do this together! Snap out of it!"

"…"

"Mahiru!"

"… … Gu …"

And then the line went dead.

She was acting strange at the end. Had the real Mahiru reacted to Guren's words? Was she still in there, somewhere?

He tried calling her back.

She didn't answer.

"Pick up."

She still didn't answer.

"Pick up!"

The phone just kept ringing and ringing.

"Dammit, pick up!"

But she didn't answer.

A ray of light suddenly burst into the classroom.

The seal from the *fuda* plastered to the window had been broken. Light from outside pierced through, filling the room.

Guren's eyes were adjusted to the darkness. He was momentarily blinded. His pupils, however, contracted immediately, and he began to make out what was happening.

A fully armed soldier dove in through the window. Guren reached for his sword, which was still near at hand, and lifted it into the air, ready to fight. He suddenly realized who the soldier was.

"Shinya?"

"Guren! Stay where you are!" Shinya shouted, tossing a handful of *fuda* into the air. "We're here to save you!"

Several more soldiers came leaping through the window. Mito and Norito were among them. They were both holding some sort of katana in their hands.

"Guren!"

"Are you okay?!"

Mito had been seriously wounded earlier, but now she was up and walking around like nothing had happened.

"..."

Guren realized why. They were all using cursed gear. The demon inside Guren responded to the demons in Shinya and the others.

The curse was coursing through the bodies of Shinya, Norito, Mito, and the other troops. Its power must have healed their wounds.

Guren eyed the demon-enhanced soldiers carefully, gauging their moves.

They were fast. But not as fast he was.

The amount of demonic poison in their systems was probably just a fraction of that injected into Guren. A weak, stable, and rational dose, for those who weren't aiming for anything greater, as Mahiru had put it.

But they were strong enough. Guren would probably lose if he tried to take them on all at once.

For the moment he remained in his seat, unmoving.

But he felt the demon...

He felt Noya awaken.

—*Kill them,* Noya said. *Kill! Kill! Kill!*

Guren resisted him.

—*Kill the soldiers. Kill your friends. Kill the humans!*

Guren resisted with all his strength.

The soldiers surrounded him.

"We were tapping your phone earlier," Shinya said. "It sounds like you've still got a grip on—"

"No, the demon is waking up," Guren hissed. "If you're going to restrain me, do it fast!"

Norito, who was standing next to Shinya, grimaced.

"Ah, dammit!"

"Try to hold on!" encouraged Mito. "Don't give in to your desires!"

Norito and Mito rushed toward Guren. They grabbed him by the shoulders and held him down. Apparently, they had already experienced battling with their own demons.

Noya, meanwhile, continued to scream over and over in Guren's mind.

—*Kill! Kill! Kill! Kill!*

"Kill!!"

The word suddenly tore its way out of Guren's mouth.

Glaring at Mito, he pulled himself free from her grasp.

"Not on my watch!" she shouted angrily.

She reached for him again, but Guren punched her square in the face.

"Agh!"

"Mito!" yelled Norito from behind them.

He tried to put Guren in a headlock, but Guren responded by head-butting him hard.

"Ngk!"

Norito's nose shattered, but the bones repaired instantly. The regeneration was clearly inhuman—the power of the demonic curse.

He was still weak, though. Much too weak for Guren.

Guren grabbed Norito by the throat. Snapping his neck would be easy. Just a little squeeze.

"S-Stop!" Guren shouted, and for half a second his hand froze.

Shinya took advantage of the moment to attack from the side. He kicked Guren's arm away.

"Stay calm, Guren," he said. "I'll have you restrained soon."

"Just hurry it up!" Guren screamed.

Shinya reached out with his right arm. He was holding a *fuda*. It was covered with writing Guren had never seen before.

Instinctively, Guren began to dodge.

"Hold still!" Shinya ordered.

"Nrggh…"

Guren grimaced, tensing all the muscles in his neck. The demon wanted him to dodge the *fuda*, draw his sword, and cut Shinya into pieces. Guren was doing everything he could to resist.

Shinya smiled.

"Nice job, Guren. It looks like we beat it."

Shiyna reached for Guren's face with the *fuda*.

The moment it hit Guren's forehead, its magic began flowing into his body.

The spell was designed to affect the mind and nervous system.

Guren's body began jerking and twitching. The demon was trying to resist the magical poison. Guren could sense Noya's voice waning in his head.

"Guren!" shouted Mito. "Come back to us!"

She was holding a spike in her hand. She swung it at Guren. There was some sort of chain attached to it.

Guren dodged out of the way. He glanced around quickly. All of the soldiers were holding the same spikes. Guren suspected if they hit him with one of those spikes, he would be immobilized.

That was what he wanted. But…

"…"

Instead of surrendering he leapt into the air. He struck his sword into the ceiling and hung on, standing upside down.

He quickly took stock of the soldiers beneath him.

There were twelve of them in total, counting Shinya, Mito, and Norito, and they were all equipped with the same katanas.

Those swords were weaker than Guren's own weapon but were still cursed gear. Guren probably wouldn't be able to kill them all.

So then, what next?

What should he do?

"I guess one *fuda* wasn't enough," said Shinya, staring up at him. "I don't know how much of the demon's curse Mahiru stuck in you… But listen, Guren. I'll use as many *fuda* as it takes. We'll have you back to your senses sooner or later. Just try and cooperate with us, all right?"

"What's the point of trying to deny the truth with your little *fuda*? Those desires inside you, those are the real you. You can't deny that!"

Shinya glared at Guren. "Was anyone speaking to you? I'm talking to Guren. Keep your mouth shut, demon."

"You're the one who should keep your mouth shut, human. What you really want is more power, yes? Enough to ensure no one can steal your next fiancée from you. Enough so that you don't have to grovel before Kureto Hiragi."

"…"

"Go ahead, let your anger take control. Say that you want power. If you do, the demon inside you…"

But Shinya wasn't about to get riled up so easily.

"Have fun while you can, demon," he said, grinning. "We humans are going to find a way to make you obey. And once we do, your kind will be our slaves for all eternity."

For a split second, Guren sensed that the demon inside him was afraid. For the first time, he realized that demons feared humans. It might even be a weakness they could exploit. For now, however, he was unable to control himself.

Shinya closed his eyes. He held two of his fingers up in the air to focus and began chanting.

His defenses were wide open. Whatever spell Shinya was casting, it seemed to need a lot of time to complete.

Guren would kill him first.

Mito and Norito, however, stood in the way. They held their katanas awkwardly, unused to wielding a blade.

"We won't let you hurt him," Norito said. "We know that's not what you really want."

Speak for yourself, thought Guren.

"For a change, we're going to be the ones to save you!" promised Mito.

What would a weakling like her know about it?

Guren smiled, his mouth spreading open in a fiendish grin. He could feel the fangs touching his lips.

"Curse yourselves while you die, humans, for risking your lives on something so pointless!"

He swung his sword. His blade clashed against Norito's.

"Ngh!"

Norito's sword arm was weak. If Guren just carried through with his strike, he could chop Norito in two…

Suddenly, Mito joined the fray. She swung her own sword against Guren's, adding her strength to Norito's. Guren felt his blade lose some of its momentum.

It was two against one. But Guren was stronger than the two of them combined.

Mito gritted her teeth. "Nngh… I won't lose! And I'll never regret risking my life to save one of my friends!"

Friends, she said.

Friends.

"Nonsense!" roared Guren.

"Yeah, it's the kind of nonsense you would think of," reminded Norito. "Which is why we're here now risking our lives for you!"

Norito suddenly leaned his head to the side. As he did so, Shinya stuck his hand out. He was holding a *fuda*.

It was the same kind as before. If Guren let it hit him, he'd be immobilized.

He took a step back, but as soon as he did so, Shinya's hand disappeared. His whole aura seemed to vanish.

Norito grinned. "That was an illusion, by the way," he said.

Crap!

Guren glanced around quickly, searching for Shinya.

But he wasn't there. At some point, while Guren wasn't looking, Shinya must have...

"Over here!"

The voice came from the ceiling.

By the time Guren turned to look, it was already too late. Shinya's face was just inches from Guren's.

When Shinya stuck another *fuda* on Guren's neck, he felt the strength suddenly drain from his body. Shinya grabbed him by the hair and held him close. Guren twisted his arm around, trying to stab at Shinya, when...

"Stop, demon!" Guren shouted.

His body froze for an instant just like it had before.

Shinya smiled and shouted, "Just hit both of us together!"

At his order, the soldiers began to throw their chained spikes. As they hit and pierced through both Shinya and Guren, the chains began twisting into intricate shapes beneath their feet, like some sort of mandala.

Guren didn't recognize the pattern. But he had a feeling it was designed to bind the demon.

"It's over now, Guren," Shinya declared. "Go, make your demon submit, and then come back to us. Back to humanity!"

Guren's eyes met with Shinya's.

"..."

Then it all faded to black.

"..."

When Guren opened his eyes again, he was back in that place.

The blank, white space.

Waiting, in the middle of that whiteness, was the demon.

It was in the shape of a beautiful young boy.

With lily white skin.

Scarlet eyes.

And scarlet hair.

His entire body was wrapped in chains that bound him to the earth.

It was Noya. His strength had dwindled to almost nothing. Guren stared down at him.

Staring back, Noya said, "It's not very nice of you to gang up on me like that..."

"That's what you get for being such a loner," countered Guren.

"Really? But I thought you were the loner. I mean, you've never believed in anyone. That's why you sought me out. Because no one else would help you."

Noya had a point.

"Why don't you let me out of these chains?" the demon said. "If you do, I'll make you even stronger than before."

"..."

"In the end, humans are alone. That's why they need power. Use me, become unstoppable!"

Noya reached his hand out toward Guren. But his hand shook. It was weak and ensnared in chains.

Guren stared down at the demon's hand.

"Yes, you're right…" he said. "Humans are alone."

"So set me loose…"

"But to grow strong, they need to form a herd. They need to rely on friends."

"But you don't really want to rely on anyone, do you?"

Guren was silent for a moment. The part of him the demon was trying to use, the part of him that was conceited…

The part of him that wanted to show off…

The part that was stubborn and self-satisfied…

He pushed them all deep inside before he spoke.

"I'm too weak," he said. "If I don't learn to rely on others, I'll never get anywhere."

"…"

"People risked their lives to save me. I have friends. I have followers. I'm not like you. And I'm not like Mahiru."

"Sooner or later they'll betray you," the demon said.

"So?" said Guren. "My life should have ended today. So what if I get betrayed in the future? What other lives do I have to lose?"

"…"

The demon didn't have an answer to that. He sank a little further into the ground, dragged down by the chains.

He glared up at Guren and said, "Before long, a day will come when you realize I'm the only one who's on your side."

"Get lost, demon."

"That day will be glorious. The day when you lose every last bit of hope…"

Suddenly, Noya fell silent and turned around, peering over his shoulder. There was nothing behind him. Just the endless whiteness.

Yet he seemed to be staring at something. "Ho-ho… I didn't realize that time was already so near. Fine. I guess it doesn't matter, in that case. I'll be quiet for now."

"What are you talking about?" asked Guren.

Noya smiled at him gleefully. "It's nothing. You'll come looking for me again, soon. That's all. Good night, Guren. Until we meet again."

Guren had no idea what Noya was getting at. But the demon suddenly stopped fighting. He was dragged away by the chains, sucked down into the ground out of sight.

All of a sudden...

Guren's senses came crashing back.

For what felt like the first time in ages, he was fully in control of his own mind.

He was still a little tired from battling with the demon. But his mind and spirit, at last, were clear.

It seemed Kureto really had found a way to tame demons.

The power Guren possessed now was much more attenuated than when his desires had raged unchecked. But the demonic curse was under his control this time, instead of the other way around.

"..."

Glancing down once more at where Noya had been sucked beneath the ground, he closed his eyes.

Moments later...

◆

Guren's eyes opened.

He was back in the classroom.

Shinya was holding onto his collar. He had a worried expression on his face.

"Are you...back?" he said.

Guren stared at Shinya.

"..."

For some reason he felt too embarrassed to answer. Just hours ago they had been shouting all sorts of crazy things at each other. Like "I believe in you" and "I'm going to risk my life to save my friends." Now they were so close their noses were practically touching.

Guren couldn't believe Shinya had really risked his life just to save a friend. It was stupid.

"..."

He frowned uncomfortably, not sure of what to say.

Shinya, however, smiled. He could see from Guren's eyes that he was in control of himself now.

"Seriously, I know how you feel," Shinya said. "What the hell were we thinking, risking our lives to save someone just because we're friends? But hey, what's done is done. For now, I think a 'thank you' will suffice? Go on, then. Say it. Anytime."

"..."

"Come on, Guren, I'm waiting. I want to hear you say 'thank you.'"

Guren frowned. "I don't remember asking you to save me..."

"Hardass," teased Shinya, laughing.

Mito was also there. When she noticed that Guren had regained consciousness, her eyes glistened, and tears spilled down her cheek.

"Guren!" she yelled, rushing over to hug him.

She was crying. Again. Guren never knew that she was such a softie.

"Thank God!" she said. "Thank God you're all right!"

Even Norito looked like he was on the verge of tears.

Mahiru's illusion—the one that intensified their emotions—should have already run its course. But everyone was being so dramatic. Guren wasn't sure how to handle it.

"Fill me in on the situation?" he said instead.

He pulled free from Mito. Shinya was tangled up together with him in the chains, and it took a while for them to separate.

"Seriously though, where's my 'thank you'?" Shinya kept asking while they worked to free themselves.

Guren ignored him. Once he had finally created a little breathing room between himself and his friends, he glanced around the room. Several other soldiers were also there. They were all busily rushing back and forth to check on the condition of the school.

He turned his eyes toward the schoolyard. There were a lot more personnel out there than before. There were also a cluster of transport buses. The place was practically swarming with troops.

"Is the bulk of the Imperial Demon Army here?" Guren asked.

"They're here to protect you," Shinya said, smiling. "You're an important asset now."

"Protect me? You mean protect the cursed gear project, don't you?"

Shinya nodded. "I guess so. The whole world has their eyes on us. The Hiragis released a public statement and let the rest of the world know that they've succeeded in creating cursed gear."

Apparently, the power plays had already started.

"Hmph…" grunted Guren, nodding.

The statement had probably also brought an end to the recent war.

No doubt, groups all around the world had already been researching cursed gear. Everyone knew how strong it could be. Strong enough to completely alter the balance of power amongst the world's magical syndicates.

The Imperial Demons' announcement that they had gotten their hands on the demon's curse meant that the world's syndicates would begin trying to cozy up to them, either afraid of being crushed by the magic's strength or angling for a piece of the pie. It also put the Brotherhood of a Thousand Nights at a sudden disadvantage. It was even possible that the title of "most powerful magical syndicate in Japan" had transferred from the Thousand Nights to the Imperial Demons. Unless the Thousand Nights had pulled something of their own.

"Have the Thousand Nights made a move?" Guren asked.

Shinya shook his head. "Not yet. But their attacks have ceased entirely. The bigwigs from both groups were supposed to meet to negotiate, but I heard that got called off too."

That made sense. The Imperial Demons had just thrown a huge trump card on the table with this cursed gear. If the groups met now, the Thousand Nights would be at a major disadvantage.

Of course, Mahiru had been feeding information to the Thousand Nights as well. There was no telling what they would do next. For now, however, it seemed the night's battles were over.

Guren glanced toward the broken classroom window. It was the one Shinya and the others had come leaping through.

They had come back for him. Just like they said they would.

Had come back to rescue their friend.

Their classmate.

Idiots, the whole bunch of them.

Guren stared out the window. Outside, past the broken glass, the moon hung in the sky. The night wasn't over.

The bodies had already been cleared away. There was no smell of blood, either, just the sharp scent of disinfectant.

Guren glanced at the clock. The time was 4:00 a.m. That meant about an hour had already passed since Shinya and company burst into the room.

From Guren's perspective, the time he had spent in his own mind had seemed like a matter of minutes. In reality, it had been a whole hour before the demon was sucked underground.

All that time Shinya had been by his side, stuck to him in chains, while Mito and Norito had sat nearby like dopes, with tears in their eyes.

The big bunch of idiots. Guren kept his eyes averted from them.

"..."

He knew what he had to say.

"Ahh, dammit," he muttered. "You guys saved me, all right..."

His voice was so tiny that it even surprised himself. Shinya, though, had heard him.

"Eh? What's that?" he said.

"..."

Guren wasn't about to repeat himself.

"Did you just say we saved you? Is that what you said?"

"..."

"That you're so overcome with gratitude you might cry? Maybe even wet your pants?"

"I didn't say that!"

Guren turned around. The trio was laughing. While they had smiles on their faces, katanas that held demonic poison hung from their belts. They'd given up their humanity in order to save Guren.

"It's my fault," he said, staring at their swords. "If I hadn't—"

Norito didn't let him finish. "You're the one who saved us first. We were just returning the favor."

"Yes!" said Mito. "You don't need to apologize to us."

"Come to think of it, you're right," Guren agreed, glancing at them. "You two should be thanking me."

"Whaa?!"

Norito and Mito both burst out laughing.

Shinya, meanwhile, took a step away from the pair and said, "You didn't save me, though. That means you still owe me one, huh?"

"That goofy smile you're always wearing gets on my nerves too much for me to owe you anything."

"Is that your way of saying you're jealous that I'm more handsome than you?"

Guren laughed. "I'm pretty sure you've already noticed, but I'm the one who's most popular with the ladies. Remember? Even your woman picked me."

"Hmph." Shinya glanced sideways at Guren. "After all the trouble I went through to save your ass, that's the way you talk to me?"

"It's the truth."

"How about I toss you out that window?"

"You and what army?"

Mito glanced back and forth between them.

"Umm… What are you two talking about?"

Guren glanced over at her. A few hours ago, when Mito had been on the brink of death, she had said all sorts of crazy things about being in love with Guren. But that probably hadn't been her speaking. It had been a fever dream brought on by Mahiru's illusion and the fear of death.

"Me and Shinya were both fighting over the same girl," Guren said. "But I won."

"Huh?" For a second, a look of surprise flashed across Mito's face. In the next instant, though, it was gone. "Ah…really? Not that it has anything to do with me!"

It seemed Mito was back to her old self after all. Not getting all spun around by breathless romance and stupid crushes. Mahiru's illusion had faded.

Norito glanced at Mito with a smile on his face.

"But in the end, Guren got dumped too," appended Shinya.

"He did?!" There was a hint of happiness in Mito's voice.

"Okay, enough of this nonsense," Guren said.

"Hey, you're the one who started it," Shinya pointed out.

Ignoring him, Guren asked, "Where are my bodyguards?"

Sayuri and Shigure had been up on the roof the last time he'd seen them. Afterward, the school had been sealed shut. The door to the rooftop had also been sealed, apparently, so they had probably escaped over the side. Either that or they had gotten stuck up there and were waiting.

"They're being watched over…by my brother…" answered Shinya.

Guren immediately took his phone from his pocket and dialed Kureto, who picked up.

"Kureto," Guren said.

"Ah, you're finally awake…"

"Where are my guards—"

"I'm in the teacher's lounge," Kureto said, cutting him off. "Come see me in person if you want to talk."

Kureto hung up. Guren stared at his phone for a moment, then began walking.

"Hey, Guren!" yelled Mito from behind.

But Guren ignored her and exited the classroom.

◆

The teacher's lounge was dark. All of the desk and chairs had been cleared away.

Kureto stood in the middle of the room.

Guren stopped in the doorway, and Kureto glanced his way.

"Guren, there you are…"

"Yeah."

"You wanted to speak with me?"

"I did…"

Guren glanced at Kureto's waist. A katana was strapped to his belt. It was the same kind of sword that Shinya, Norito, Mito, and the others had been wearing.

The weapons had been developed with amazing alacrity. Guren suspected Kureto had reduced the level of the curse's poison drastically to ensure a large margin of safety, just like Mahiru had said. Still, the cursed gear was a very dangerous thing to be in Kureto's hands. After all, he was heir apparent to the Hiragi Clan.

The next head of the Imperial Demons was now wielding a demon sword.

"It was the wrong decision," criticized Guren. "What happened? Was the lure of power just too strong for you to resist?"

Kureto laughed. "That's rich coming from someone who toyed with power at the bidding of some woman, all without an iota of scientific evidence or experimentation."

Guren laughed as well. "Good point… This hasn't been a fun night."

"Haha."

"By the way, Mahiru had some things to say about you earlier on the phone."

"You mean when she called me a coward afraid of taking risks who's only capable of creating weapons with a 'large margin of safety'?" Kureto asked. "I was listening in."

Apparently, Kureto had heard everything.

"Actually, I was talking about when she called you a limp-dicked virgin," Guren said.

Kureto furrowed his brow in mock confusion. "I don't recall that particular insult," he said, laughing once more, before drawing the sword from his waist.

Its blade was black. A demonic weapon.

"We've managed to rein in the impulses of the curse," explained Kureto, staring at the blade. "We've created a version where we can control its power. It's a rational weapon, with a large margin of safety. And what's the problem with that? What could you and Mahiru ever hope to accomplish wielding weapons you can't control?"

Guren had no answer to that. Kureto continued.

"What could you ever hope to accomplish consumed by power and on a constant rampage? Who could you protect like that?"

"..."

"We're not a pack of apes anymore, Guren. Humans only begin to make progress when we use reason to control our desires. You agree, don't you?"

Guren nodded. "That's the first thing I've heard you say that's ever made sense to me."

"Hmph. I only ever say sensible things."

"Either way, you still made the wrong choice today. You shouldn't be wielding that sword. The demon curse poison is too dangerous to let into your—"

"We were already carrying out our own research into the curse," Kureto cut him off. "Once we got our hands on Mahiru's data, and the demon's blood from your research lab, the development process was practically complete. The risk is very low. We've completely restrained the demonic impulses."

Like lightning, Kureto drew his sword from its scabbard. He swung straight at Guren.

Kureto's speed was incredible, faster than Shinya and the others.

Guren drew his own sword—and blocked the strike.

Their blades clashed. The sound of metal against metal filled the air.

Guren was lifted off his feet and thrown back to the wall.

Kureto pressed him against it. His strength was incredible. He was much, much stronger than even Guren.

Pushing on his sword, Kureto forced Guren's arm back until the blades were just a hair's breadth from Guren's skin.

"..."

Then, leaning in close, Kureto brought his face next to Guren's.

"What do you think, Guren? You see what humans can do when they keep their reason intact?"

Straining against Kureto's blade, Guren said, "You're still weaker than I was when the chains were off..."

"So? What can you do all on your own?"

Nothing, that was what. Guren knew that better than anyone.

Shinya had saved his life. And Mito, and Norito. They had saved his life.

More importantly, before Guren had made his choice—a choice he knew was a mistake—he had called Kureto to ask for help. He already knew then just how powerless he was on his own. So why was Kureto saying all this?

"What are you trying to prove?" Guren asked, meeting Kureto's gaze. "Haven't I displayed my loyalty enough at this point?"

"True... You've bowed down to my authority. As have Shinya, Mito, and Norito. I've even made the Thousand Nights submit."

Guren noticed that Mahiru wasn't on that list. "And Mahiru?"

Kureto didn't reply.

"Haha. So you're just being a sore loser over Mahiru now?" provoked Guren.

Kureto glanced at him, withdrew his sword, and took a step back. Walking to the center of the teacher's lounge, he opened his arms in a shrug, still holding the sword in his hand, and said, "Is that what you think?"

"How the hell should I know?"

"Hahaha." Kureto returned his sword to its sheath as he laughed. "When the demon tried to tempt me," he said, "I wasn't thinking of Mahiru. My desires lie elsewhere."

"Where would that be?"

Kureto shrugged his shoulders. "Is there any reason for me to tell you?"

Obviously there wasn't. "About my guards," Guren changed the subject.

"Are you sure they're the only people you should be worrying about right now?" asked Kureto.

Guren's eyes widened in surprise. Anger and fear welled up in his chest. He felt the chains binding his demon groan, ever so slightly.

Kureto was referring to Guren's family. The Ichinose Clan.

Not just his family, but also all of the Ichinose Clan's followers in the Order of the Imperial Moon.

All of those people might be dead thanks to tonight's incident. Guren had been meddling with cursed gear. No one was allowed to conduct such research without the Hiragi Clan's permission.

Kureto smiled. There was something infernal about his expression.

Guren glared at his grinning face.

If Kureto had killed them...

If Kureto had really killed them all...

"..."

...Guren didn't know what he might do.

He had thrown everything away in order to save Mito, Norito, Shigure, and Sayuri. He had even thrown away his own humanity.

Swept up by his immediate desires, he'd sold out his own family without thinking of the consequences. Obviously he'd known something like this could happen. Still...

"...I trusted you," Guren hissed.

It sounded foolish. Kureto grinned at him in amusement.

"So you did. It was a very stupid and irrational thing to do."

"…"

"Not the sort of thing a person qualified to lead would do. Now, thanks to you, all of your followers have been sentenced to death…"

"You son of a bitch!"

Guren attacked immediately.

Kureto was faster. He parried Guren's strike.

Not letting up, Guren followed with a second and a third strike, but he just couldn't land a hit on Kureto. His body wasn't moving fast enough. The chains implanted in him were keeping the demon in check.

That had been the point. The magic holding Guren's demon at bay must have been designed specifically to make him weaker than Kureto. Guren tried to unshackle the chains.

"Don't do it," Kureto warned, without missing a beat. "Hold on to your reason. This is your weakness. Anytime someone else is hurt, you promptly lose your cool."

"…"

"What I said was a lie, by the way. Your followers are actually under my protection."

"…"

"The clan leaders wanted to 'exterminate every last Ichinose rat,' but I told them you had only been researching cursed gear under my orders. I protected your people."

Guren's family, his bodyguards, and his followers had all been saved by Kureto if he was telling the truth.

"So now you want to take credit for everything?"

"Not really," Kureto denied, looking straight at Guren. "I don't need to take credit for something like this. It would have absolutely no effect on my position."

That was true. From the moment he was born, Kureto had been destined for the very highest rung of power in the Hiragi Clan—as long as no stronger sibling stepped in to take his place.

But then…

"Why did you protect my family and the Imperial Moon?" Guren asked.

"Because I want you," Kureto replied simply.

"..."

"Thanks to my maneuver, you're completely loyal to me now, aren't you? You owe me a debt of gratitude. One that ranks higher than your promises to Mahiru, your own ambitions, or any desire for power."

"I don't see what you need my loyalty for," Guren said. "You already hold all the cards. What strength could I have that you need?"

"If I seem to hold all the cards to you, it's only because you're gazing up at me from a position of weakness."

"..."

"We're more alike than you think. There is always more that I need to accomplish than the resources at my disposal allow. I never have enough followers or time. But unlike you and Mahiru, I am too rational to consider that to be a good justification for meddling with forbidden magics."

Guren glanced down at the sword in Kureto's hand. "Looks like you're meddling to me."

"I'm willing to take some risks when it's absolutely required. If I hadn't, we would have lost the war. But I only take risks within reason. I would estimate your strength, when you were out of control, at about nine times my current level. But even in your rampaging state, thirty men armed with these swords would more than suffice to slay you."

"..."

"That also means we can kill Mahiru now. Her days of being invulnerable are over."

"But it's thanks to Mahiru that these weapons got developed in the first place," remarked Guren. "This is all probably still going according to her plan."

"Do you think so?"

"I do."

Kureto tilted his head and appeared to consider the possibility. "I think Mahiru expected the Imperial Demons leadership to hold the

Ichinoses responsible for what happened and to exterminate your clan. Mahiru was raised by our clan. She spent her whole life with us. She knows full well that's how we tend to react."

" ... "

"Your clan would have been wiped out. In turn, your grudge against us would have grown even stronger than it already is. The power of the demon's curse favors such dark impulses. The death of your family would have made you stronger. That's what Mahiru wants. To force you to grow stronger, by driving you to desperation. You should have never let that woman get her hateful claws into you, Guren."

So that was why Kureto had bothered to save the Ichinose Clan from annihilation. It was to sidestep Mahiru's plan. He just couldn't bear losing to her. He wanted Guren? It was a big fat lie.

"Am I still supposed to feel gratitude toward you? Everything you did was in your own interest," Guren accused.

Kureto laughed and said, "You better. I meant it when I said I wanted you. You're a valuable asset."

Whatever.

Kureto had already gotten his hands on the power of demonic curses. The Hiragi Clan had just grown stronger than ever, and the Ichinose Clan could never beat them now. There had been barely any opening to begin with. Guren knew that, which was precisely why he'd begun messing with forbidden research.

" ... "

He may have been slower in getting to the starting line, but in the end he had done the exact same thing as Mahiru.

"Well," he asked, "what are we going to do next?"

"Ha. You're starting to sound like a proper follower for a change."

"Get bent."

Kureto laughed, then answered Guren's question. "We're going to kill Mahiru. And I'm tasking you with that mission."

" ... "

Guren glared at Kureto, who slowly sheathed his sword as he spoke.

"Obviously you can't refuse. I have too many hostages for that. Sakae Ichinose, Sayuri Hanayori, Shigure Yukimi… Hmm. I don't know any other names, but all of your followers are my hostages now."

"…"

"Don't glare at me like that. It's not like anything in particular has changed. This is the way things have always been. Everyone you hold dear could have been killed before at any time, without a moment's notice."

"…"

"It never happened simply because you never stood out. As long as you were just another mongrel, you were easy to overlook. But today you stood out. You stood up and wielded power, stepped into the arena. Now you have to accept the consequences. You can't grow stronger if you're going to cling to everything you hold dear."

What Kureto said was true.

Nothing had changed. It was the way things had always been.

Taking up the cursed sword hadn't altered anything. Individual strength could only get you so much.

It was why Mahiru had thrown everything else away, even her humanity. Otherwise, she could never grow strong on her own.

Because in this rotten world—or at least, the twisted kind of world that awaited someone born into the heart of the Hiragi Clan—personal happiness wasn't an option.

"Where are my guards?" Guren asked.

"You do have good people working for you, I'll give you that," commended Kureto. "In exchange for canceling your execution, they both agreed to be guinea pigs for further experiments into the demon's—"

Guren reacted instantly. He rushed forward, grabbed Kureto by the collar with his right arm, and lifted him into the air.

The blood rushed to his head.

He'd kill him!

Kill him!

He heard the demon—Noya—whispering faintly in his head.

—I told you. You should have taken my hand like I said.

Kureto didn't resist. He stared back at Guren with an amused expression.

"Even without drawing my sword, I'm stronger than you," he noted, still grinning. "Unless you're planning on letting your demon run loose again?"

At some point, Guren had been surrounded by a few dozen soldiers who were each wielding a cursed sword. They drew their blades.

Kureto raised his hand to stop them.

"We're fine, stand down… Guren isn't going to hurt me. He can't let his demon loose, not with all of the hostages I have."

"…"

"Besides, what would killing me accomplish? Even if I died, the Hiragi Clan would live on. Nothing would change."

"…"

"There's no need to let our demons run loose. Thirty men equipped with cursed gear can kill Mahiru without us suffering a scratch. As long as it's not for selfish, private desires, cursed gear is already powerful enough as is."

"You think that's all it will take to defeat Mahiru? She's been sharing information with the Thousand Nights—"

"My father has already formed a pact with the Thousand Nights," interrupted Kureto. "From now on, the Imperial Demons and the Thousand Nights are going to work together on developing the demon's curse. We will solidify our might and crush the other magical syndicates in the world. With the power of the demon's curse on our side, it should be easy."

"…"

Mahiru probably hadn't foreseen that outcome.

Guren, himself, had never guessed that Japan's two largest magical organizations—the Brotherhood of a Thousand Nights and the Order of the Imperial Demons—would one day join forces.

But things had changed. Thanks to the overwhelming power of

cursed gear, the two had joined hands. And now they were thinking of mowing down all of the other syndicates that stood in their way.

The Hiragis had set their sights higher than ever before.

Unless, perhaps, Mahiru had predicted that too?

"The war is over," Kureto said. "And now the next fight is beginning. But Mahiru is in our way. She's amassed too much information. We need to kill her. And that task falls to you."

"And if I don't kill her, then you're going to kill my entire clan and family?"

"Your clan has nothing to do with this. Mahiru is dangerous. She needs to die. Surely you understand that now as well as I do."

"…"

Guren did understand. Already, too much blood had been spilled because of her.

"But you're the ones responsible for what happened to her," he submitted.

Because of the Imperial Demons' experiments, Mahiru had been born cursed. Later, she had undertaken experiments of her own in a desperate bid to save her younger sister, Shinoa. As a result, she had been possessed.

That didn't seem to matter, though, to Kureto, who snorted, "What's your point?" just as Guren had anticipated.

His question had been a stupid one. That was just the way of the world. Sometimes bad things happened, and you couldn't expect those in charge to take responsibility. You just had to manage somehow, on your own.

Either become stronger.

Or get swept up by something more powerful than yourself.

Or die.

"You made the right choice," assured Kureto. "You chose to rely on me, in the end, rather than the demon's curse. I plan on living up to those expectations. I want you as my follower."

"Heh. If you already trust me, then what do you need hostages for?"

"I didn't say I trust you that far."

"…"

"Besides, you're the type of person who rises to the occasion when your own people's lives are in danger. Let me make one thing clear. If you ever betray me, I will kill every last one of your people without hesitation."

"…"

"Now choose once again. Which is more important to you? Mahiru, or the lives of every follower of the Ichinose Clan?"

Mahiru or the Ichinose Clan? Guren recalled the events of the previous night.

He had made love to Mahiru in her cozy apartment in Setagaya.

He had tried to tell her that he would protect her.

You can't protect me. Not yet. You know that, don't you?

She'd been close to tears as far as he could tell from her expression.

You already have people to protect. People other than me.

In the end, she had just looked resigned.

If you can give me some proof, then I'll come with you. If you really love me, and want to be with me…then kill your friends. Kill all of them.

But of course, he couldn't do that.

He'd tried to tell her he would protect her. But he wasn't strong enough, wasn't prepared for it.

"If you want to protect your friends, then kill Mahiru," ordered Kureto, interrupting Guren's thoughts. "You have one month. If you haven't killed her by that time, I'll start by killing your father."

"…"

"If another month passes and you still haven't done it, I'll kill a hundred of your followers."

"…"

"But I have faith that you'll manage to kill Mahiru before then. You're very talented. By the way, we've already taken a sample of your blood. The research will continue. If they discover anything, I'll have them share it with you. There's nothing else left for you to do here. Go home and rest."

Kureto turned his back on Guren. Apparently their conversation was over. The Hiragi scion began speaking to one of his soldiers instead.

Guren stood rooted in place. In the end he was still powerless. He wasn't sure if he was angry at himself or just disgusted.

If he didn't kill Mahiru, then his family and followers would die.

Nothing had changed. The status quo had persisted one hundred percent. Guren was almost tempted to laugh. He'd decided to meddle with forbidden power, to sprint like a hare. But in the end...

"What have I got to show for it?"

If anyone was laughing now, it was Mahiru.

At last, Guren turned away. He exited the teachers' lounge.

His friends, whom he had risked his life to protect, were waiting for him out in the hallway.

Shinya Hiragi. Mito Jujo. Norito Goshi.

"..."

Apparently they had heard everything.

Mito stepped closer, reached out to touch Guren's hand, and called his name. He brushed her hand away.

"Happy?" he said, sneering at himself. "Just as you wanted, I'm finally one of Kureto Hiragi's lackeys, body, mind, and soul."

Mito's face clouded over. Guren shook his head.

"I'm sorry..." he told her. "Forget I said anything. I didn't mean it."

He continued to walk past her.

"Guren!" she called after him, but he didn't answer.

His heart was too banged up for that.

Norito was watching him. He didn't say anything as Guren walked past, and instead just patted him on the shoulder.

Guren felt warmth at his touch, and anger and self-loathing.

They were trying to comfort him. To be there for him. But Guren couldn't help hating himself for inspiring so much pity.

Shinya stood behind the other two with a somber look on his face.

"Don't look so gloomy," he said. "After all, nothing's really changed, has it? Things are just back the way they used to be."

"I'm not being gloomy," Guren retorted. "This is just how my face looks."

"Haha."

"I'm gonna head home, if you don't mind."

"Of course. We'll stop by your place later to hang out."

"I don't want you there."

"Hey, come on. We're friends. We just risked our lives for each other, remember?"

"There are no such thing as friends."

"Then maybe you should quit saving people."

"..."

"Quit saving Norito and Mito's lives, if you don't really mean it."

"..."

Casting a sidelong glance at Guren, Shinya said, "Me, I knew what I was doing when I saved you... You say there's no such thing as friends? Get real. We are friends. And it's your fault. You're the one who brought trust and friendship into the crazy world we live in. You've got a kind of madness that Kureto and Mahiru can't even begin to dream of. So now..." Shinya stretched his hand out toward Guren. "Take responsibility for what you did. You have to lead us—lead this team—properly. There's not a whole lot of things to believe in in this world. But we're ready to follow you."

Mito also stepped forward. She stood next to Shinya and placed her hand on top of his.

Norito followed. For once, he wasn't being flippant. His expression, as he added his hand, was serious.

What they were doing right now was madness. To say that they were following Guren, instead of the Hiragis, was tantamount to treason. All three, however, did it without flinching.

"..."

Guren stared down at their hands.

Friends.

Friends…

It was naïve. A childish, vacuous word. He could hear the demon whispering in his head.

—*Friends? You don't need friends, you need to kill them. If you don't, you'll never catch up to Mahiru…*

Maybe the demon was right.

If Guren took their hands now, what would Mahiru say? Maybe she would laugh at him again and call him a weak fool.

But Guren didn't care. He wanted to take their hands.

Because he wasn't Mahiru.

And he wasn't Kureto.

At the end of the day, he was the type of person who couldn't abandon his friends to get ahead. Still…

"You know I'm not as strong as Kureto or Mahiru."

Guren had been learning that lesson the hard way ever since his first day at First Shibuya High School.

He lacked resolve. The guts to sacrifice his comrades, family, and friends to progress.

He stared at their hands.

"I might not be able to protect any of you…" he warned. He lifted his head up and looked into their faces. "I think you're all making the wrong choice—"

"We don't care," Shinya shut him down.

"Even if it's a mistake, we choose you," Mito seconded.

"After everything that's happened, we're hardly gonna turn back now," Norito chimed in as well.

If Guren wasn't going to come to them, they were going to come to him. They reached out and forcibly grabbed his hand and added it to theirs.

Guren stared down at their joined hands.

"…"

He wasn't sure why, but he started to grow a little teary-eyed. It was pretty ridiculous.

In the end, Guren was pretty simple. The warmth of their hands made it all better. He was so weak.

He sighed, trying to muffle his emotions. Putting his free hand to his head, he made a face like he thought the whole thing was silly.

"Being with you three is really exhausting..." he muttered.

And they laughed.

The Seraph of the End

Twelve days later.
September.

Guren was sitting at the dining room table in the apartment where he lived, resting his chin in his hands. There was a sleepy expression on his face.

The apartment was pretty noisy at the moment.

Sayuri and Shigure were cooking something in the kitchen.

Norito was sitting on the couch and reading a comics magazine.

Meanwhile, Shinya and Mito were sitting in front of the TV and playing a video game. In the game they each controlled a pixelated character. The point was to lay down bombs to destroy blocks and to catch your opponent in an explosion. The game was a retro one they had bought used at a game shop. But just as Mito, Shinya, and the others had never even played shogi before the other day, it was a brand-new experience for them. Lately they had been playing it every day. They just couldn't seem to put it down.

At first Shinya had been the best at it, but Mito had picked up a console for her home, too, and had gotten good at it pretty fast. Right now it looked like she had Shinya on the run.

"W-Wait, Mito, hold on. Give me a chance!"

"Heehee... You're not getting away this time, Shinya!"

"Noooooooo!" Shinya screamed.

Guren glanced their way.

"You're gonna rupture my ear drums," he muttered.

Norito leaned over the sofa and glanced at Guren.

"Hey, Guren. Check this out," he said.

Guren turned his way.

Norito had opened up the centerfold in the magazine he was reading. He was pointing it at Guren. A naked woman had her legs spread wide with just a leaf covering her crotch.

"Nice, right?"

"Go home."

Norito laughed. He went back to reading his magazine.

What he saw in comics was a mystery to Guren.

"Master Guren, the curry and rice will be ready soon," Sayuri said, standing in the kitchen. She was wearing an apron.

Shigure carried in a bowl of salad and several plates and began setting the table. She glanced at the cup in front of Guren.

"Would you like me to bring you something to drink?" she asked.

"I'm fine," answered Guren.

Norito, Mito, and Shinya all piped up.

"I'll have cola!"

"Shigure, would it be all right if I had black tea?"

"Orange juice for me, please."

The nerve of them.

"They can all just have barley tea," Guren said.

"No way!" his classmates complained.

Shigure glared at them and made a face. She went back into the kitchen and began preparing the *mugicha*.

Ten days.

The three had been over at Guren's every day during that time. Not…because they were friends. It was because they were all part of the same team. The squad that had been ordered by Kureto to assassinate Mahiru.

Shigure and Sayuri had finally begun to warm up to them on account of their having saved Guren.

"Shigure? How much longer until the food's ready?" asked Mito.

"You're going to have to ask Sayuri," Shigure said.

"Sayuri?"

"Let's see, if everyone's not too hungry, I'd like it to simmer for another fifteen minutes."

Mito nodded. She glanced toward Guren with an excited grin.

"All right, then! That gives us just enough time for one more round. This time with me, Norito, Shinya, and Guren!"

All Mito seemed to care about lately was that game. And to make matters worse, four could play it at once.

"I think you're addicted," teased Norito.

"I can't help it, it's so fun."

"Maybe, but you've played it so much the rest of us can't beat you anymore."

"Norito, I could send you a console and a copy of the game."

"No thanks."

"I will, too."

Norito glanced at Guren and rolled his eyes.

Mito wriggled with excitement as she reset the game. She picked 4P from the menu, and the character selection screen popped up.

"Guren, this is your controller. You sit here," she said.

Shigure and Sayuri, meanwhile, were staring at her from the kitchen. They had sour expressions on their faces. They seemed unhappy about something.

"If you two want to play, it's fine with me," Guren said.

Sayuri responded with an exaggerated pout.

"That's not why we're frowning," she said.

"Really?"

"I don't even have to play that game with you. I already know my delicious curry and rice is the real key to your heart."

"Say what?"

Guren shrugged his shoulders and turned back around. The game was already starting.

"I made your character pink by the way," Shinya said, chuckling.

"So?"

"You're supposed to get mad like a little kid and say, 'Pink is for girls, I'm a boy!'"

"Man, you're a pain in the ass."

"Teheh."

Guren stood up from the table and walked over to the TV.

"…"

Obviously, there were more important things they should be doing. The situation, after all, was pretty dire:

His father, Sakae Ichinose, would be executed in eighteen days unless he killed Mahiru.

Sayuri, Shigure, and other members of the Ichinose-led Order of the Imperial Moon were being used as daily test subjects for research into the demonic curse.

Clearly they didn't have time to spare to be joking around and playing games.

But Guren had put aside time for precisely that.

His reason was simple. They needed to control the demons lurking inside them.

Cursed gear wasn't perfect yet. The latest research, however, suggested that in keeping the demons at bay, a strong attachment to one's humanity was paramount.

Camaraderie, family, friendship, laughter.

These were the sort of things that helped keep the demons under control.

On the other hand, desires, wishes, efficiency, determination…

Those were the aspects of a person that demons could most easily take advantage of.

Which was why they had begun doing this.

Although it might not seem like the best use of their time, it was important to have a little fun.

To hang out.

It was a way to create strong, long-lasting senses of attachment to their human sides.

"..."

Of course, the six of them weren't purely human anymore.

They were demons.

They had fused with demons.

Guren's friends had given up their humanity in order to save him.

"..."

But there was no use in thinking about that now.

Guren picked up his controller and got ready to control his pink avatar.

"Okay, here we go!" said Mito.

A fierce, bomb-wielding battle began on screen.

"Ahhh!"

"Oh no!"

The four of them shouted like maniacs while they played.

It really was a pretty stupid use of time. Guren had to admit, though, that he was having fun. Despite the circumstances, it felt nice to kick back and waste some time.

Guren's pink character scurried left and right, bomb in hand. He still didn't understand the controls very well and ended up dropping a bomb in the wrong spot. If he didn't move, he was going to get caught in his own blast.

"Ah! Urrgh!" moaned Guren, trying to run away in a panic.

"Hahaha. You're really terrible at this," mocked Norito.

While he was laughing at Guren, however, Norito ended up killing himself with one of his own bombs.

"AGGHHHH!"

Guren smirked at him. "You should see your face."

"I don't even care."

That left three of them: Shinya, Mito, and Guren.

Shinya and Mito were both really good at it and were going after each other.

Guren, meanwhile, was too busy running away from his own bombs for his character to join the fight. He kept dropping them by accident.

"Ahh! No! No!"

Shinya had managed to blow up Mito's character. "All right!" he said.

That left just the two of them.

Guren's had barely moved from his starting position.

"Oh ho…" chortled Shinya. "I think I see an itty-bitty mouse. Maybe I should step on it."

"Huh? Just try it. You know I'm gonna win in the end."

Even as he taunted Shinya, Guren made a big mistake.

He'd dropped a bomb in front of his character, and now he was stuck. There was a wall right behind him.

"Ah!"

The pink character spun around, desperate to flee. But he was completely trapped, and there was nothing he could do.

The bomb exploded.

He was dead.

G-A-M-E O-V-E-R.

"…"

Shinya, Mito, and Norito fell over onto their sides, holding their stomachs in laugher.

Shinya, in particular, was laughing so hard that tears came to his eyes. He patted Guren on the shoulder and said, "Y-You… You're too funny!"

Guren started to lose his temper. Smacking Shinya's hand away, he said, "Hold on a second, I want a rematch!"

Just then, though, Sayuri called out from the kitchen.

"Dinner's ready!"

"Okay!" the three guests responded and stood up. They were still laughing.

Guren watched them go before turning his eyes back to the screen. He started the game back up to practice a little on his own. He couldn't seem to get the hang of it, though.

"Hey, Guren," said Shinya, glancing over his shoulder. "The curry's getting cold."

"I'm coming, I'm coming," he said, standing up.

The time was 8:00 p.m.

September 2nd.

The weather was a little chilly tonight. Summer was coming to an end.

Pretty soon it would be fall.

And then winter would come.

According to Mahiru, the world was going to end on the 25th of December—Christmas.

A catastrophe.

The apocalypse.

But it was hard to believe something like that could happen. On the surface at least, things looked pretty calm.

Guren switched the TV channel from the game input to the news.

Apparently nothing very significant had happened that day. The only news playing were fluff pieces. When it came down to it, however, you couldn't trust the media. The war between the Thousand Nights and the Imperial Demons had occurred in Shibuya and all across Japan. But according to the coverage, it had been an "accident" brought on by widespread power failures.

The fighting had been extensive. Scores had been killed. Regardless, the news had barely mentioned it.

It just went to show what Japan's two largest magical syndicates could do once they joined forces. The entire country was now under their thumb.

Research into the demon's curse, meanwhile, was barreling forward. In just these past ten days, their capabilities had progressed by leaps and bounds.

The research had come so far now that ten men, in control of their senses and equipped with cursed gear, were probably enough to kill Mahiru. Perhaps Guren's squad could take her out on their own.

Shinya, Mito, Norito, Sayuri, Shigure, and himself. Guren figured it would take them about ten minutes to kill Mahiru.

That was how powerful cursed gear had already become. Killing Mahiru was no longer an issue.

But had all this progress been a part of her plan? Was it unexpected? Guren wasn't sure.

"Master Guren?"

It was Shigure.

Guren glanced her way. Everyone, other than Sayuri and Shigure, was already sitting around the table eating their curry and rice.

"Is something worrying you?" she asked.

Guren's two bodyguards didn't know that the head of the Imperial Moon, Sakae Ichinose, was going to get killed if they didn't defeat Mahiru. There was no need for them to know.

Shinya and the others looked over at Guren. A hint of sadness filled their eyes.

Guren shook his head.

"It's nothing. Come on, let's eat!"

"Yes, sir!"

Sayuri went rushing into the kitchen to fix Guren a new plate.

Just then, Guren heard a thunk. A piece of mail had been inserted through the slot in the door.

Orders from Kureto.

They had been waiting for the package to arrive.

Kureto's instructions would probably contain Mahiru's latest whereabouts. She had already been spotted in locations throughout Japan. Yet every time Guren and the others were dispatched to grab her, she was already gone.

Still, they were closing in on her, little by little.

She could only run for so long. Both the Thousand Nights and the Imperial Demons were out searching for her.

Under the circumstances, it was a miracle that she had managed to avoid capture for twelve days.

"I'll get it," Sayuri said.

Guren waved her off and headed to the front hallway himself. He opened the mailbox attached to the slot in the door. Inside was a plastic bag with a bundle of documents.

The bag was stained with blood. Fresh blood that hadn't even dried yet.

In other words, they weren't orders from Kureto.

"Ah!"

Guren jerked the front door open.

Just as he expected…

There was a girl standing outside. Her sailor-suit school uniform was splattered with blood. It was Mahiru.

Mahiru Hiragi.

Her eyes were pitch black.

But she was beautiful, all the same.

She stared at him with those bewitching eyes. Eyes that were sad, lonesome, and as black as night.

"I just couldn't stay away," she said.

Guren called for his cursed sword, which had been left lying in the hallway. Immediately it flew into his hand.

"If you don't kill me, your father is going to die, yes?" Mahiru said. "What are you going to do? Are you going to kill me?"

" … "

"Remember when you tried to tell me you'd protect me? Are you going to kill me anyway?"

"Hey, Guren," Shinya called out from down the hallway. "What are you doing out there? The curry's growing cold!"

Guren turned around to look.

It was just a ploy. Shinya already had his cursed sword out and was rushing down the hallway toward them. Sayuri, Shigure, Mito, and Norito were close behind. They knew what was up.

Mahiru flashed Guren a sad smile.

"I guess you're going to kill me, then?"

In response, Guren stepped across the threshold.

"Guren," Shinya shouted at him from behind, "don't go out there alone! We'll fight together!"

But once Guren was outside…

"Guren!"

…he shut the door, drowning out the voices of his friends.

Mahiru didn't draw her sword. Instead, she spread her arms out wide.

"As long as it's you," she said.

"…"

"Draw your weapon, and stab me through the chest. I've already accomplished most of what I wanted. I'm ready."

Killing Mahiru was the right thing to do.

She was already lost. She had gone so far there was no coming back from it. Countless people had died because of her.

It was too late. Too late to forgive her. And if Guren didn't kill her, then his father would die. As well as every single member of the Order of the Imperial Moon—people who believed in the Ichinose Clan and followed them.

Killing her was Guren's only choice.

His face wrinkled as if he was about to cry. He drew his sword and went charging toward her.

Mahiru waited, her face beaming in ecstasy.

"Come to me, Guren," she beckoned, smiling. "Kill me."

"Uh… Urrrr!"

"Kill me, so I can live on inside of you forever."

"AAHHHHHHHH!!"

The door swung open behind them.

"Guren, don't!" hollered Shinya.

"Guren!" screamed Mito.

"You idiot!" yelled Norito.

Guren's two bodyguards were shouting at him as well.

"Master Guren! Master Guren!"

His sword pierced Mahiru's body, going through her shoulder. He continued to run, forcing the blade all the way through. Still pushing her in front of him, he leapt off the building from the exterior balcony.

They were on the twenty-fifth floor.

Even with a demon inside, a fall that far was sure to kill them.

Mahiru stared up at him as they fell.

"Why didn't you stab me through the heart?"

"I told you I would protect you. But I can't. I'm too weak. It's my fault. But...at least we can die together."

Smiling at him softly, Mahiru said, "This makes me so happy."

Guren held her close. She didn't resist. She clung to him, pressing her chest against his.

"I'm sorry, Mahiru," Guren said.

Mahiru shook her head. "No, don't say sorry. I'm the one who should apologize."

Then, grabbing him by the neck and yanking back hard, she reversed their hold.

Her strength was incredible.

"Ngh!"

Guren's body was wrenched free from her.

She was smiling. Her eyes weren't black anymore. Her senses seemed to be intact.

"This makes me love you even more...but I'm afraid a lovers' suicide is out of the question. I'm entrusting the future to you. When everything is in hopeless ruins, I want you to be the last ray of light shining on the world."

Mahiru drew her sword. She thrust it into the wall of the apartment building. The blade made a screeching noise as it cut through foot after foot of wall, slowing their descent.

Mahiru flung Guren into the wall, hard.

"Agh!"

Guren's body was embedded into the concrete. His organs burst, and blood spilled from his mouth, but heedless of his injuries he shouted after her.

"Mahiru!"

But she continued to fall toward the ground without him. Her leg broke when she landed, but it regenerated immediately.

She wasn't a person anymore. She wasn't human.

Mahiru glanced up at him and spoke.

"Go back upstairs and read the love letter I left you ♪"

She had to be talking about the bundle in the bloodstained plastic bag.

Apparently, Kureto was already aware that Mahiru was there; down on the ground, a swarm of soldiers rushed toward her. A close watch was being kept on Guren's building at all times in case Mahiru showed up.

There had to be at least twenty soldiers, all of whom wielded cursed swords.

According to everything they knew, that should have been enough to take her down.

Yet, pirouetting through their ranks, Mahiru cut through them like a banshee. In a matter of moments, the soldiers were reduced to mere lumps of flesh and gore.

Once she had killed them, she wiped the blood off her blade and onto her skirt. Then she returned the sword to its sheath.

She was a monster. A beautiful monster.

In the next instant, she was gone.

Guren was helpless to stop her.

Pulling himself free from the wall, he climbed back into the building through a balcony. He was on the fifth floor. He'd fallen pretty far.

He used the elevator to return to his apartment.

Shinya and the others weren't there. They had probably gone

chasing after Guren and Mahiru.

Mahiru's "love letter" was still waiting for him in the front hallway.

A love letter wrapped in a bloodstained plastic bag.

Guren tore the bag open and began reading it.

The cover read:

The Seraph of the End—the project being carried out by the Thousand Nights that will bring the world to an end

Guren flipped through the pages. The names of countless children were listed inside. They were being experimented on in locations across the country.

Yuichiro Amane
Mikaela Shindo
Shiho Kimizuki
Mirai Kimizuki
Yoichi Saotome
Tomoe Saotome
... ...
... ...
... ...
... ...
... ...
... ...

What followed was a description of a weapon of mass destruction that dwarfed even the demon's curse in scale: a log of loathsome experiments that could obliterate the world in a matter of heartbeats.

Guren stared at the pages.

He started to feel dizzy.

And then he heard the sound again.

Tick, tick, tick.
The sound of desires.
Of human desires.
Like a second hand moving forward, inch by craven inch.
Toward the end of the world. Toward a world of blood.
This, then, is the tale of the human race shortly before its demise.
Catastrophe looms, so close now.

This is the tale of how desperately humanity cried out for life in those last moments before the trumpets of the apocalypse sounded and brought down the hammer of fate upon the world.

Hello. It's me, Takaya Kagami! How did you like Book Four of *Seraph of the End*?

The story of how the end happens is really starting to unfold now.

I'm writing the manga (which happens after the world ends) and the novels (which are set eight years earlier) at the same time. But lately, I've been writing a lot of scenes for the manga that feature the novels' main characters. (I'm talking about the issue coming out in Jump SQ the month after this installment of the novel is published. It should be Volume 7 of the manga...I think!) Anyway, I got pretty excited seeing Team Guren show up in both. I know I'm the one writing these, but I can't help it. Just look at how many scenes they're getting!! (LOL)

About the writing process, I already had a pretty clear idea going in of Guren's story and how the world is going to end (if I didn't, it would be pretty hard for me to write what happens eight years later). I planned to dive in and take a straight course through the plot. But Guren, Mahiru, Shinya, Kureto, Mito, Norito, Sayuri, Shigure and all the other characters have really taken on lives of their own, and they keep trying to change the world in their own little ways. So the more I let the setting from eight years earlier percolate, the more the story from eight years later also starts to change. So even though I'm the one doing the writing, I get to feel surprised sometimes. When I'm working on *Seraph*, I can't help but think how glad I am that I got involved in this project. I'm really grateful to all of you for your support, which is what lets me write in the first place. I just can't thank you all enough.

And while I'm thanking people, let me fill you in on what's new. Both this book and *Apocalypse Alice 3* (*Mokushiroku Arisu 3*), from

Fujimi Fantasia Bunko, are coming out this month, which means I've been trapped in deadline hell! I spent the whole month screaming: "No more! No more! I can't!" But in the end I somehow made it. In any case, I'm actually writing this afterword on the same day that I finally finished *Apocalypse Alice 3*. So I guess that really makes this the afterword to *Alice* too! (No, not really! LOL)

Uh oh—it looks like I used up the last page making stupid jokes.

Next up is the sixth volume of the manga, and Book Five of the novel!

Thanks for reading *Seraph of the End*, everyone. Until next time!

Takaya Kagami
Website:
"Healthy Living with Takaya Kagami"
http://www.kagamitakaya.com